RUNNING INTO THE DARKNESS

DARKNESS

Deepest Darkness Book One

D. A. Bale

Running into the Darkness is a work of fiction. Characters, names, places, incidents, and organizations are a product of the author's imagination or are used fictitiously. Any resemblance to actual persons living or dead, business establishments, events, or locales is entirely coincidental.

Running into the Darkness
D. A. Bale
Copyright © 2011 D. A. Bale
Published by D. A. Bale
http://dabalepublishing.blogspot.com

Cover design by Genevieve LaVO Cosdon, LaVO Design
www.lavodesign.com

ISBN: 1495975428
ISBN-13:   978-1495975424

ALSO BY D. A. BALE

The Deepest Darkness Series:
Piercing the Darkness

The Study
a novelette

DEDICATION

As always, everything I do is for Tyler.
My son, may I inspire you to reach for your dreams.
Let no one stop you.

ACKNOWLEDGMENTS

This book would not have been possible without the time, patience, grit, and merciless teasing of the GK Brainstormers. You know who you are.

CHAPTER 1 – A BLOODY MESS

The storage room door burst open and toppled boxes of gauze across the glaring white floor. Samantha Bartlett awoke as the torrent pelted her, then stared through glazed eyes as the new wild-eyed resident doctor came into focus.

"Incoming multiple wounded!"

The brain fog dissipated as Samantha peeled herself off the linoleum and shot down the hallway to ER. If only to have more than a catnap – cats themselves wouldn't survive on the naps she took. The instructors had spoken about it in medical school but living it was something else entirely. The life of New York residency – always looking for sleep in all the wrong places.

"What's happened?" Samantha asked.

"Several stabbings – one shot, and another who isn't expected to survive the ambulance ride."

Controlled chaos greeted them as they rushed around the corner into the unit, the scent of sterility invaded by blood and sweat. Wounded were shuffled through triage, vitals checked even as gurneys were wheeled through the trauma center. Blood trailed across the unit as staff swarmed each body and connected patients to oxygen and cardiac monitors. Questions and commands overcame the screams and reverberated throughout the room.

"I need a suture tray over here."

"What're his vitals?"

"Blood pressure is dropping."

"Strap down his arms."

"We need to intubate now!"

Second year residency starting now. Samantha snapped on gloves and jumped into the fray with her team as they cut off the bloody shirt. "What do we have here?"

The attending nurse rattled off statistics. "Male, approximately 50-years old. Multiple gunshot wounds to the chest and neck."

"Do we know what happened?"

"Altercation at a hotel known for prostitution. Girls over there say he's a john gone wrong. Got the pimp and hotel owner after apparently filleting one of the other girls. A couple tried to stop him."

"Blood type?"

"A-positive."

The cardiac monitor pulsed a steady rhythm. "Blood pressure is weak but stable." She probed the wound in the neck. Bullet didn't appear to have hit a vital artery. "Get a line in him and shoot me a picture so we can prep him for surgery."

"Yes, Dr. Bartlett."

Police officers herded the other hookers into a holding area as Samantha turned her attention to her patients. Prostitution – sad business. What desperation would drive someone to even consider such a life, much less participate in it?

An occupied gurney sat unattended along the wall, a stained sheet haphazardly tossed over the body of a female. A dark red stain seeped through the sheet, and almost imperceptibly the sheet moved up then down. Samantha's heart raced with stark realization.

The girl was still alive.

She dashed to the gurney and called out for a nurse. As she pulled back the sheet, she swallowed the rush of horror that rose in her throat. The victim – the prostitute. Parts of the chest, face, and arms had been sliced all the way into muscle as if someone had tried to conduct vivisection on a living human being. Blood oozed like lava from the layers of tissue. The paramedics hadn't even untied the poor girl's hands. Samantha sliced through the rope with a scalpel.

"Find a vein, we need a vein."

Together they searched the bloody mass for an adequate vein, the arms eaten up by heroin tracks. The nurse finally located one in the leg, inserted the IV and got the blood line connected while Samantha loaded up and injected albumin. A weak and unstable pulse registered as the nurse hooked up the cardiac monitor. No time to prep for surgery. The girl would never survive the elevator ride, however if they could just stabilize perhaps she'd have a chance.

"Five cc's of epinephrine," the nurse stated as he handed over the syringe.

Had to work fast. No time to be neat. Those deep cuts needed attending to before the adrenaline took full effect. She had to suture multiple layers instead of one at a time. "Increase IV drip and keep a close watch on that bag. Do you have a standby?"

"Yes, Dr. Bartlett."

Though the task seemed impossible, she started piecemeal at the neck on a long and deep puncture, sutures broad and wide as she began the arduous process of stitching the poor girl back together, searching for perforated vessels or organs. The slices of skin and tissue were precise, as if the john had a knowledge of anatomy. The detectives would want to know later. As the flow of fluids into the body increased, the ooze of blood turned into a stream. The pace of the monitor intensified. They needed at least to match the inflow with the outflow to have even a millimeter of chance at saving her. Samantha focused on maintaining a steady hand.

"Dr. Bartlett, I need your assistance please." Dr. Gibbon, the attending physician, tried to draw away her attentions.

Not tonight, please not tonight.

"I'm with a critical patient, sir." She continued suturing and spoke to the nurse. "Have a crash cart standing by." The unsteady beep of the monitor screamed the precarious situation of her patient.

"Dr. Bartlett, you will assist me now."

Ignore him, ignore him.

Samantha gritted her teeth and persisted in attempt to save her patient. Sweat dribbled into her eyes while anger knotted her stomach as she fought to hold back an avalanche of expletives.

The monitor flat lined. "Defibrillator!"

The nurse handed over the paddles.

"Clear!"

The body convulsed as blood spattered from the wounds. No pulse. She warmed up the paddles and shocked the girl a second time. Nothing.

The nurse had another syringe ready before she even asked. "Five cc's of epinephrine, doctor."

Samantha snatched the syringe and injected the contents into her patient, blood pulsating in her ears. She willed the girl's heart to start again, but the steady high-pitched whine of the monitor only mocked her efforts.

***

The dingy wall housing Dr. Gibbon's plaques, framed degrees, and awards ridiculed her with their accumulated honors and years of service to the medical community, but the years and accolades had only hardened his soul to the human condition. Would he even listen to reason this time?

Dr. Gibbon's dark eyes seethed as he looked up from his ancient, cluttered desk. "There is no question that your skills surpass any second year resident I've worked with, but there is no room in this respectable institution for those who do not follow orders from their superiors."

Respectable? In whose eyes?

"Sir, I was with another critical patient when you called. What was I supposed to do – leave her to die alone?"

"She was dead-on-arrival."

"But I had a pulse on her. Didn't you hear the monitor?"

"No, you were just trying to make another one of your damned points. There was no way she'd survive."

"Making a point? She was very much alive when I found her shoved off to the side."

The vein in Gibbon's temple throbbed as his face flushed red. The room reverberated as he pounded his fists on the desk and towered over her.

6

"She was just another prostitute."

"And I suppose you are the morality police? I, sir, take the Hippocratic Oath seriously with *all* of my patients, not just the ones who advance my career and enhance my reputation."

Dr. Gibbon's face contorted as he pointed to the door. "Get out of my hospital!"

CHAPTER 2 – HELLO AND GOODBYE

The crowd opened before her as the girl exited the hospital. She appeared alone in a sea of people. As if preparing to cross the street, she glanced in both directions, stared at her hands before stuffing them into her jacket pockets, and glared at the sidewalk.

The night lit up as if it were day through the special sunglass lenses. He stared at her.

Look up. Look up. What's she waiting for?

He brought her image closer into focus then zoomed in on her face. He would be ready for that split second opportunity.

As if on command she jerked up her head and jutted out her chin defiantly before stepping into the crosswalk.

Just like her mother.

The familiar scar trailed across her jaw line in plain view. With a press to the nose piece he captured her image and transmitted the signal. Then he double-tapped his ear and spoke as he blended back into the frosty night air.

"It's her."

***

The echo of the pounding gavel indicated another sale by Carlisle's, the premier auction house of New York. Late evening auctions for such a prestigious firm were rare, but exceptions transpired on occasion to accommodate the schedules of wealthy repeat patrons. Even so, business made Ben late for this important event, not to mention the Saturday evening traffic worming their way to the latest Broadway offerings.

Personal excursions were a thing of the past. The opportunity to schlep in close proximity to both the rich and scum of New York humanity remained sporadic at best since he'd accepted his present position. Tonight he'd satisfy two urges in one overnight hustle. Hopefully the first hadn't made him too late for this one.

After he registered and entered the spacious auction room, momentary eye contact and an almost imperceptible nod told him he'd arrived just in time. Since he had no intention of staying for the remainder of the sale, Ben took residence against the back wall near the doorway to await his purchase.

The painting was nothing really, just a tiny blip on the radar by comparison to the work currently on display and bidding upward of two million. But he had to obtain the historical piece to hang in his office, if only for the irony. The boss would find the congruency quite humorous.

The gavel slammed down again, closing the current sale at a crisp $2.4 million dollars. The voluptuous redhead, his eyes and ears at Carlisle's, set a new canvas in the easel. With practiced flourish, she removed the cloth like a matador at a bullfight, exposing the image of the ship languishing among jagged icebergs. The attendees released their collective breath of disappointment, most burying their heads in their catalogs while others glanced away and yawned or checked messages on their cell phones.

He'd get it for a song.

A mere seven minutes later and fifty-three thousand dollars lighter, he waited in the back of the limousine, irked that he'd gotten into a slight bidding war with a phone handler whose client was probably some idiotic history buff. Frustration melted away when the package passed through the doorway into his hands, the redheaded handler with it. Fifty-three thousand dollars was forgotten as she slid onto his waiting lap, her tongue snaking its way deep into his mouth.

A small price to pay to mix pleasure with business.

***

Snow and ice swirled around the New York night sky and pelted like tiny pieces of hail. Hail.

Hell on earth adequately described her existence. The biting wind whipped around the skyscrapers of downtown Manhattan, cutting through her worn mustard-brown jacket.

Samantha tightened the belt and drew the worn lapels up around her frozen cheeks and hunched down into what little warmth the flimsy coat provided. A hat and gloves would come in handy on such a night.

The congestive throng threatened to sweep her from the sidewalk into the street among the honking cabs and cursing drivers. At least they were all snug in their vehicles with someone to speak to, their rumbling bass keeping par with her chattering teeth. Sleek stretch limos glistened in the streetlamps, no doubt ferrying the well-to-do to their Connecticut cottages and svelte downtown apartments or a game or concert at Madison Square Garden.

Samantha shut her mind to the swelling pity-party and focused on putting one foot in front of the other while keeping her head down from the raw wind. A nearby subway vent steamed its frosty breath. She paused to savor the warmth it provided before being crushed forward again by the wave of bodies working their way toward the nearest subway entrance.

The scent of grease and grime flowed up from the tunneled depths as she made her way down the stairwell. Thankfully the aching wind could no longer rip through her bones down in the pit known as the New York subway system. The clink haunted her ears as she dropped a precious token into the turnstile. At least she wouldn't be heading this way again soon. Good riddance.

Huddled at the platform with the masses, Samantha continued the mental barrage as she waited to board the next train, repeatedly blowing her warm breath into frigid and reddened hands. Exposed fingers felt as if they would shatter if someone so much as touched them, difficult to avoid in the pressing crowd.

Grandma would be disappointed if she ever found out that she couldn't control her blasted temper enough to hold a residency in even the most meager of New York City hospitals. Thoughts of Gramm riddled her mind, longing to see her after all of these years, but she just couldn't bring herself to return home. Gramm wouldn't dare set foot on a plane and come to New York – that reasoning she well understood. Almost ten years and a lifetime of heartache had passed since she'd shaken the dust of the Kansas prairie from her feet and loaded her belongings into that old Chevy Camaro for the long trip to New York University.

She'd tried, but the ghosts of the past haunted her previous visits so that she always cut them short. There was no way she could go back now. New York was home. The weekly calls satisfied them both.

The stench of wedged bodies and sweet perfume coupled with the grease of the pit brought Samantha back to the present. Her head swam and pounded as they pressed en masse into the rickety silver beast slithering along the tunnels. Luck finally smiled as a seat opened up for the long ride to her apartment.

The night shift always presented the most striking characters on the trip home: businessmen working all hours, Broadway attendees, dock workers, partiers with tattoos and body piercings in areas she didn't even want to think about, pimps with hollow-eyed prostitutes. She'd seen enough traumas of street walkers to last a lifetime and harden the average soul.

Dr. Gibbon's words flashed through her mind. Anger reared again against her chosen profession. Doctors with years of standing saw the prostitutes not as flesh and blood with names but as numbers, mere things to be thrown away. Was she the only one who saw them as members of the human race? Pimps saw them only for the cold cash their bodies brought. The average person saw right through them as if they weren't even there, except the johns who secretly needed to use them to satisfy their own urges. Then the stupid girls who survived their trips to the emergency rooms would go right back onto the streets all bandaged and bruised, returning like dogs to their own vomit.

There goes the emotional turnstile. Emotion always got in the way – and therein presented her biggest hurdle. Time and again her instructors cautioned her to turn off the spigot. If she didn't stop wearing her emotions, no matter how talented she grew, the industry would end up chewing her up and spitting her out. Try as she might, Samantha was either controlled by sorrow over circumstances she witnessed or the anger which welled up at feeling utterly helpless. Now she couldn't even control her emotions enough to keep a paying residency position. At least she still had the clinic in which to keep her sanity, but volunteer work didn't cover personal expenses.

Twenty-seven, unemployed and riddled with more debt no normal human being should carry. Samantha sighed. If she said anything to Gramm, the woman would bend over backward, mortgage the house, find her a job at a local hospital and beg her to complete her residency in Wichita. However, New York offered the opportunity to hone her surgical skills among the best hands in the world. She couldn't pass it up. But she'd blown it – blown it big. Monday morning she'd have to fess up and try to explain the latest snafu in her residency requirements.

The train finally released her from its grasp just as she'd achieved normal human body temperature. Samantha had almost forgotten how desperate the late February cold had felt forty minutes before until she stepped from the grease pit into the aching wind. Tenement buildings with homeless living under the stairwells lined the road as she stumbled to the one called home. With stiffened fingers she maneuvered her key into the lock, slipped into the dark and dingy alcove to gather her supply of mail before trudging up rickety narrow stairs.

Good old 1104, with the rusting bathroom sink and creaking walls that kept out only the faintest noise. Pretty amazing digs for a doctor. If only for the university dorm again. It wasn't for the sparsely furnished room itself she pined, but the bubbly roommate with whom she'd shared it. They'd managed to room together during the last four years, but fellowship and residency didn't allow for anything but long persistent hours. Slowly all of her classmates had drifted back to their little corners of the world. Oh to have time for a friend.

An overnight envelope laid just inside under her front door. The return address caught Samantha's eye – Mr.

Eddis' law firm out of Wichita. Maybe he'd discovered something left over from her parents' estate. If so, it couldn't come at a better time. She ripped through the envelope and drew out a five thousand dollar check, but the memo line cut her celebration short – ESTATE ADVANCE. A cloud of unease settled over her as she scanned the enclosed letter, the words swimming before her eyes.

Gramm was dead.

CHAPTER 3 - FIREBALL

The boarding pass wavered noticeably as Samantha passed it to the attendant, sweat gathering on her brow even as she made her way down the cold tunnel and stepped across the threshold into the 737. The air stale, her knees weak. The flight attendant must have recognized her dazed state and therefore helped her locate and settle into the assigned seat.

Until that moment she'd kept her promise never to fly. Even now Samantha knew she could leave the plane and rent a car, but covering that distance in her present state would only make for another funeral. Anyway last night's macabre call to Mr. Eddis confirmed the need for haste only a plane trip offered. She dug around her purse for the prescription she'd picked up on her way to LaGuardia, begged a water from the attendant, then washed down four pills instead of the prescribed two.

Just to be sure.

Her eyelids drooped even as the plane taxied then

lifted off the runway, her stomach fluttering as the plane banked toward Kansas and what awaited. The thoughts had long been buried with her parents, but the old memory surfaced in a dream as Samantha slept away the long plane ride.

***

She'd been five years old then as she stared at her reflection in the big glass window. How she hated the long brown ringlets Gramm had curled that morning. Brown poop, that's what they looked like. Then pink – of all colors she could have chosen for her dress Gramm had chosen pink, a girlie-girl color. She scratched at the crinoline skirt and practically danced a jig trying to reach the spot where the tag itched. Momma would never have made her wear such a thing to the airport.

"Samantha, stop dancing around and stand still," Gramm commanded.

Prim and proper, that described Gramm. Sit up straight and lift the chin. Everything in its place and a place for everything – or was it the other way around? Gramm's white gloved hand clutched the navy handbag while she adjusted the white pillbox hat then applied yet another coat of bright red lipstick.

Samantha focused her attention back to the runway and leaned her forehead against the cold glass. The wild wind off the Kansas plain blew the snow across the concrete. Gramm had called it the 'tarmac'. Sounded like something from McDonald's. *Yes ma'am, I'll have a Big Mac please, hold*

the 'especial sauce and add some tar. She giggled, imagining
Daddy saying that in the drive-thru. Maybe they'd stop
there on the way back to Gramm's house for some real food.

As the glass fogged over, Samantha leaned closer and
smashed her nose against the window, puffing and filling
the surface with steam. She grew lost in her world of stick
figures as she smeared the fog into shapes.

"Samantha Jane Bartlett! Stop that this instant and
come be seated."

Samantha rolled her eyes and dragged her shoes
across the carpet, knowing it would drive Gramm bonkers if
she didn't pick up her feet. Scuff marks on the white patents
would surely send her flying higher than an airplane. When
Samantha plopped down in a chair she made certain to leave
an empty seat between them. The space disappeared as
Gramm moved over and patted her knee.

"They'll be here soon, Samantha dear. Just try to be
patient."

The speeches began on the importance of Momma
and Daddy's trip to D.C. while Samantha slumped in her
chair and scratched against the plastic back. Gramm droned
on and on about how nice it was that her Samantha could
visit her in Wichita and that she didn't get to see her little
Samantha enough, blah, blah, blah. But then Gramm said
something that caught her ear.

"Boeing merged with Stearman here in Wichita years
ago. Your father had such an opportunity knock at his door
that he packed you all up and whisked you off to Seattle

when you were just a baby."

"You mean I was born in Kansas?" Samantha asked.

Gramm smiled and patted Samantha's cheek with a scratchy gloved hand. "But of course, my dear."

Too much to stomach. She was a good Seattle girl, not some hokey from the sticks.

Glancing at her watch then staring out the window, Gramm interrupted Samantha's drear thoughts. "I'll bet that's your parents' plane coming in for a landing."

Samantha shot out of her chair and plastered her body against the glass, ignoring the chill. Gramm stood beside her without scolding and said something about a 737, but all Samantha could see was the plane that carried Momma and Daddy. They'd never left her alone with Gramm for two whole weeks. Her heart pounded as the plane's nose turned toward them and scooted along the concrete.

Then she stared in confusion as a huge orange ball took the place of the plane. The building rumbled and swayed beneath her feet like they were having an earthquake, but they were in Kansas not Washington. People screamed as the explosive power swept across the tarmac and hit the glass enclosure. The windows crackled and erupted as Gramm swept over her and cradled her body beneath her own.

As the flying glass settled and the winter wind blasted through the building's shell, Samantha craned her neck to see balls of fire fall from the sky. Sirens wailed as emergency trucks raced over and surrounded the fire, spraying pink foam all around the area. Fluffy like Daddy's shaving cream. Pink like that Pepto stuff Momma would take when her stomach hurt. Pink like her dress.

Her chin burned. Samantha freed an arm and scratched at it, blood oozing down her arm and dripping bright red spots on her dress. She never liked pink anyway.

***

Turbulence jolted Samantha awake, her pulse pounding in her ears as her past closed in on her present. Instinctively she scratched at the thin scar trailing across her chin – forever the reminder of the promise she'd made never to set foot on a plane.

After the day of her parents' death.

CHAPTER 4 - HOMECOMING

The Kansas wind buffeted the taxi as it rounded the corner and slid to a stop. Samantha stared through the frosty window at the old home where Gramm had raised her, the white paint weathered by several Wichita winters, and the concrete walk cracked and buckled by the strong root system of the old elms. Knowing Gramm, a painting contractor had already been retained to repaint the house come spring. Gramm always looked ahead to what needed accomplished.

Samantha tentatively stepped to the icy walk, took her offered suitcases from the taxi driver and paid him from the money Gramm's attorney had kindly forwarded. Then she began the long walk up the sidewalk to the airplane bungalow home. Gramm's trimmed rosebushes lined the porch, their unencumbered branches almost shivering as they awaited the warmth of spring. The porch swing swayed and creaked in the frigid wind. She and Gramm had shared countless ice cream cones nestled there together and read books to one another. Joe Roberts had also kissed her for the first time in that swing.

Shame washed over her at all of the missed opportunities since then, of the fears she'd allowed to keep her apart from Gramm and all of those for whom she'd once cared. Why did the past have to infect every fiber of the present? As Samantha slipped the key in the lock she hesitated, the years long wasted away since she'd last used it. With a begrudging click, the key turned and the heavy front door swung open with a familiar creak. She confronted the past left behind but never forgotten.

The green living room carpet had been removed and the old hardwood floors refinished, no doubt because of all the cherry kool-aid Samantha had spilled. The floral furniture remained as did the lace curtains lining the windows. A faint scent of lavender tickled her nose as she walked into the dining room. Same old Gramm. A chill passed over her at the thought – in all the times she'd considered visiting, never had she imagined returning to an empty house. Her insides felt as hollow as the eyes of New York's prostitutes.

Samantha trudged up the stairs to the loft, surprised to find Gramm had not touched a thing since she'd last left. The loft – her space. She'd always kept it lined with navy curtains and filled with as many noisy friends as she could cram into the wide room. Her posters still covered the walls: basketball, football, race cars and any other sport to drive Gramm nuts, things devoid of femininity – one of her many areas of rebellion. Samantha swallowed her tears, set the suitcases beside the bed, and quickly returned downstairs.

Gramm's room had only changed slightly since

Samantha's departure. Floral curtains draped the windows and a matching comforter spread across the bed. The manufactured scent of roses hung in the air. She sat at the edge of the bed and gently stroked the silken pink flowers. Real roses from Gramm's garden always replaced the fake ones come late spring.

The kitchen had been renovated, the only room in the entire house that reflected any real change. Samantha couldn't believe after all those years of arguing for a dishwasher that Gramm had finally put in one. Well no wonder. Her granddaughter wasn't around anymore to help with chores. Shame again gripped her as she imagined Gramm taking care of everything all by herself in her increasingly fragile state. She felt like such a failure as a granddaughter.

A six pack of Dr. Pepper sat on the top shelf of the new refrigerator, the date indicating they'd expired. Gramm didn't touch soda pop, said it contained no nutritional value, and she'd always refused to buy it. After Samantha had secured her first paying job she'd triumphantly brought home two cases of Dr. Pepper with her first paycheck and thereafter kept them in a dorm-sized refrigerator in her room to share with friends. Gramm must have bought the cans when Samantha had talked about coming home for Thanksgiving several years ago. In the end, she'd just not been able to bring herself to accept that train ticket. Though it seemed almost a sacrilege, Samantha removed a can and poured herself a glass.

The bookshelves in the dining room contained various

photo albums, and after a pensive deep breath she selected
several then sat at the table perusing their history. Hours
passed as she sipped flat Dr. Pepper and reminisced over
photos covering her life with Gramm. A picture of Gramm
stood out as she turned the page: a smile. She'd always had
such a pretty smile but rarely ever used it after that tragic
day at the airport. Samantha had been about nine, and they
were sharing ice cream cones in the swing. Ever the ornery
one, Samantha had plunged her ice cream into her own nose,
leaving a mess trailing down her chin. For a moment she
thought Gramm would be mad, but instead Gramm had
laughed at her antics. Recognizing the moment, Samantha
had grabbed her camera and snapped the picture.

Tears ran hot, puddling on the picture's plastic cover
and blurring the memory. The setting sun cast long shadows
through the room, her sobs echoing throughout the empty
house.

"I'm all alone."

CHAPTER 5 - FAREWELL

Her brown hair stood out against the sea of gray during the graveside service. The early March cold penetrated the tent as Samantha sat unaccompanied in the front row, the eyes of Gramm's friends boring into the back of her head. The hours she had spent trying to pin her hair up in a French roll had made her arms ache, but she was determined not to embarrass Gramm during their final goodbyes.

The pastor droned on, while Samantha's thoughts were centered only on what lay within the silver casket. Due to the accident, Mr. Eddis had ordered it closed when making the funeral arrangements. The hit and run had engulfed the car in flames. How many bodies had she seen come through ER over the years and smelled the stench of scorched flesh? Samantha fought to keep the rising anger at bay.

Now's not the time.

The accident required investigating, something the

police department was supposed to do. Someone had left her all alone in the world – not even allowed her to say goodbye to Gramm. Samantha hung her head and quickly dabbed at her nose with Gramm's lace hankie before gently cradling the silken square against her cheek. Lavender wafted from the folds and new tears threatened to flow.

That's your own fault, girlie, for not coming back sooner.

The service ended. Samantha knew she should be the first to rise, but she didn't want the moment to end. She didn't want to say that final goodbye. Eventually others stirred behind her and began to move aside. Time stopped as she stared at the casket for God knows how long until the funeral officiant came to lower Gramm into the ground.

"Wait," Samantha begged.

After gathering the enormous bundle of pink roses from her lap, Samantha tentatively stepped forward and laid them upon the casket. Just touching it sent a shiver up her spine.

The cold metal seemed to bite her cheek as she leaned against it and whispered, "These are for you, Gramm. I got them just for you. They're your favorite." Emotion knotted her throat and the tears she'd been holding back all day spilled over onto the casket. "I'm so sorry."

Gentle hands encircled her arms, and Mr. Eddis drew her away. Always there for her family, paunchy Mr. Eddis had handled the estate of her parents and been a stalwart figure in their lives ever since. Well at least Gramm's life. Samantha was glad to accept the aged attorney's helping hand. The limousine waited as Mr. Eddis guided her toward it without a word. As he opened the door for her, one of Gramm's friends intercepted her. The shrill voice grated on Samantha's already raw nerves.

"Lovely little show you put on for us all, *Miss Samantha*. I'm sure Sylvia would have appreciated it more in person though. How can you even call yourself her granddaughter?"

Mr. Eddis placed his bulk between them. "Mrs. Hall, this is neither the time nor the place for your outpouring of affection. Perhaps another time?"

With a snort Mrs. Hall scuttled away, taking her withered face back to torment her husband. Samantha had always hated the little pig and couldn't understand why Gramm had considered her a friend. Wearily she collapsed into the limousine. Mr. Eddis peered over his glasses and offered condolences before shutting the door. Once again she was alone.

The blue tent stood stark against the wintry background, the edges flapping in the wind. A lone man in a black suit stood near the corner, his eyes not on the busy workers but staring at the limo while they pulled away. As they lazily wormed their way past weathered headstones and family mausoleums, Samantha's curiosity piqued. Was the man part of the funeral home crew? Why did he wear sunglasses on an overcast day? Questions ceased as a familiar sight arrested her attention.

"Stop!"

Samantha recognized the twin vaults even though she'd missed far too many visits over the years. Time to make up for lost moments.

"I'll only be a few minutes," Samantha called to the driver.

The wind blustered across the landscape and moaned through the barren trees. Samantha hadn't felt the keen wind as much in the tent. She picked up her pace as she neared the graves. Twigs traversed here and there across them, but the vaults showed little weathering after more than twenty years. Nothing but the best for Gramm's only child and son-in-law. The flower cups yawned empty and barren. She'd fix that come spring. Caring little for her dress and etiquette now, Samantha knelt on the hard ground near the head of her mother's grave.

"It's been a long time, Momma and Daddy." It seemed funny talking to the headstone, yet a strange comfort warmed her heart despite the coldness of the ground. "I haven't been a good daughter to you because I didn't take care of your mother the way I should've. I know you'll take care of Gramm – a lot better than I ever did."

Samantha never had much use for religion – always felt it was a crutch for the weak. Considering it now seemed a bit of a contradiction, because no one could ever accuse Gramm of being weak. Anyway the idea of them being together again in some sort of afterlife offered a measure of comfort.

"I know I can't change what has happened, but this I

promise you. I will find out who killed Gramm and make sure they face justice.

"No matter what."

***

It didn't matter the time of day or night, the precinct never stopped buzzing with activity. Computer keyboards clacked as officers pecked out their reports, and the oddest ring tones jingled throughout the room. Some people were still so juvenile.

During the day it was the political game, the 'clean' or white collar crimes they pursued, homicides, domestics, or traffic incidents. The night was different, when the scum of humanity showed itself in rapes, robberies, prostitutes, brawlers, and the really graphic and grisly murders. The occasional lull came after sunset, the time of day when traffic slowed and normal people were home, and the daytime criminals took a break before the night-timers crawled from the shadows.

Detective Joe Roberts leaned back in his chair and allowed his mind to wander from the file on his desk. The pencil eraser went straight to his mouth, a bad habit for sure, one he'd tried to break years before, but sometimes it was the only way to keep from talking out loud to himself in the tough cases. This family had suffered more than their fair share of turmoil, and now this. How much could one person endure?

He should've gone to the funeral, paid his respects and said farewell in person. One problem.

She'd be there.

Depending on her mood he would have either been welcomed or his presence considered an intrusion. No need to risk a scene. Truth be told, he should've just manned up and called Sam the moment her plane landed and let the cards fall where they may. He never could win with her anyway.

Time slowed as an unusual movement near the stairwell caught his eye. He'd expected it, figured it would only be a matter of time until she sought him out, but he didn't think she'd arrive on this day. He'd actually allowed himself the luxury of imagining what she looked like after all these years, however the sight of her still caught him off guard. Though the hint of dark circles ringed her eyes, Sam had never looked more beautiful.

When they were younger she'd been very athletic and way too skinny but he hadn't really cared about that in high school. However, his tastes had matured over the years. Some guys liked stick figures, but Joe preferred a woman with some meat on her bones and soft curves. He admired Sam in the simple jeans, black t-shirt, and the familiar worn jacket as she spoke to his colleague across the room. Her brown hair was pulled away from her face in a ponytail, but he remembered the silkiness of her dark locks when he'd run his fingers through them while...

Joe sat up and hunched over his desk to focus his attention back on the task at hand – the file, the pictures, his notes. Maybe this wasn't the best file to have open on his desk with Sam in the room. With a flick of his fingers, he closed the file and glanced up.

Into Sam's brown eyes.

"Hey, Joe."

"Good to see you, Sam."

A moment of awkward silence passed between them. How ridiculous. He'd never felt uncomfortable around her in all the years they'd known each other. No need to start now. Joe got up and came around his desk, then enveloped Sam into his arms. She melted into his embrace as if the years were mere weeks. He hated to break the silence but felt she needed to hear it.

"I'm sorry about Gramm."

Her body stiffened. Joe recognized the sign as the tough girl stance, that Sam's personal wall was being built high against the world to keep the hurt away from her heart. Some things never changed.

"Thanks," Sam finally responded and pulled from his arms.

"I thought about coming today."

"Why didn't you?" Her dark gazed pierced him.

"Well I didn't want to be…"

"Bothered?"

"A distraction."

"Don't flatter yourself."

The girl could still get under his skin and irritate the living tar out of a rock if necessary. The most ridiculous part of it all, he *let* her do it to him. Nearly ten years had passed and still they so readily picked up right where they'd left off. Well his profession had also taught him how to build walls of protection.

"I was here, you were there. I checked in on her occasionally. Your grandmother treated me like family."

"Is that a slam?"

"Just the facts, ma'am."

The corner of her eye twitched, the only sign she allowed to let him know he'd gotten to her. For a moment she tensed as if she might explode, then her body relaxed. She closed her eyes and rubbed the scar on her chin.

"She told me about your visits. Look, I didn't come down here to start an argument."

The moment over, Joe returned to his chair and attempted to slide the file off his desk with practiced ease. The professional wall remained. "What can I do for you then?"

Sam never missed much. "That's her file." Her strong grip tugged at the manila folder.

Joe laid his hand over hers to keep her from opening the file. "It's not pretty."

"You're forgetting – I'm a doctor."

"Well, Dr. Bartlett, you've never had to work on family or friends, have you?" If there was any way to spare her additional trauma he'd do it in a heartbeat. He softened his demeanor. "There's a reason Mr. Eddis requested a closed casket."

A lifetime of pain glistened deep in her eyes for a spare second before she released her grip on the file. The wall of protection wavered. Would the girl ever let anyone in?

"Tell me one thing," Sam continued as she sat down.

"I'll try."

"Was it really just a simple case of hit and run?"

"It's rather looking that way. Why?"

"If that's all, then why are you investigating it?"

"I asked to, Sam."

He allowed her to digest the information. A myriad of questions played dodgeball in her mind – he could see it in her eyes, the twitch of her cheek, the purse of her lips, and the continued stroking of her scar. Even with her level of intelligence, Joe could still read her thoughts and know her mind by a mere glance at her face. It always drove her nuts. At times it drove them closer together.

In the end it drove them apart.

"Well is there some reason the FBI would be

involved?"

That question came out of nowhere, and completely surprised him. "There's no reason for them to be."

"You still have friends there, yes?"

"Yeah, but what does that have to do with your grandmother?"

"There was a guy at Gramm's funeral today who looked the part, that's all. I thought afterward maybe you sent him to question me, but he never did."

Odd – no reason for his buds at the Bureau to be involved, and they certainly had more tact than to show up at a funeral for questioning. No one had called him for copies of reports or pictures from the accident, and if they had an angle on anything he'd be the first they'd contact. They knew he was worming his way toward the Bureau, the ultimate professional goal in his line of work.

"Maybe he was with the funeral home," Joe offered.

Sam sighed. "Probably."

The phone call startled them both. Joe picked it up and spoke with the chief briefly before settling the receiver back in its cradle. When he stood Sam followed suit.

"Chief Snowe needs to chat. Was there anything else you wanted to check on for now?"

"No, just wanted a rundown, that's all."

"If anything comes up you'll be the first to know."

"Sure – thanks, Joe."

He caught her hand as she turned to go. "It was good seeing you, Sam."

She smiled half-heartedly. "You too."

Sam's shoulders sagged, as if any hope she'd carried into the precinct had bled out. The girl really needed to relax and let her hair down instead of carrying the entire world on her back. Maybe she'd consider dinner with him, just old friends catching up. First thing in the morning he'd call his buddies at the Bureau and find out if they were working cases with any possible connection to Gramm's accident. Then he'd call Sam and see about dinner.

But Joe didn't hold out much hope of success – on either front.

CHAPTER 6 – GIVE AND TAKE AWAY

Warner moaned with pleasure as he continued thrusting hard and gripped the carved headboard of the canopied bed for support. The girl was so tight, far too long since he'd had a virgin. Most girls these days were so loose he could ram them up to their eyeballs, but this young thing he'd only get to those mountainous tits that glistened with his saliva. They hardly jiggled with each thrust – the real things, not those gelatinous implants so common among women these days.

Tits had always been his weakness. Warner always had to concentrate to stay focused on the face of the well-endowed and maintain decorum in public. However, he hadn't had to keep his hobby a secret from the old crone for more than twenty years, the only stipulation being never to use their bed. That thing hadn't seen action in so long he considered it a jinx, and they rarely slept together in it. He was happy to romp about other rooms throughout the mansion.

Sated and spent, Warner collapsed between the mountains and massaged their peaks once more. With a farewell suck he withdrew from the girl's spent casing and robed himself, glancing in the mirror momentarily to smooth his speckled gray hair before slipping on his glasses. He winked to the reflection and flashed a smile. Even at sixty-four, he was still a handsome devil with stamina to boot.

Seating himself on the bed's edge, Warner took the girl's hand and kissed it. "You have been such a pleasure to me this evening, and I will reward you accordingly, my dear."

She stared back at him with dark haunted eyes and replied, "Thank you, sir."

The eyes caught him for just a moment, and a spark of guilt twitched his cheek. Her parents had practically laid her in his lap as they sought his attentions and concessions for their contract bid, dangling their daughter's virginity like bait – and he'd bitten. Well what could he do? As a man, he had certain cravings that begged to be fed.

Warner strode from the room, pausing only to speak to his assistant stationed with the security detail. "Clean her up and give her the usual obligatories. Make sure she takes that blasted pill then escort her out of here." As an afterthought Warner followed up, "Make no promises to the parents, Forsdale."

"Yes, Mr. President."

With that said, U.S. President Frederick Douglas Warner left them to their business of cleaning up after his conquest.

***

A flash of his badge gained entry to the raging Alexandria, Virginia nightclub, joining the press of bodies writhing in rhythm to the throbbing techno beat. Scantily clad women and men slid their sweating bodies against him and pressed groins to his in seductive invitation. But he hadn't come to dance.

He had a job to do.

The strobe effect gave him a headache until he passed into the hallway and through the elevator doors. Even two floors below he could feel the music's pulse through the elevator shaft as he pulled the weapon from his pocket and the doors opened. The attendant never knew what hit him.

After tucking the body away in an alcove, he followed the horseshoe-shaped hallway and counted off the closed doors in the scarlet infused low light. A quick check of his watch outside number nine, and then he made his move. With an almost imperceptible click, he entered the dim room and closed the door.

She rode her john hard, neither one immediately aware of his presence. Damn shame she was on top because he'd have to take her out with him. Then lady luck smiled.

Recognition flashed in the man's eyes the moment his target rose up and glanced over the prostitute's shoulder. He took aim.

"Eric, what the…"

"Time's up, Congressman."

The spit of the weapon silenced the public servant forever. Together they rolled the body from the bed before the stream of blood stained the sheets. Then the prostitute enveloped his mouth with hers and drew him to her naked and sweaty form as she clawed at his jacket and shirt buttons. He couldn't get out of his suit fast enough.

"I got your message," he panted in her ear and pressed her down to the bed.

She responded, "I thought you weren't coming."

"Give me a few minutes and I will." He smiled.

Their undulating bodies pounded against the mattress in increasing fervency, the scent of fresh blood heightening the passion. Too damn long since he'd gotten a good piece of her heated action. The other girls could never get him to the unending fever pitch and change it up often enough to maintain his interest. But she hurled her pelvis up to match his – their rhythm in perfect sync – until his pleasure liquefied.

She nestled up to him as their breathing slowed and bodies cooled. Eric curled a finger around a strand of her red hair and sighed before he spoke.

"Next time make sure you're not on top when I arrive."

She sat up, her stare boring into his green eyes. "You wouldn't."

"You know I'd have no choice."

Her shoulders slumped in resignation. "What about

him?" She nodded toward the Congressman's body.

Eric slipped into his pants and gathered his shirt and jacket. "Your responsibility this time."

"What?"

He paused at the door. "Oh, and don't forget the other one in the alcove."

She glared at him then licked her lips. He'd leave her wanting more.

Eric smiled. "Don't wait so long until next time."

CHAPTER 7 - A DISCOVERY

"You'll get a much better price for the house if you get it on the market now. April is the biggest residential home sales month of the year."

Faithful Mr. Eddis puffed on a stogie while he urged Samantha along the steps necessary to process Gramm's estate and move on with life. The scent of tobacco soothed, a familiar part of Mr. Eddis' ways – like the grandpa whom she'd never known.

Daily Samantha struggled with torturous thoughts of selling Gramm's house and going back to New York City. Once the house fell into another family's hands, she'd truly have no place to call home. Part of her missed New York. The hustle and bustle had breathed into her at a time she'd needed it – or so she'd thought. Selling the house would sever any and all connections to Kansas, but most of all to Gramm.

"I know, Mr. Eddis, and you've been so patient with me through all of this. I truly don't know what I would have done without you and Mrs. Eddis this last month. It's been nice having home cooked meals."

It reminded her of the meals Gramm had prepared for her without fuss. Once again she berated herself for the times in high school when she'd skipped out on meals without calling. Gramm had eaten alone many a night after waiting and worrying. No wonder she'd be so upset when she finally shuffled in after midnight.

Mr. Eddis came around the walnut desk and sat beside her on the chocolate leather divan, taking her hand in his and patting it comfortingly just like Gramm used to do.

"Forgive me, dear. My lawyer hat sometimes gets in the way. I think we've discussed enough business for today. You hold onto the house as long as you need, and I'll take care of the taxes out of the estate until you decide the time is right to move on with things. That way you can scuttle on back to New York and finish up that medical residency."

Samantha took the offered tissue. "Oh, I don't have to worry about getting back to New York right away." She shrugged sheepishly. "Truth be told, there's been some issues with my residency placement, but they'll hold my status for up to six months."

"Perhaps something local? I could make a few calls."

"I'm really not ready to think about my future yet."

Mr. Eddis stared. "I suppose this also has to do with your desire to find the culprit responsible for the crash?"

Too many evenings spent at the Eddis home allowed him a hint at her purpose. Regardless of the starting topic, most of their dinner conversation ended up centered on the investigation.

Mr. Eddis continued, "How 'bout I call Mrs. Eddis and tell her to set another place at the table tonight, hmm?"

The man could be so sweet and understanding. How on earth did he end up a lawyer?

"I appreciate it, as always, but I just need a little quiet time."

"Which is it tonight – swinging by the precinct or the hospital?"

Samantha couldn't stifle the laugh that erupted. "Have I become that predictable? I thought I might stop in at the hospital to hold some babies."

To see new life entering the world even when others passed out of it gave her a sense of joy in the midst of the heartache. Some of the older nurses remembered Samantha from the summers when she'd volunteered as a nurse's assistant. They welcomed her willingness to hold and cuddle the drug-addicted newborns for hours on end, their wails of agony screaming life to Samantha's ears.

Several hours of crying babies passed before Samantha continued her weekly ritual and headed to the cemetery. After a brief stop at Gramm's grave to restock the flower cup with fresh pink roses, she took up residence at the now familiar headstone of her mother, leaning against it as if it were her mom's steady shoulder. She sighed, remembering the warmth of her mother's arms but having to make do with cold hard reality.

"Still nothing new to report, Momma. I've worked 'em over pretty hard, but the police have come up as empty as me. Joe just won't cooperate. You know, forensics was pretty interesting when I took that course during medical school, but when it's your own family?"

Lightning flashed off in the distance. She'd waited for a Kansas thunderstorm since she'd arrived. Gramm used to come out and sit with her on the front porch to enjoy the sound of the downpour and the roar as the wind tossed the rain and misted their faces. A pleasant shiver passed up her spine as she noticed the familiar scent of approaching moisture.

"Looks like we're going to get a thunderstorm tonight. It's funny, I don't remember having them in Washington. I do remember it rained a lot but not a thunderstorm."

The sun dipped behind the clouds and the wind increased. As Samantha finished up her musings, the sky deepened with the approaching storm and thunder rumbled. A flash of lightening brightened the sky momentarily as she said her goodbyes. Something caught her eye as she turned.

The next flash illuminated a man in the distance standing beside a lonely tree. His outline appeared just visible after Samantha's eyes readjusted to the gathering darkness.

Pull it together, girlie. Just a man visiting family like you.

She was too jumpy. Must be the storm.

***

The manila envelope burned against his flesh, as if reminding Joe of the dishonorable duty he undertook. If the chief found out, all hell would break loose across the City of Wichita – maybe even the entire state. He'd probably get demoted back to street cop too, but the potential disgrace did nothing to deter him as he pulled out of the precinct parking lot and flipped on the headlights.

At first Sam had been the one to stop by the precinct or call him every couple of days to see if anything new had shown up on the radar. In the beginning she'd remained subtle, but as the weeks went by and her frustration grew, demands for copies of the file contents were nothing short of blatant. She had to know he couldn't just hand over investigative material, but in Sam's case emotion always outweighed logic.

Apparently the logic disease had infected him too. When he'd first started the duplicate file, it was under the auspices of running it over to his buds at the Bureau to see if there were any connections between his case and one of theirs. But if he were even a hint honest with himself, this plan had been percolating in his mind all along.

He wanted to see Sam. He wanted to spend time with her. He wanted to worm his way back into her good graces. He wanted her to stay.

He wanted her – plain and simple.

Lightning flashed as he rounded the corner and pulled up to the old familiar house. The house remained as dark as the sky. Sam wasn't home.

Joe stared at the windows of the upper loft and remembered the times he'd climbed the backyard tree onto the roof. They'd laid out there all hours of the night and gazed at the stars. Sometimes they'd made out, but the rough shingles kept his hormones in check. Then there was the fact that her grandmother's room rested beneath them, and older people tended to be light sleepers.

One afternoon burned in his memory. He'd stopped by to see if she'd wanted to go grab a burger, but since Gramm hadn't returned from grocery shopping he'd decided to wait until she arrived home. In the meantime, Sam wanted to show him the storm shelter – she always referred to it as the 'fraidy hole – and in the cool darkness they'd nearly gone too far. Even now, he could still remember the softness of her beneath him, smell the scent of her skin, feel the intensity of their youthful passion.

The crash of thunder brought his racing heart back to the present. Joe unbuttoned his shirt and pulled out the thick manila envelope moistened by his skin. The air hinted at the approaching rain as he dashed to the front porch and inserted the thick envelope between the screen and door.

***

After swinging through a drive-thru, Samantha headed back to Gramm's, the first tinges of rain sprinkling the windshield as she pulled into the drive. An envelope fell out when she opened the screen door, and she recognized the handwriting immediately – Joe. The warmth of the envelope told her she'd missed him only moments before, and a strange ache nudged her heart as she entered the dark house and flipped on the lights before pouring the contents onto the table.

The dining room table lay littered with the array of newspaper clippings and reports which she quickly scanned through, but the photos were what arrested her attention. They depicted the burned-out car, skid marks, and a group of bystanders. But it was the up-close charred remains that stopped her cold. Tears blurred her vision.

Joe had tried to warn her. The guy was too honorable for his own good. She wished she hadn't yelled at him. If only she'd been at the house when he'd arrived. His arms were needed. Joe always gave the nicest hugs at just the right moment. But only emptiness consumed her.

Thoughts of Joe's warm brown eyes still curled her toes. When they'd been young, she'd loved running her fingers through his sunny hair. Then his desire of becoming a police detective came between them. In her short life she'd already endured enough loss, and the idea of waiting up late at night, wondering if he'd ever come home, was too much to contemplate. There always seemed to be a good reason to break up with every guy she'd ever dated – at least at the time. Since then medical school and residency hadn't allowed for much of a social life, much less a real date.

The storm gathered force and the sky opened up with a blaze of lightning and a peal of thunder. Samantha flicked on the TV to check the weather report. Another surprise of Gramm's was an updated television and, of all things, cable even after the countless arguments of *but all my friends have cable* they'd had over the years. The lame excuse had never worked on Gramm.

With the TV blaring in the background, Samantha sorted through the clippings for the hundredth time. At least that's how it seemed. The coroner's report, newspaper stories, obituary, registration of the Saturn, pictures of the scene – it all required Samantha to put on her forensic investigative hat and put aside the fact that what she read about and saw had involved Gramm.

Something in the pictures from the crash scene kept drawing her back. Samantha retrieved Gramm's magnifying glass she used to put around her neck in order to read and crochet very fine patterns. In the scenes, the setting sun made it difficult to distinguish much among the gathered spectators. Then again newsprint wasn't known for its clarity. The flames were still being extinguished in one, the edge of the crowd still visible. Another showed the firefighters and police cordoning off the highway.

What is it? What is it? Gramm, help me see whatever is bugging me.

After more than three hours bending over the photographs and clippings, Samantha gave up for the night, kneading her aching neck to release the tension. The storm had turned into a steady rain, and after checking the weather report one last time, she headed up the stairs to turn in for the night.

A nagging feeling tugged at the back of her mind about those pictures. Reading in bed didn't distract her. Two chapters sped by and Samantha had no idea what she'd even read. In frustration, she slammed down the book and flicked off the light. Sleep would be hard coming.

As her mind drifted and body relaxed it came to her. Samantha shot straight up in bed, the iridescent numbers on the clock reading one thirty-seven. It was him – the guy in sunglasses standing by the tent after Gramm's funeral. That same guy was in two of the camera shots at the crash scene.

Samantha leapt down the stairs and slid into the dining room, flipping on the light as she stumbled to the table. She drew the photos close under the magnifying glass. Goose bumps chased each other up her spine as the man in sunglasses peered out from behind the fire truck in one and near the front of the bystanders in another.

"Well hello, Mr. Shades."

CHAPTER 8 - SOMEONE'S WATCHING

"Damn it, Joe! You know I'm not crazy."

If Joe didn't do something and stop treating her like some sort of imbecile Samantha would go right over his paper strewn desk and strangle him. Yeah right – in the middle of the police department. At least they wouldn't have to drag her too far to book her into jail for murder.

The precinct boiled with activity, phones blaring and people yelling across cubicles looking as bleary eyed as she. Samantha had barely slept after her discovery last night and couldn't wait to get in front of Joe's face. Maybe she should've gone through with her initial instinct to call him in the middle of the night. A sleep-deprived brain might have made him a little more compliant. Now he just looked at her with those soft brown eyes as if he were placating a kitten down from a tree.

"Keep it down, Sam," Joe whispered. "I'd be in a heap of hot water if the chief knew I'd given you copies of those reports. Don't know now why I even did."

"And I don't know why I actually expected you to do something about this," Samantha hissed.

She even sounded like a cat. *Get it under control, girlie.*

Samantha took a deep breath. "You've got to admit, it is a bit odd that this same man from the scene shows up just a week later at Gramm's funeral."

"But you don't even know if it's the same man," Joe countered.

Samantha felt about ready to jam the guy's nose into the pictures scattered on the desk. Might balance out the little crook left when he'd gotten his nose broken in that fight in high school.

"Look at the dark slicked back hair, the squared jaw line – at Gramm's funeral he was in a black suit but I think here it's a sport coat. But the shades. Why would he wear sunglasses that time of the evening and then at Gramm's funeral when it was cloudy and dreary?"

Joe rubbed his temples. Usually that meant she had him right where she wanted him, but he wasn't the same old Joe from high school.

"Come on, Sam. You admitted earlier you didn't get but a glance at him the day of the funeral." Joe's voice softened as he laid his hand on top of hers. "Things were real tough for you that day, I'm sure."

The warmth of his touch created a knot in Samantha's stomach. Jerking her hand away, she gathered her purse and stuffed the envelope and its contents back in it, the chair almost toppling over as she stood.

"Yeah, something you couldn't possibly understand."

Samantha stormed out of the office and fled down the stairs of the city building, Joe's protests dying in the background. The Wichita wind felt good on her face, the air clean and crisp after the night of rain. Though too angry to cry, nothing she did stemmed the warm tears from gathering beneath her eyelids. She drew her jacket tighter. A brisk walk would do her good.

Maybe she should stop by and talk to Mr. Eddis. His law firm sat just a short jaunt down Main Street and would make a good stretch of the legs. Perhaps he might listen to her conclusions on *her* investigation. Obviously she wouldn't get too much more out of Joe and his cronies – taxpayer money simply wasted. Good thing she hadn't mentioned the guy at the cemetery last night, or else Joe would have called the men in white to bring a straight jacket.

The wind roared around the corner of the city building. Perhaps a cut through the alley would shorten her walk to Mr. Eddis', but would he be available? His schedule was always constricted. Did she have any real purpose in seeing Mr. Eddis and wasting his time with her ramblings? No question he'd hear her out because he knew how much this meant to her.

Thankfully the alley offered protection from the biting wind, but instead of the sun's warmth she walked in shadow. The shadows brought Mr. Shades to mind.

Samantha tried to capture the image of him from the funeral again, but Joe was right. She'd only caught a glimpse of him in passing and hadn't thought anymore about him for a month. Then the pictures had brought it all flashing back. Last night it had seemed so clear.

Rocks clattered. A glance over her shoulder and she stood immobile, her limbs frozen as if winter had returned. Shades walked along the far end of the alley. He didn't act as if he were afraid of being discovered. To the contrary, he acted as if he wanted her to know he was there. For a moment, Samantha wanted to charge up to him and bash his head against the brick wall, demand to know who he was and what he had to do with Gramm's death. Then something inside her screamed.

Run!

Samantha took off like a shot. She'd always been a good track runner in high school, star of the hundred yard sprint. Took second in state. Well this would be a bit more than a hundred yards. As she exited the alley, she didn't even bother glancing behind as she practically flew across the street and dodged light traffic.

She yanked the heavy glass door open, the burst of adrenaline too much as the wind fought to keep it closed. The curtains in the glassed-in foyer hid her as she searched for any sign of Shades. Her breath came in gasps as she filled her lungs.

Gotta get back in shape, girlie.

With a sense of satisfaction, Samantha realized she'd

outrun the creep. The satisfaction melted into frustration as it occurred to her – she may have lost her chance at finding out who the guy was, and more importantly what he had to do with Gramm's accident.

And what he wanted with her.

CHAPTER 9 - A NOTE

Paranoia settled over her as Samantha glanced back and
forth past the gravestones and scattered trees of the
cemetery. After the strange morning and the near run-in
with Shades, she decided it best to have a talk with Momma
while plenty of daylight remained.

When she'd shown up at Mr. Eddis' office, he'd been
patient and attentive while she'd spoken of the eerie
encounter in the alley, showed him the photos from the
crash, and told of seeing Shades at Gramm's funeral. But in
the safety of his law office, Samantha hadn't felt the rush of
panic any longer and instead berated herself for not
following through on her first instinct to confront the guy.

All through her ramblings, Mr. Eddis tapped his lips in
thought. He'd asked a few questions and even wondered if
she felt it best to have someone look after her for awhile,
suggested a security system at Gramm's house and added it
would be a nice sales benefit when the time came. But it had
all seemed a bit strange and overbearing to think she, of all
people, would need such *protection*. That was what

Hollywood stars had to deal with, not near medical school dropouts.

After leaving the law firm, Samantha had aimlessly driven for hours until making her way to the lonely cemetery. The antsy feeling returned. It didn't make sense for someone to bother her, dare she even say *stalk* her. Her head pounded from the rushing thoughts.

After telling Momma of the day's strange events, Samantha calmed again and leaned her aching head against the cool marble. She imagined leaning against Momma's shoulder again like when she was a little girl. Longing rose within her.

"I miss you both so much, Momma. I never had a chance until now to stop long enough to tell you. Don't think I could have put into words what I felt back then anyway. But since Gramm died…"

The tears came in unending torrents.

***

With a start, Samantha awoke disoriented and chilled. The cemetery. Momma and Daddy's graves.

As her head cleared, she remembered the drive to the cemetery and her conversation with Momma. Her racing heart stabilized. She stretched her stiffened limbs and back, gathered up her purse and headed to the car. Head down into the wind, she stuffed her hands into her jacket pockets to warm them.

A slip of paper brushed her hand, and Samantha drew the small square from her pocket. She couldn't remember putting anything in there this morning, and she didn't make shopping lists. Besides, she always put notes in her purse so they wouldn't blow away.

Fear crept over her like an icy hand as she unfolded the note and stared at the unfamiliar handwriting.

Find the key.

As she quickened her pace to her car, she was certain of only one thing.

Somewhere nearby he watched.

CHAPTER 10 - SECRETS UNRAVEL

The month of April dragged closer to May while Mr. Eddis continued working Gramm's estate. If not for the note, Samantha would have thought the whole of events with Shades had been a dream. Nothing had happened since the eerie moment in the cemetery and the alleyway chase, but she continued to be watchful.

The television blared in the background about the body of a missing Kansas politician, but the pictures of Shades hanging on the dining room wall drew her focus. He stared back from the image as if taunting her with his presence. Who was he? Where did he come from, and most importantly, what did he want with her?

A key. *Find the key*. Did he actually mean a physical key for a lock or a key like for a map? What did he want her to find this mysterious key for? Not until Samantha decided to rummage around in Gramm's room did she begin to find an answer to her questions.

In the top linen drawer Samantha shuffled through

Gramm's personal effects, expecting at any moment to hear Gramm's familiar outcry against snooping. She'd give her arm to hear the righteous indignation of Gramm's voice. But never again.

I miss you so much, Gramm.

A safe deposit box key surfaced from beneath a lavender sachet. The tag referenced number 2386. Gramm had always kept her accounts with a small locally-owned bank, so she figured that was the best place to check.

***

A quick call to Mr. Eddis on the drive over confirmed he'd already filed a copy of the death certificate with Gramm's branch. The branch manager said since she wasn't on the safe deposit box as a signer she couldn't remove anything just merely inventory it. Fine with her.

After providing her with an inventory sheet, they set up camp in a privacy booth. The shouts of an angry customer echoed through the branch, his pounding on the counter displaying obnoxious disregard for others. The manager excused herself momentarily and said she would send another employee over if she couldn't come back right away.

Samantha laid everything out on the table. Wasn't much, just a few jewelry boxes, bonds, and what appeared to be an insurance policy of sorts. Mr. Eddis needed to know about the policy and bonds, however nothing about the contents suggested anything unusual. Upon picking up the box for one last glance she heard a rattle. Slipping her hand all the way toward the end, Samantha wrapped her fingers around a metal object partially taped to the side.

A key.

Samantha's heart raced. The manager hadn't returned or sent anyone else to replace her. Before conscience engaged, she slipped the key into her purse and continued compiling the inventory list.

Someone knocked at the door and entered to replace the manager, a young thing hardly out of high school. Harmless enough. With a belying calm, Samantha opened the jewelry boxes to be certain of their contents, steadied her quaking hand and finished the list while little Miss Prom Queen admired the few pieces of Gramm's nice jewelry.

Once completed, they replaced the contents and the box while Samantha secured her copy of the inventory sheet. With the key snug in her purse, she left the bank and called Mr. Eddis.

***

Samantha puttered east along the highway, Gramm's deviation puzzling. Gramm had never banked out of town in her life, at least not that she'd ever known, the location more than inconvenient. A search of Mr. Eddis' records revealed another safe deposit box for Gramm in the nearby small town.

No telling if either of the safe deposit box keys were the key mentioned in the note from the cemetery. She didn't even care anymore. It wasn't like she planned to turn either one over to them. Who the hell were *them* anyway?

This time she'd not get the same opportunity to take anything found in the box. Couldn't ask for the stars to shine on her twice in one day. Mr. Eddis didn't need to know of her clandestine activities in taking the second key from the safe deposit box, so tomorrow she'd nonchalantly drop off the inventory list from both banks to show her reasoning for her questions. It would be enough just to see whatever the box contained. No rush.

The service representative asked her to sign in to enter the box.

"But I'm not a box holder, just needing to inventory for the estate," Samantha explained.

"Well according to our records you were registered and signed as a box holder almost eight years ago. You are Samantha Bartlett?" The lady eyed her momentarily.

"Last time I checked. Here's my driver's license, but I don't remember signing anything."

Apparently satisfied with her signature and identification, the representative smiled. "It's amazing what one can forget in eight years."

Samantha bit back the rising retort and managed a smile. No need to bite the hand that feeds. The employee set her in a privacy booth and shut the door. Just for safety's sake, Samantha snapped the door lock into place and stared at the box. It was smaller and much lighter than the previous one. Something slid when she tilted the box.

Inside she found a cellophane sleeve encasing a tiny

silver device, almost square and very thin like a miniature thumb drive. The casing appeared metal with a slight opening at one end, fitting easily into the small of her hand. Samantha held it up to the light but could see nothing through it. She tried to pry it apart with her fingernails but broke a nail instead.

Enough time wasted. Samantha tucked the item back into the sleeve then into her purse and had the representative put away the box. The drive back to Gramm's presented more questions. She needed some answers before her head exploded from overload.

The car practically skidded into the driveway. Samantha scoured the bookshelves and desk drawers while she tried to decide where Gramm would keep a note or list. Then it came to her – Gramm's Bible. Important papers were kept there for some strange reason.

With no concern for sacrilege, Samantha grabbed the Bible off Gramm's nightstand, flipped it over, opened it up and shook the hell out of it. Several slips of paper tumbled to the floor, but the item that caught Samantha's eye was a small envelope yellowed with age. The envelope flap crackled as if it hadn't been opened in a generation.

A blood test.

On her.

The date read May 26th, ten days after her birth. The words of the notice gave her a jolt.

Her Daddy – wasn't.

CHAPTER 11 – MR. PRESIDENT

Chief of Staff, Benjamin Forsdale hustled down the hallway toward the Oval Office, the rooms he sped past aflutter with the morning's activities. Staff cowed and offered their morning greetings as he stormed through the secretarial pool. The President would not be happy with this news.

The new redheaded bombshell was absent from her station. Ben coughed to hide the smile that momentarily crept to his lips. His pulse quickened. The scene merely awaited behind the closed door. Placing the folder beneath his arm, Ben opened the door to the Oval Office and slipped inside.

She was doing more than a lap dance with her little black skirt wrapped up around her waist, her tight ass straddling the President and grinding hard. Warner had her blue blouse wide open, suckling her enormous tits like a ravenous pup. Ben knew when she'd showed up two Mondays ago that Warner would have her. He certainly hadn't wasted any time.

The hottie started with a squeal when Ben slammed the door. Warner grabbed her hips as she started to rise and smacked her back into place. She recovered from the surprise and moaned with desire.

Warner growled as he lifted his face from his landscape of pleasure, "A moment, Forsdale."

"Yes, Mr. President." Ben turned to face the wall.

The activity behind him resumed and doubled in intensity, the breathing and grunting coming in rapid gasps. From his vantage point Ben listened and imagined himself in such ecstasies. His dick swelled and grew hard. For a moment he wanted nothing more than to whip it out and foam the wall, but someone had to maintain their composure in this office. As the groans and suckles behind him grew, Ben forced his thoughts to the folder's contents and slowly the pressure against his zipper eased.

The breathless pleasantries behind him escalated, and Ben knew the time had come.

"Oh, Mr. President," the girl cried.

After Warner spent himself and scurried the young thing off to clean up in the side office, Ben left his musings and sidled up to the President's desk.

"Ah, Forsdale, there's no better way to start the morning than to follow breakfast with a tit chaser," Warner laughed, as he slipped on his glasses and smoothed his hair.

Ben joined him. "Well when you're done with this one, I

wouldn't mind if you put in a good word for me."

Warner winked. "As always." The President lit a stogie and relaxed in his chair. "So what's on your mind today, Mr. Chief of Staff?"

Ben became serious as he briefed the President. "First off, Vice President Durksen's office has requested a meeting this afternoon."

"The man doesn't know when to let up," Warner mumbled. "Fine. What else?"

"We're 99% certain at this stage – Congressman Rains was just the latest victim. The Elite have surfaced again."

Anger turned Warner's eyes coal black. The artery in his neck throbbed as he ground out the cigar. "What are the bastards up to now? Where have they emerged?"

"The last couple of months show New York, Virginia, and Kansas."

Warner muttered as he closed his eyes and rubbed his temples. Ben marveled at the President's incredible capacity to recall almost every incident in his entire political career. The political arena activities forever found a resting place within the man's mind and were retrieved by simply sorting through the files of his brain cells like a librarian sorting through an old card catalog. Ben toyed with the folder as he waited for the expected.

With a start, Warner slammed his fists on the Resolute desk and hissed through clenched teeth. "They're trying to get to *her*."

Ben smiled with satisfaction and placed the open file before the President, who scanned the top page and the photograph. Warner stated coldly the only thing to be done.

"Take care of it, Ben."

"Yes, Mr. President."

Tucking the folder beneath his arm, Ben once again strode from the room and called to the secretarial pool.

"Get me a secure line to the FBI."

CHAPTER 12 - THE KEYHOLE

Wild ivy trailed across the gravestones like the veins of a corpse. Samantha could hardly forgive herself for her absence since the awful discovery in Gramm's Bible, but her stomach churned every time the questions of her parentage returned. Answers – she'd so wanted answers to her questions. Now all she wanted was to forget the past, but it clung to her mind like a never-ending fog. Life remained stuck in a vortex pulling her backward.

Carefully Samantha cleared away the primrose vine and deposited the daisies into the canister between the two headstones. A long-ago memory cut through her murky thoughts – Momma tending the pink calla lilies amid clusters of white daisies swaying in the breeze, the warm Washington sun streaming down on her white hat. Momma had always worn that white straw hat when she gardened.

Protects my dewy skin from wrinkles, she had said.

"Here're a few daisies for you, Momma," Samantha said stiffly. "I picked them myself from Gramm's garden."

The other grave beckoned beyond an unshed veil of tears – *John William Bartlett*. A knot formed in her throat, but still she couldn't bring herself to say or even think the word 'Daddy' ever again. Had he known? The question slashed through her heart like shards of glass. Momma had always said anyone could be a father but it took someone special to be a daddy. She never realized the impact of those words until the discovery.

"How could you have done this to me, Momma?" Samantha whispered through gritted teeth. "To…to your husband? Even Mr. Eddis knew the truth."

As the dam breached, anger overtook her with a flood of raging turmoil as she paced back and forth. "What was it? An affair? Is this why you left Kansas? Were you trying to keep the truth from…him? Why didn't you ever tell me, Momma? Me! Do you know how humiliating it feels to discover that everyone else knew but me?"

Tears spilled hot down her cheeks. When Mr. Eddis had acknowledged her findings she'd felt as if she had been struck across the face. But he held no further answers to her bitter questions. If not John Bartlett, then who? Gramm had held onto that stupid paternity test all these years, but to what purpose? She was nothing but a bastard child, the product of a woman she no longer knew – perhaps had never known. Had she ever really known any of her family?

The sun glinted off the smooth carving of the headstone, the glare stinging her already blurred vision. Something appeared out of place. The carved cross above Momma's name stood out as she swiped again at her eyes. Caution whispered on the summer wind before realization struck. Samantha dug into her purse and drew out the tiny mysterious chip discovered in Gramm's safe deposit box.

The angle of the sun glinted momentarily off a sliver of metal in the carved edge of the cross, the gray coating blending into the marble except where it had since worn. Tentatively Samantha leaned closer, slid the chip from the cellophane sleeve and pressed the open end into the slot with an almost imperceptible click.

It fit perfectly.

A marble panel of the headstone slid aside to reveal a tiny screen like a computer touchpad. Samantha glanced around, and chills raced one another up and down her arms even under the heat of the Kansas sun. How had Gramm hidden such a thing in a headstone? For what purpose? What provided power for it after all these years?

Samantha shook her head to stem the questions. For a moment she didn't want anymore revelations rocking her fragile world, but the questions clung to her mind like cobwebs. Maybe if she took a risk, she might find answers to satisfy her once and for all and be rid of the past. She slid her finger along the pad. With a hiss like a dying breath, the screen withdrew and the headstone panel closed.

Nothing happened.

The wait seemed interminable. Maybe the funeral home had some new gadgetry on their headstones for some ungodly reason. Samantha felt like an idiot. What did she expect – involvement in a spy game?

Just as she dismissed the cloak and dagger thoughts, a small steel box ejected from a compartment beneath the flower canister. It appeared thin and rectangular like a small cash box. Samantha's heart pounded.

"Momma, what is this?" Samantha whispered. "What's going on?" Her mouth felt like she'd swallowed a package of crackers. "Should I be afraid?"

The whisper in her mind spoke a dreadful answer.

With a quick hand Samantha grabbed the box, slipped it under her T-shirt and snapped shut the compartment. Nonchalantly she rested her hand against the headstone over the cross and bowed her head as if to say goodbye. Shades very well might be watching. As she drew her hand away, she grasped the tiny chip and dropped it back into her purse while she fished out her car keys.

Samantha clutched her purse to her abdomen and tried to remain calm as she strolled to the car. But behind her purse, she gripped the little box that contained something she instinctively knew would bring another wave of change like the crash of a squall line.

CHAPTER 13 - THE FACE OF DEATH

Samantha fought to focus on the road as she careened a circuitous route along Wichita's highways and back to Gramm's house. Her palms left sweat streaks all over the steering wheel.

Get a grip, girlie!

After plowing into the driveway, she slipped into the house through the back door, clutching the precious cargo. The house was dark in the growing dusk. Shadows crept along the walls like silent stalkers.

Shades.

Samantha tore through the house and drew the shades and curtains to stem the shadows. She willed herself to breathe normally and listened. All was quiet on the home front. Still she didn't dare turn on the main lights and instead clicked on a small lamp perched on the dining room desk.

He might be out there.

The box clanked in the stillness when Samantha placed it on the desk. It glared in the light of the lamp. Her body shuddered. What could be so earth-shattering to have caused someone to hide the contents in her mother's gravestone? Images of the fireball that had taken her parents exploded in her mind. She scratched her leg as she remembered the itchy crinoline skirt that day then rubbed the old scar. Nothing about her life made sense anymore. She watched it go by as if through a kaleidoscope, everything topsy-turvy, twisted, and wrong. If only to go back to New York and pretend nothing from the last couple of months had occurred – impossible.

With trembling hands she pried the steel lid off. Papers yellowed with age nested inside. Carefully Samantha sorted through the small pile: birth certificates, a marriage license, drivers licenses and passports. They contained her parents' pictures but had someone else's names.

Her parents must have involved themselves in some crazy ID scam or mafia group. But that didn't ring true. Maybe CIA. No matter how angry Samantha felt with them, they couldn't have been thieves and murderers – could they?

An envelope remained. The flap cracked in her hands as she tentatively slid out the pages of a letter. She could almost hear her mother's voice as she read the words in a familiar script.

My dear Samantha,

If you are reading this letter then my sorrow is complete. If we do not return safely, the Elite will send you the appropriate documentation. Our involvement started innocently enough, or so we thought. We felt we were doing a great service to our country, but more and more I have questioned that decision.

Our demise was probably swift and painless, so don't concern yourself with what we likely didn't feel. No matter how it happened, we have loved you always. You brought such joy into our lonely lives. I only wish it had lasted longer for all our sakes. Now you must know the truth.

Your dad and I were not able to have children. For many years we had tried but were unsuccessful. That's how we knew you were likely his.

I interned in his office during summers home from college and eventually was offered a full-time position. He was merely a state legislator then but powerful and very charismatic. Your dad thought the world of him.

It happened during the fall campaign for governor. We'd always heard he was a bit of a womanizer, he had such charm, but I was still a bit naïve concerning his ways. I'd never seen him act improperly in the office. That's why I went ahead and accepted his offer to work on the campaign trail.

The weeks of travel left everyone exhausted but enthused as we neared the end. That's when it happened. No one responded to my cries for help as he raped me. Your dad wanted to kill the man when

*he found out, but no DA had the spine to touch the
case. Then we found out you were on the way, a ray
of light in our darkness. We had hopes you were
truly ours, but the blood test told a different story.*

*Samantha, stay far away from him. Do not
attempt to contact him for I shudder to think what
he may do, but the truth must be yours to bear now.
John Bartlett will always be your daddy, but
biologically you are the child of Frederick Warner.*

The blood drained from Samantha's face as the letter
fluttered to the floor. She couldn't read anymore. She felt
faint. Sick. Her *father* was now the President of the United
States. Her breath came in gasps and hiccups.

Hold on, girlie. Don't pass out now.

Through the physical nausea and mental pain, Samantha
gulped in a foul breath. She willed herself to slow her
breathing but the stench remained.

Natural gas.

The box. The documents. Samantha stared at the letter
on the floor as if disembodied. How long had she breathed
in the noxious fumes? Shades must have seen her collect the
box from the cemetery. He'd followed her home, rigged the
house. They were going to kill her – silence her just as they
had her parents.

Samantha staggered to the living room and ripped the
rug from the floor. She couldn't let Shades see her trying to
leave. He probably waited outside for her to set foot on the

front porch to slam a bullet through her skull. Well she'd fool him. He'd never expect her to remain inside the house.

The old 'fraidy hole was still there. Quickly she flung back the trap door leading to the concrete storm cellar built under the front porch, then stumbled into the stairwell's darkness.

Her ears rang, felt the heat from the explosion before passing into unconsciousness.

***

Joe stared at the charred remains that had once been Sam's home. The embers glowed in the darkness, the hiss of steam echoing as the fire department flushed the hot spots. The surrounding homes had taken quite a beating as well. Looked like the one behind might be saved, but the two on either side were toast. The neighbors across the street had all their windows shattered. The explosion must have been enormous.

Joe tried to make notes for the investigation, but he couldn't push aside thoughts of Sam. No trace of a body thus far, but her car, or at least the remains of her car, had been tossed into the dining room of the house next door. No body there either.

The nub of the pencil eraser popped back into his mouth as he tried to focus. If she'd gone for a walk the explosion would have brought her back before now. Out with friends? Well Sam wasn't known for keeping too many friends these days – except the Eddises, but the couple hadn't seen her for several weeks. If she'd gone back to New York he'd have known. Something didn't add up.

If the explosion had been caused by a natural gas leak, as the fire department suspected, she may have asphyxiated before realizing a problem. However, natural gas had a unique scent she would've recognized, unless she'd been taking a nap. Even so, they'd still found no trace of remains in the obliterated heap.

Joe allowed his mind to go where he'd not allowed before. Had he missed something important? Had someone actually targeted Sam and her family? What of this mysterious guy with the sunglasses that had so gained her attentions? Was the explosion a means to eliminate evidence – evidence that he'd provided? If needed, where would Sam have hidden it?

The 'fraidy hole.

He grabbed a flashlight and the heavy work gloves he kept in the car. Running over to where the front porch used to be, Joe slipped on the pair of gloves before hefting debris from the general area.

"Some help here," Joe yelled to the firefighters.

Someone turned the floodlights in his direction as two other firefighters reached in to assist. The smoldering debris warmed up the gloves fast, but Joe didn't allow the pain to stop him while there remained even the slightest chance she'd survived.

The memory made Joe's heart pound with hope. They'd almost lost their virginity that evening in the old storm bunker. That had been the closest Sam had ever allowed him to see into her soul. Just a brief glimpse of her agony before hormones had overtaken him. Why hadn't he let her talk instead of trying to get it on with her? Sure taught him a lesson that night, especially when her grandmother came back from the store.

"Hey, there's concrete under here," called a firefighter. "Looks like some stairs."

They'd uncovered the passage, but the cement was cracked and broken over the stairwell. After working to clear the fallen chunks, Joe found the remainder of the stairs mostly intact. He flicked on his flashlight and started down.

"The walls are probably weakened, Detective. We should reinforce it before anyone goes down there."

Joe ignored him and continued down the damp stairwell. He'd probably get an earful from the chief in the morning. The acrid air filled his lungs. A haze hung around him and stung his eyes.

"Sam?" His voice merely echoed.

Was she down here? If so, what condition would her body be in? It always felt different being on a scene when you knew the victim. Anxiety sat like a rock in his stomach.

Miraculously the walls and ceiling appeared secure as the door squealed in protest. No fissures or gaping holes in the cement. Whoever had built this shelter definitely knew what they were doing, but a good foot of water pooled on the floor. The possibility of Sam drowning hadn't even entered his mind.

"Sam, answer me!"

Joe coughed as he scanned the room, shining the flashlight across the floor while he sloshed the grid. Back and forth he crisscrossed the room, hoping his feet would run into something then alternately squelching that hope if it meant they'd drowned her. The light glinted off the water until he arrived back at the stairwell. His bittersweet hope was lost as another flashlight shimmied down the stairs and shone into his eyes.

"She's gone."

CHAPTER 14 - AN INTRODUCTION

The lights blurred. It hurt to breathe. The room spun. A distinctive steady beep in the recesses of her consciousness drew her up from the dark pit.

Samantha blinked in an attempt to still the spiraling room. The bright lights glared. As her awareness grew, she felt the presence of an oxygen mask covering her nose and mouth. Where was she?

A face materialized. The dark cropped hair. Chiseled features. Piercing blue eyes. Something about him seemed familiar.

Samantha attempted to speak, her voice raspy and hollow. "Where am I?"

The man acknowledged her. "You have decided to rejoin the land of the living, I see." His voice was deep and all business.

After he wrote something on the chart and read the monitor beside the bed, he pressed his hand to her forehead.

His starched lab coat quivered like butterfly wings each time he moved.

Butterflies.

Samantha's mind drifted. She saw her mother in a white straw hat walking through a meadow, butterflies flittering all around her. Her mother reached out and allowed them to rest along her arms. Samantha ran to join her, but the butterflies kept getting in the way. They gathered and swarmed, turned gray then black. The black hole opened up and she felt as if she were falling, falling, falling.

She awoke with a start. He hovered at her side.

"Samantha?" His blue eyes were deep like the ocean waves below Washington's cliffs. They held the tiniest speck of concern.

"Are you a doctor?" Samantha asked. The oxygen mask fogged over.

"Just call me Dr. Marcus." He returned to business again.

The environs appeared stark and sterile like an operating room at one of New York's finest hospitals. But she'd gone back to Kansas, hadn't she?

"Where am I? What has happened?" Her tongue felt thick and clumsy.

The memories came crashing back. Gramm's death. The cemetery. The box. Ringing in her ears. An explosion. She tried to throw back the sheets and scramble from the bed but collapsed from the effort. The pain in her arm sent a shockwave through her body like a lightning bolt.

"Your residence is a medical facility in downtown Wichita."

Dr. Marcus grabbed her good wrist and searched for a pulse. He continued, "Someone didn't do their job well in constructing the entrance, but we've already dealt with that. There was a bit of a breach, and it allowed smoke to enter the safe room. We were almost too late in reaching you."

Fog muddled her brain. Samantha stared at him in confusion and pressed her hand to her temple when he released it. One phrase pierced the fog like an arrow.

"Safe room? H-how do you know about the 'fraidy hole?"

He again bent over the chart to scribble something concerning her condition and checked her IV bag. What was her condition exactly? The room swam. Fatigue clawed its way through her body like a lioness in the shadows waiting for her prey.

"Because we built it."

Dr. Marcus strode from the room as Samantha lapsed into unconsciousness.

***

The media circus had already begun as Joe pulled into the parking lot of Castor Construction's administrative offices. The vultures. One could hardly blame them though, when word crossed the airways of the CEO's death – shot down in broad daylight in his own office.

Chief Snowe directed him to park at the side of the building, and he got out. "Let me distract the media while you run upstairs."

"Got it, Chief."

Death had surrounded him for years, but he didn't look forward to the job at hand. Sam's death last week had hit him hard, and he'd had a difficult time shaking it off. Truth be told, her passing had hit him harder than even his own mother's six years ago. Mom's life and body had deteriorated slow and steady – cancer. They'd had time to deal with the reality, had time to say goodbye. Mom had been at peace.

Sam was another story. The longer she'd stuck around town, the more he'd allowed himself to toy with the idea that they'd make another go of it. He'd convinced himself that she just needed time to deal with Gramm's passing, that she'd eventually take his calls when she was ready. He could wait.

Where had waiting gotten him?

Police personnel greeted him as he made his way through the maze and into the far office. Albert Castor's body sat slumped in his chair, blood splatters surrounding the bullet hole in the window behind him. Good luck finding that slug. After Joe gave the okay, the medical examiner bagged and tagged the body. Nothing on the desk appeared to be disturbed, just a set of blood-spattered blueprints Mr.

Castor had been reviewing. Joe collected the notes from the secretary's interview and scanned them for any appearance of inconsistency. He'd follow up with her before he left.

Considering the recent demise of his father, Joe was surprised to see the elder son present and being interrogated in the far corner. Manny Castor stood to inherit a vast sum of money, not to mention the power of the largest construction conglomerate in the Midwest. Though the man's eyes remained focused on his interviewer, Joe felt the coldness of the dark, beady gaze watching him out of the corners of his eyes. He'd never backed down from a challenge before, direct or subtle.

Joe interrupted and stuck out his hand. "Mr. Castor? Detective Joe Roberts."

The beady eyes directed their full attention toward him but a hand remained unoffered. "Detective."

"Excuse my intrusion, but wouldn't you be more comfortable conducting the interview down the hall?"

"I've spent more time in this office over the years than my own, Detective. My father's death doesn't change that."

"Were you in here when the assailant arrived?"

The man had the audacity to smile. "One of the rare and, dare I say it, lucky moments when I was not."

Joe glanced back over the notes from the secretary's interview. "The secretary said you'd left this office a few minutes before the shooting, that she'd heard a sharp disagreement about the same time."

"Yes, to grab another set of blueprints for comparison to the ones on my father's desk. We were arguing about a problem on a previous project."

"Where is the other set of blueprints?"

"I hadn't located them before I heard the shots."

"And you didn't see anyone run out of the office?"

"No."

Manny Castor wasn't going to give them any information, even if he knew something – and Joe would bet his measly pension the man knew more.

Much more.

***

Two men stood talking near the foot of her hospital bed while several others stood silent near the doorway. Sleep had dissipated the fog in her head. Then she remembered his name – Dr. Marcus.

The doctor spoke. "How are you feeling now?"

Samantha watched him with focused eyes. "Better, I guess."

Dr. Marcus didn't write anything on her chart but only watched her, stared deeply into her eyes as if groping her mind. Samantha's flesh crawled but she stared back in defiance. Dr. Marcus' lips curled into a smile.

He leaned toward the other man and whispered, "See, she'll do well indeed."

Narrowing her eyes, Samantha firmed up her position. "Tell me what's going on here or so help me, I'm calling the entire damn nursing staff."

The other man, much older and almost frail looking, shuffled around the bed and came alongside. "You may call me simply Debrille."

Debrille's beady eyes looked like someone had bored holes into his head with an ice pick. His voice sounded pinched with a bad French accent, stature short, and his gray hair cropped like the doctor.

Debrille continued, "I am arrived from a long journey, my dear, to offer you a once in a lifetime opportunity."

"Okay, *Simply Debrille*, first tell me where I am. I don't recognize this hospital."

Samantha glanced again. Wasn't any of the Wichita hospitals she was familiar with. Wait, Dr. Marcus had said something about being downtown. Perhaps Riverside.

A smug smile glanced off of Debrille's face. "You are in a state-of-the-art facility of my own making. I have many such facilities scattered around the world. In this part, we have done much work these past few decades."

"I don't understand."

Debrille settled himself into the nearby plush armchair. "This may take some time to explain."

He removed his red tie and held it into the air. One of the doorway goons captured it then returned to his post.

Debrille continued, "I have dedicated my life to rooting out corruption – invested and spent my fortune many times over to create an underground labyrinth of research labs, medical facilities, housing units, and safe houses connected to the world above. I prefer to surround myself with the best minds and hands to assist in carrying out my quest. We can move about in corporate and political circles the world over, protect the common man from the corruption of the powerful, then slip away into the night without a trace. We are seen when we wish to be seen."

His eyes bored into Samantha's. "How would you like to avenge yourself on the man who put you into this bed?"

Samantha hesitated. A dull ache crept up her neck and gripped the base of her skull. "What are you saying? You know who caused the explosion?"

Debrille snapped his fingers. Dr. Marcus slipped a photograph from the clipboard and handed it to Samantha.

"Do you recognize this man?" asked Debrille.

Samantha's heart went cold at his words. The photograph quaked. Tears of rage sprang to her eyes. Samantha held in her hands the photo of a leering rapist – a picture of President Frederick Warner.

Her father.

Without thought of the pain in her arm, Samantha

ripped the photo in two, then again, and again until the tiny pieces pooled upon the sheet. She stared at Debrille through a veil of tears.

"How do you know this? How do you know who I am? How did you know where to find me after the explosion?"

Debrille sat upon the edge of the chair, his body trembling, his fervor increasing with each word. "Because *I* ordered the construction of the safe house where you were found. Your parents worked for me. *He* killed your parents and your grandmother. *He* ordered your death. Now you must work for me.

"Because he will stop at nothing to silence you."

CHAPTER 15 - THE ELITE

The coldness in Samantha's soul gave her unstinting clarity of thought. Her mother's letter came to mind.

"You are the Elite." It was not a question anymore.

Debrille smiled, a sickening, twisted band of flesh. "Bravo. Bravo, my dear. You have the sharpness of your mother's mind. Perhaps her quickness too? Yes, second in state in the hundred yard sprint."

"I can't even begin to grasp how you know this about me, *why* you know this about me."

"We make it a point to know and understand everything about our own. We have protected you for many years, you see."

"Protected me? From what?"

"From your biological father."

"Don't ever call him *that* to me again."

Debrille chuckled and glanced again at Dr. Marcus. "I like her spirit. Yes, a temper just like his."

She didn't have to ask who Debrille meant by *his*.

"You see, my dear. We have watched your activities for many years, kept you outside of his radar. Covered your tracks. He never knew you had gone off to school in New York, but he found out about you again when you came back. You had to be taken out, you see, to keep you from being a thorn in his flesh. Now he and the entire world believe you to be dead."

Dead.

The word hung ominously in the air. She'd been surrounded by too much of its reality recently – hell, pretty much for her entire life and career.

"But surely someone saw you pull me from the fire – the rubble."

They couldn't have accomplished extracting her from all of that mess without being seen. It'd been just about dusk at the time of the explosion, plenty of light for the neighbors to see the activity. They would've all been searching for the cause of the noise and damage. Miracle this gang found her and got her out before the fire department arrived. Joe might be looking for her even now.

"No, my dear. We move underground. You were rescued via a connecting tunnel and brought here out of sight of any human eyes. The only thing anyone above will find is the rubble and assume you were consumed by the explosion."

The thought came down on her chest like a crushing weight. The world thought her dead. Joe thought her dead. No ties any longer to the land of the living, she'd become a mere wisp in the wind.

"How did you know I would even be down there?"

Debrille raised his brows matter-of-factly. "You are your mother's daughter."

Oh sure. That settled it in everyone's mind but her own. "What happens now?"

"It is very simple."

Debrille lit a cigarette and drew on it, blowing out the smoke like a deep and dangerous thought. The smoke dissipated the moment it went into the air. Good filtration in the ventilation systems. State of the art.

"As you now have no further ties to your world, we wish you to join ours."

"Join the Elite?"

What had her mother said about them in her letter? How she wished she still had that final link to Momma. But it, as well as her life, was now ashes to be blown about at the whim of a wind.

"Yes," Debrille stated. "There is now nothing to stop you."

"But I have bills, huge student loans that Gramm's estate

will never be able to repay."

"They are already paid, my dear. The wire has already been routed and re-routed to cover those costs. It is but a pittance in order to have you with us. Dr. Marcus will be able to continue whatever training you have need of in the field of medicine…as well as other areas of necessity."

Dr. Marcus stared at her, his blue eyes cold and unfeeling like an impenetrable wall. How would it be to work with such a man, to become such a human being? Something about him seemed so oddly familiar: the angle of his jaw, his chiseled chin. But exhaustion overwhelmed her again – her mental capacity stilted by all she had learned.

Debrille interrupted her tangled thoughts. "We need you, Samantha. You need us. It is time to carry out your revenge on the man who raped your mother, killed the Bartlett family, murdered your grandmother, and attempted your life."

Samantha stared at the pile of torn fragments, the photograph of that hated man. A beast. Anger surfaced hard as ice and beat against her ribs, begging to be released.

As she continued to glare at the pieces, Samantha replied, "I accept."

The matter settled, Debrille erupted from the chair, belying his earlier frail appearance, and strode from the room followed by an entanglement of guards. Dr. Marcus alone remained to change her IV bag. Afterward he wrote on her chart and checked her pulse before he spoke.

"I've given you a sedative in this bag to help you sleep a little longer. Helps to repair that broken arm and your weakened lungs."

Samantha rolled her eyes at him. "I'm well aware of the need for rest, doctor. I was near the top of my class, as I'm sure you know."

A brief stare glanced from his eyes, the hint of a smile on his lips. "I'm looking forward to continuing your training." Then Dr. Marcus left the room.

The steady beep of the monitor echoed in her mind as the medicine took effect. Her jumbled thoughts drifted to the photos on Gramm's dining room table. Two faces came together in her mind as darkness swelled around her.

Dr. Marcus was Shades.

CHAPTER 16 - AN END

The limousine turned down the cemetery lane. Samantha stared through the dark veil as the familiar twin vaults came into view. A chill passed over her at the sight of fresh earth mounded over the surface of the nearby ground. A new granite stone graced the head.

All bore the last traces of Samantha Jane Bartlett.

She tugged at her earlobe. The sting that greeted her drilled the reminder home. Now she belonged to the Elite.

"You'll get used to it," offered Dr. Marcus.

Samantha glared at him through the veil. Marcus only stared at her with a bemused expression on his lips, but his eyes remained flat, devoid of emotion. What a shame to waste gorgeous blue eyes on such a creep. When she'd agreed to join the Elite she hadn't realized they would implant the microchip in her earlobe. GPS, microphone, whatever it all was – now she was a freak, a walking satellite transponder allowing Debrille to track her every move, fill her head with his irritating shrill voice whenever he pleased. Was this how schizos spent their every waking moment? No wonder psychological medicine had never appealed to her.

"The damn thing hurts worse than my stinking arm," Samantha retorted as she rubbed the air cast.

"Well *it* will be the only thing coming off in another two weeks." He thumped the cast.

She wanted to deck him. Several weeks gone and the man rarely let her out of his sight. His presence irritated her already. Besides the jerk had an explanation for everything.

He'd arrived at the scene of Gramm's accident to see if she could be rescued. Claimed to have had nothing to do with it. Said Warner had targeted Gramm to draw Samantha back into the open. The *good* Dr. Marcus had deposited the note in her coat pocket to urge her toward learning the truth. They'd known Warner was closing in on her. She didn't know what to believe. Samantha didn't trust the man farther than she could spit, something Gramm had failed to teach her.

As the limousine rolled to a stop, Dr. Marcus slipped on his shades and exited, walking around to her side and opening the door. If she hadn't had the cast on her arm, she would have opened the door herself right into his crotch.

Take that family jewels.

The summer heat hit her like an oven. Her lungs still ached from the smoke inhalation, and heat only exacerbated it. Even so, it felt good to see the sun after weeks underground. How many long months before she would see it again after this?

She slipped the black sling over the cast and stepped from the limo.

"Remember, Samantha Bartlett is dead," stated Dr. Marcus.

"Screw you, Shades," Samantha muttered.

"We'll get to that soon enough."

The twin graves stared her down as Samantha covered the distance as if she were in an ever-stretching tunnel, the walk never so far on previous visits. The wind fluttered the veil, everything muted and dark like a gathering storm. *Her* grave rose to greet her in mocking welcome. Mr. Eddis had likely buried ashes scraped from the explosion.

Poor Mr. Eddis.

The presence of death hung over her like a black cloud. She turned her back on the macabre mound.

"Momma, it's not really me there. I'm here. I'm still breathing," Samantha whispered. Tears sprang to her eyes. "I'm following in your footsteps, though, so don't worry about me. I have a chance to set things right, but to do that I'm going away for a long time. A very long time." Samantha stared off into the distance. "I don't even know how I'll ever return."

Tapping behind drew her attention. Dr. Marcus urged her toward the waiting limo in some stupid Morse code or something he beat out on the window. He could wait a little longer.

"Shades is having a conniption fit over there, so I better go before he zaps me with an electric shock treatment. I'll probably need one before this is all over."

Samantha pressed her gloved hand to the stone. A familiar ache seeped into her heart. The sun soaked through her black attire as if she were near the fires of hell itself.

"I miss you so much right now, wish you were here to help me make sense of all this." She choked back the lump in her throat. "I'll get Warner, Momma, for what he did to you and Gramm – and what he only thinks he did to me. I can't let him do this to anyone else ever again."

With a glance at the second grave, Samantha walked back to Shades and the waiting limousine. Samantha Jane Bartlett had indeed died, her life at a sudden end. Yet the phoenix rose from the ashes to swoop down upon an unsuspecting man.

She would have the last word.

***

Joe drove around the bend and watched as a lady in black turned away from the graves and returned to the waiting limo. Something didn't sit right with him. Strange. Was this a friend of Sam's from New York come to pay her respects, or an old co-worker unable to make the funeral?

As the limo pulled away Joe parked his car and stepped

out. He'd only take a moment of the city's time. In this heat the flowers would shrivel up in a matter of hours, but that didn't stop him from offering the token. He should've kept in touch more. Then he'd gone and pissed her off when he had blown off her idea about that guy in the photos at the accident scene. Somewhere, somehow he'd missed something, and it ate at his gut. Now he missed her.

As he placed the small bouquet of red roses near the headstone, Joe stiffened. His brain awoke with a start. He stared after the limousine as it turned from the cemetery back toward K-96. Then it clicked. She hadn't been there to visit Samantha's grave.

The lady in black had stood gazing over Mr. and Mrs. Bartlett's graves.

CHAPTER 17 - A NEW BEGINNING

The sleek, high-speed underground train came to a halt and opened upon a plush underworld. If this was hell, Samantha decided her stay wouldn't be too bad. No glaring white walls like she'd been subjected to in the hospital setting beneath Wichita. This was first rate elegance in a most uncommon backdrop.

An enormous cavern vaulted up like a giant, ancient magma bubble as they entered what Shades called their commons. Strategic ambient lighting provided a view of the vast chamber. The floor and walls at the lower levels were tiled with elaborate and colorful motifs like the work from an Aztec or Incan temple, while furniture resembled something more of an oriental nature in deep red, orange, and hushed amber tones. A narrow river skirted the tiled floor near the far wall, its rush cutting deep into the hard basalt stone and echoing throughout the cavern.

Dr. Marcus remained silent as he led her through a labyrinth of smaller rooms and carved hallways until turning onto a corridor ending in a waterfall. In fascination,

Samantha watched as the waterfall parted to reveal enormous carved oak doors while a stone ledge rose from the pool below to connect the walkway. Before they even reached the doors, her earlobe buzzed and Debrille's voice echoed inside her head.

"You may enter."

She felt like a wireless radio receiver.

The double doors opened upon a paneled entry hall with a six-tiered chandelier chattering overhead. Similar oak doors to the right swept open as Debrille made his grand appearance like a king greeting his subjects.

"Ah, my dear. So good to see you again."

Debrille strolled up and embraced Samantha as if she were a long lost relative. The move turned her stomach.

"So where are we now?" Samantha asked. "An hour doesn't get one very far from the heart of Wichita."

Debrille seated himself in a curved leg chair like something from a medieval movie set. The guy obviously thought himself royalty surrounded with this set-up. He flipped open a scrolled table drawer, then lit and puffed on a stogie.

"Those things will kill you eventually," offered Samantha.

Debrille stared hard at her out of those beady eyes and drew long on the cigar before lazily blowing smoke at her.

"We are in my chambers, my own little workshop if you will, deep beneath the Chesapeake Bay."

Geography had never been Samantha's strong point. "Near the Gulf? That train traveled faster than I thought."

Debrille raised an eyebrow and turned his gaze upon Marcus. "You are going to have your work cut out for you with this one."

Little Hitler man had a way of making her feel like an imbecile every time he opened his mouth. Marcus seldom spoke but when required monosyllabic, which probably suited Debrille just fine since he had enough hot air for both. Even after knowing them only a few weeks, Samantha wished the doctor would grow a set of balls and stand up to their ringleader.

Debrille turned his attention back to Samantha. "The Chesapeake is fed by the Potomac which runs through the greater Alexandria, Arlington, and Washington D.C. areas."

Samantha felt as if her heart dropped into her stomach. *He* was close. Too close. "D.C.? You mean we are in D.C.?

"More or less, my dear." He smiled and drew again on his stogie. "Now, onto more important matters." Debrille's tone changed to that of a drill sergeant. "You must understand that from now on, Samantha Bartlett no longer exists. You are part of the Elite. You are ours. The microchip implanted in your earlobe will allow us to track your whereabouts at any given time via satellite."

Samantha interrupted. "Yeah, I know. The *good* doctor

here already instructed me in that function."

Debrille's eyes bored like daggers into hers. "And you will never interrupt me again."

Samantha rolled her eyes and muttered, "Sorry."

With a sniff Debrille resumed his rant. "Let me put this another way." His voice grew cold. "We own your hide, my dear, and you will do exactly as instructed. No questions. No attitudes. You are expendable, and if you get out of line at anytime, the *good doctor* here will dispose of you faster than you can say you're sorry."

Like a bear with all four paws in a trap, reality snapped over her mind and sank deep into flesh. They had her. They controlled her. Escape – impossible. Marcus returned her stare with icy blue eyes.

They owned her.

Debrille stood and stamped out the smoking cancer stick. "Marcus will run you through all courses of your training for the next eight months. Your mind and body will be fine-tuned to perfection, and if he is not satisfied in that time your training will be terminated.

"As will you."

CHAPTER 18 - HARD BODIES

President Warner delivered his stump speech beneath the New Mexico State Seal outside the State Capitol building in Santa Fe, or the 'Roundhouse' as referred to by the local populace. Governor James Newman, his cohort since their crazy Harvard days, flanked his left while the First Bitch draped his right shoulder, most likely with that pasty and adoring smile about to crack her plaster-like veneer.

Warner had lived for the moment in college, thinking those days were the best life had to offer, while James Newman had always looked ahead to a rosy future for them both in politics and with women. Though at one time he'd had a multitude of sins to bury, marriage and a mild heart attack had calmed the steamy liaisons for Newman and driven him from D.C. back to his home state. He'd even refused to come back when Warner offered him the position of Secretary of State. Even so, they never missed an opportunity to relive the old days and live vicariously through Warner's indiscretions.

The wind dusted fine sand granules over the Bradford

pear trees lining the center of the sidewalk. The Indian summer of October left the trees practically panting for water. The crowd of thousands probably felt that way also. Pity the poor Secret Service agents in their stifling black suits.

Warner continued addressing the adoring crowd. "Just as your motto states, Crescit Eundo – grows as it goes, Governor Newman has followed just that in his first term, growing the New Mexico economy, growing jobs, growing benefits for your families, growing school funding for your children. I've also led the charge at the Federal level, doubling the benefit to New Mexico's residents. Governor Newman would like to continue that growth with your vote for a second term. He has my full faith and support."

Applause stopped him momentarily as he soaked up the praise and scanned the crowd. It never hurt to put a plug in for his Presidency when he stumped for others either. The fervor in his voice rose a couple of notches.

"As I stand here before your beautiful Capitol building, first dedicated in 1966, I am reminded of its design after the sun symbol of the Zia Pueblo Indians. The symbol is comprised of a circle from which four points radiate. The Zia believe that in the brotherhood of man, we all have four obligations, those being of a strong body, clear mind, pure spirit, and a devotion to the welfare of the people. This is personified in the man to my left who I am proud to call my friend, a man who serves at the will of the people of New Mexico. A man who is willing and able to serve yet another term with your vote. Together, you and Governor Newman will continue to make New Mexico one of the brightest points in the United States of America. Thank you, and God bless."

Thunderous applause swallowed up Newman's brief comment as they embraced then lifted their hands together in victory for the photographers. Newman's re-election was in the bag.

Stumping for his friends gave Warner renewed energy and purpose. It was too easy to get lost in the shuffle of cutthroat D.C. politics, where little of worth ever got accomplished. But in the heart of America, progress remained measurable. Sometimes he missed his days as Kansas' governor, but the Presidency was the shining echelon of every serious politician's ambitions. The Presidential perks and entourage were nothing to discount, but rolling up one's sleeves and staying up all night to haggle over state matters had lit a fire in his soul that had excited him more than staying up all night to quell the fire in his trousers. However, in D.C. important legislation moved slower than a snail and frustrated the life out of him.

That continued to be his problem. Frustration always led to boredom – and boredom led to the bedroom's lustful passions. His dalliances were becoming too careless. He needed to take a break before the media caught wind of more than just dangling rumors.

After shamelessly pandering to the crowd for another twenty minutes, Warner and Newman stepped back into the Capitol and crossed over a tiled version of the State Seal, the Secret Service detail following at a watchful distance. No doubt the wife was somewhere in the mix. She always did take care of herself best.

Newman thumped Warner on the back. "Can't thank you enough for the speech, Fred. You always were the best blowhard at Harvard. Sure you two can't stay for dinner with me and the missus, that is if she's feeling up to it?"

Warner massaged his temple. "Wish I could, Jim, but duty calls me back to D.C. You remember, the city where everyone talks and does nothing?"

"Still that bad?"

"Gets worse every damn day. Sometimes I wonder why I even bothered running for a second term. *Loyalty to the party* and all that drivel, I suppose." Warner smiled. "But the perks can be quite enjoyable."

Newman laughed. "You're nothing but a hormone driven teenager, man."

A shot rang out – two – then ten. Bullets flew from every direction while agents tackled Warner as if he were the quarterback in the Super Bowl. Guns blazed with return fire. Bodies fell with a sickening thump from the second floor balcony. The firefight seemed to last for an eternity, though later he discovered it had been less than a minute.

The assassins were there one moment and gone the next, with no comrades left behind. When the shooting stopped, the Secret Service agents whisked him and the First Lady to the waiting limousines. But not before Warner saw the strafed body of James Newman lying in a pool of red with blood oozing from his mouth and eyes staring lifelessly.

Dead.

***

Three months passed in a blur of sleepless fog, the nightmare of residency nothing compared to her new daily grind. Marcus poured into her brain until it became mush.

"Samantha Bartlett is dead. Samantha Bartlett is dead."

"Then who the hell am I supposed to be?" Samantha retorted as she wiped sweat from her face.

His eyes again turned to ice. "A machine. Only a machine, which I will mold and shape, but not if you just sit there. Lift!"

The weight machine fed into the ceiling with something like fiber optic cords, thin and clear but pliable. The monstrosity took up half of the sweaty smelly gym, its smooth hiss like a rhythmic metronome. Samantha's arms ached and her legs felt like noodles every time she left the apparatus. Then it was off to the park.

The Elite had built an incredible underground park, arrayed with trees, flowers, creeks, and even the occasional chirp of birds – an oasis in the midst of hell, replete with another waterfall. Paths crisscrossed and meandered around the ten acre complex, which Marcus utilized to the full extent.

"Pick up the pace, Miss Second-in-State, or I'll give you five extra laps and no dinner before bed," Marcus called as he pranced ahead in his black biker shorts that showed off his rippling gluteus.

Too bad his shorts didn't come with a red-button remote for *squeeze here* in the front. Yeah, she'd give anything to hear his voice climb twelve octaves, the masochistic creep.

Samantha's lungs burned. "Just give me the bed," she wheezed, "and I'll gladly skip dinner."

Marcus pulled up short. "Oh I'm sorry, did I say bed? Tonight you are pulling an all-nighter with the history books again."

That did it. Samantha threw down her sweatshirt and let fly. "Listen, I've just about had it with you and your sadistic all-nighters. For three months I've worked my ass off doing everything you've asked without complaint, but I've had it up to here with the lack of sleep thing. Every minute of every day I feel like a zombie. Residency was nothing compared to this."

With one fluid motion Marcus straightened his arm while Samantha stared down the barrel of a gun muzzle. His voice was calm, controlled.

Emotionless. "Suck it up and give me five more. Otherwise, I'll be happy to let you sleep – eternally."

The room fell silent save for the cheerful bird chirps. Samantha had faced down a couple of whacked druggies in the emergency rooms before, but strange how the yelling and itchy trigger fingers hadn't frightened her like the calm demeanor Marcus displayed. Debrille had threatened it, and

Marcus obviously had no problem carrying it out. Slowly she knelt, picked up her sweatshirt, and tied it back around her waist while swallowing the fear.

But Samantha couldn't resist one last retort after Marcus had put the gun away and they started up their pace again. "Aren't we getting appropriate enough hard bodies yet?"

Marcus reached around as she jogged by and smacked her butt. She glared but kept running, his wicked smile never quite reaching his eyes.

"That remains yet to be seen."

***

The park beckoned. Samantha felt drawn to the sunlight, the mist near the waterfall. Someone sat upon the gray stones surrounding the basin, her dark hair flowing in the breeze from beneath the white wide-brimmed hat. Curiosity tugged at Samantha's heart. She knew this woman, sensed the connection they held. The lady raised her hand. A dove took wing and soared overhead as Samantha drew near. But as Samantha reached out, the woman turned to face her with the screeching image of Debrille.

Samantha started awake as the ear chip zapped her from the edges of sleep. Her earlobe felt as if it were on fire.

"Damn it, Debrille!" Samantha screamed to the coffered ceiling.

She picked up one of the history books lying on the desk and threw it toward the door. It slammed hard with an echo, pages fluttering in the air like the wings of a flock of spooked geese before settling to the ground. What did White House history and its artifacts have to do with getting at Warner anyway? It all felt like such a waste of time.

Tears pulled at the edges of her tired eyes at the thought of the dream. Her mother – she'd been sure. So why did she become Debrille? Did something in the microchip plant dreams in her head? Samantha pressed her palms to her eyes, no desire to give Debrille the satisfaction of breaking.

Her stomach rumbled. At this late hour she could take satisfaction in locating a snack to stem the pangs of hunger without anyone knowing. The continual lack of sleep and stress was definitely sending her cortisol levels through the roof, spurring on her appetite.

The door creaked as Samantha opened it and stared down the hallway from her three-room suite before slipping out, her bare feet padding along the cool tile. Granite columns lined most corridors in the never-ending complex, and they provided great hiding places from the sentries that passed. Debrille had a thing for architecture. Nearly every room she'd seen thus far had been built like a Roman coliseum, ancient castle, or a Mediterranean villa. Sometimes it was difficult to believe they were covered with earth and the aching weight of Chesapeake Bay. But she longed for the warmth of the sun to caress her face.

After skirting more of Debrille's goons and backtracking through endless halls, the commercial kitchen winked a stainless steel welcome as Samantha flicked on the light. Cookies and chips were a no-no on Debrille's strict diet so finding several packages behind one of the pantry doors was a treat. She grabbed a jug of milk from the fridge before shimmying up onto the counter and leaning against the cabinets.

Cold refreshment washed down the chocolaty goodness. Pure heaven. Strange that Debrille would keep such things around when they weren't allowed. Of course, maybe they just weren't allowed for her. Samantha gained a wicked satisfaction, as if she flipped him the bird each time she popped a forbidden cookie in her mouth.

After downing half the package and three glasses of milk, Samantha brushed the crumbs into the industrial sized sink, leapt from the counter and hid the evidence of her dirty deed beneath the apples. Ugh, she used to love apples before arriving.

The freakish obsession Debrille and Shades had with her body weight bordered on insanity. The workouts made sense, training for the mission they had for her to perform. But why the daily measurements with the weight checks? It was as if the two just got off on parading her scantily clad body around the facility for their own strange fantasies, no concern given for her sense of modesty. Had they treated her mother in such a way?

Momma. The dream hung again on her mind. Did it mean anything? Samantha remembered how they used to walk together among the garden, Momma clad in her white straw hat with the wide brim to protect her dewy skin. Their Washington home had been so remote, surrounded by acres of trees, a river careening over the hills covered with verdant grass during spring and summer and crowned with snow in winter. Samantha closed her eyes and remembered the feel of the spongy grass carpet, the softness of Momma's hand as it cradled hers so long ago.

Samantha opened her eyes, but her mind continued passing through the dreams of what once was her life until coming to the realization that the passages she walked were no longer familiar. The halls no longer held the architectural beauty of the Mediterranean, but were clinical and white.

After attempts at retracing her steps failed, Samantha pressed her earlobe to pull up the holographic display map. The blue lines glowed before her eyes in ever increasing detail until a red blip entered the screen. She had ventured into a storage facility unit. No need for fancy architecture there. A large, unmarked void appeared near the edge of the map like maybe an unfinished room.

More twists and turns led her deeper into the complex, down a stairwell then up again until she came upon a riveted metal wall. There was no right or left, up or down. The hallway just stopped upon the unmarked void. Perhaps it was the outer wall of the whole facility, but if so no need for a manmade wall when the natural basalt stone would do. A tap to her earlobe again brought the holographic map to view. The unmarked room no longer appeared. Odd.

For a moment Samantha pressed her ear to the wall and strained to listen. A low mechanical hum reverberated through the metal then something else.

A voice.

The emergency sirens blared like an ambulance careening through the hallways. The lights dimmed and red flashed as Samantha raced up the hall, down then up the stairwell as she followed the directional holograph. Her heart pounded in rhythm to her bare feet slapping along the tile, jogging right then left – no right again – until she came to familiar territory. She recalled the path to the surgical unit as they had drilled countless times. But as she slid through the stainless steel doors Samantha realized with stark clarity.

This was no drill.

Members of the unit had been shot to hell. Blood snaked along the floor as Samantha leapt into her scrubs and tore into the wash room before entering surgery.

Dr. Marcus' pleasant voice plowed through her head. "Where the hell have you been?" He was already up to his armpits in blood and flesh. "Clamp this artery before it drowns me, then open him up." He nodded toward another gun shot victim.

The nursing staff continued to wheel a steady stream of prepped bodies into surgical care as Samantha cut incision after incision and popped bullet casings as if she were dissecting cadavers. Debrille worked just beyond the window in another surgical care room specially designed for his short stature. The relentless beep of the heart monitors echoed in her head until the piercing steady whine shrilled across her frayed nerves.

They lost twelve that night.

CHAPTER 19- MORE QUESTIONS THAN ANSWERS

Joe sorted through the endless reams of paper strewn across his desk – blueprints, phone records, utility bills. The questions only mounted. Why hadn't he done this sooner?

In the months since seeing the woman at the cemetery, something nagged at Joe's mind like an irritating mosquito. It wouldn't go away no matter how much he swatted at it, and a good detective never ignored evidence no matter how elusive. Countless nights over the last few months he'd lurched awake in a cold sweat, the dream evaporating before he could grasp it and pull it into reality. Was Sam trying to converse with him from the dead? No, he was too practical for such lunacy.

Where to start – that always remained the million dollar question when he only had a hunch in his gut. The mess on his desk revealed definite anomalies, but now what? Nothing in the 1926 blueprints showed the elaborate storm bunker. If they'd built it later, no permit reflected the effort.

Then the incredibly high electric bills: two, three, four thousand for a three bedroom airplane bungalow. Impossible Sam's grandmother could have afforded such bills. Much less there was no way an eleven-hundred square foot house could use that much energy even if everything had been on and running twenty-four hours a day.

The phone rattled. "Roberts."

"Hey Joe, it's Proctor. You got a minute?"

"Always for you, Bill. What've you sniffed out now?"

Best friends since grade school, William Proctor had chosen to manage city affairs instead of following Joe into investigation, despite the fact the man had an instinct like a bloodhound. However, they still made a great team as they collaborated from their respective sides when the need arose.

"You know the house explosion four months ago?"

Joe appreciated the reference only to the incident instead of mentioning Sam directly. The memories continued to ache. Even though Bill hadn't liked it when Joe and Sam had dated in high school, he'd remained considerate of Joe's feelings. They would always be good friends for that one.

"Working on those oddities with it right now."

"Same here. Well I went way back to when the house was built and went forward from there, searching the microfilm for copies of any checks to pay the electric bill. Looks like the Hendricks who owned it from '26 until '47 always paid with cash. Then the Gibson's until '53."

"Cut to the chase, man. What'd you find?"

"Starting in '68 there was that spike in the electric consumption – not enough to throw a wrench of suspicion into anything. Before that, the grandparents paid by cash too. Then by '72 they consistently paid by check. That's when the consumption tripled, then quadrupled and went off the charts."

"You've already given me that information. What're you getting at?" Bill always loved drawing out a good story, but Joe's patience wore thin. They needed to start making some headway, anything really to make him feel like he was doing right by her memory. Then Joe could almost *hear* Bill smiling like a Cheshire cat.

"I've got a copy of a check that I think you'll find interesting. From the July 15, 1974 bill."

Curiosity coursed through Joe's veins. Summer of seventy-four, summer of seventy-four – Sam's grandfather had died in that construction accident working for Castor about six weeks before.

"Are you scanning it?"

"It should hit your email any second."

"Anything else?"

"I'll call when I find the connection."

"Thanks Bill. I'll call you back when I need your nose

again."

He set the phone in the cradle before checking his email and printing the attachment. The amount no longer surprised him, but the imprint at the top left more questions – Castor Concrete and Construction. The signature was none other than the owner himself at the time.

Albert Castor.

***

The October wind spit rain like needles against his face as Joe got out of the car. Four months and he'd refused to sign off on the demolition notice, convinced all along that more evidence only waited for him to find it in the rubble of Sam's last known place of residence. The chief had fought him and threatened to sign off on it himself if he hadn't discovered anything else by the end of the month. But now he had something tangible to back up his instincts. The connection to Castor only made it more curious.

The company had originally done a lot of grunt work for the city. With those contacts, Jacob Castor built his father's company from a family concrete operation during the Depression into a respected construction conglomerate by the end of World War Two, now employing thousands of employees across seventeen states.

So why was Castor waiting on the sidelines to complete the city's bid of final demolition on the remains of Sam's house? Odd little job for a company with more important things to do.

Joe had to tread the connection carefully. If the company had any inkling they were being considered in another investigation, however slight, whatever available crack they found to peek through would immediately be sealed shut. Also, he needed to be careful for Bill's sake. They'd met earlier under the premise of lunch to chat like old friends and swap information. Bill continued to quietly investigate the Castor company in the city's records while Joe dug through the information he provided.

The remains of the storm bunker had to provide him with something tangible soon. If he held off on Castor much longer they'd get suspicious.

Joe ducked under the yellow police tape and flicked on his flashlight as he once again went down the damp and slimy steps into the concrete shelter. The installed padlock gave him a bit of trouble before it yielded. With all the rain from the leaden sky, water again pooled on the floor but only a couple of inches. The night of the explosion water had been up to his knees.

That night continued to haunt him. No DNA traces had shown up in the ash and residue, but no one could have survived such an explosion either. Sam hadn't left the house. Matter of fact, a neighbor across the street had noticed her tearing into the driveway about ten minutes or so before. They'd located the remains of her bombed out car plowed into the side of the neighbor's house. No registered traces of DNA there either. The only other place she could have gone was the storm shelter. In a way, he'd been thankful her body hadn't been located under the water. He'd never have forgiven himself if she had indeed escaped the explosion and they'd drowned her.

A chill crept up his spine. Joe flipped up his jacket collar to ward off the seeping cold air. The place just gave him the creeps. It still stank like fire even after all these months and the water washing down the stairs. Maybe the scent just remained permanently imbedded in his mind from when he'd first been on scene.

Water gurgled. Without stirring too much, Joe turned toward the sound and shined the light along the top of the water. Nothing. He closed his eyes. No movement, no sound except water lapping against his boots. Only listening.

There – again bubbling.

The direction of the noise cleared off to his right. The explosion had probably created cracks in the concrete. Perhaps snakes had taken up residence to escape the fall cold.

With the location clear in his mind, Joe snapped his eyes open and shined the flashlight toward the northwest corner. Intermittent bubbles broke the water's surface. Careful not to disturb the water unnecessarily, Joe slunk closer and peered through the liquid.

God, please don't let it be a snake.

He could see the headlines in the Wichita Eagle – *Investigating Officer Killed By Deadly Snake Bite!* But snakes would have to poke their heads up for air, and when the beam penetrated the water Joe could see nothing but the concrete floor.

The bubbles stopped for a few moments but soon broke the surface again. No death by snake today. It sounded on occasion like water trying to make its way down a partially clogged drain. After removing his gloves, Joe drove his hand beneath the cold water and felt along the wall where it met the floor. Reminded him of the stories his grandfather used to tell about noodling along the banks of the Verdigris River. Dangerous business.

Suddenly his fingers slipped into a smooth notch beneath the concrete. He searched for the end to the notch. Roughly two feet. A crack caused by the explosion? The exposed edge felt too smooth for that. It had to be man-made.

Joe ran up the stairwell and retrieved a crowbar, screwdriver, and mallet from the car before making his way back into the depths. He adjusted the flashlight on the stairwell and shined it again toward the northwest corner. With a little elbow grease the crowbar slid into the slot and made contact with - nothing. No dirt, no concrete. His mind raced with anticipation.

The crowbar wedged firmly under the lip of the concrete, Joe stood on the other end and countered the concrete with all his weight. Even though he expected to see something, he was still surprised when a fine line appeared along the wall. It hadn't been there only a moment ago. Joe pressed his finger against the wall where the line revealed and whipped out his pencil to mark it in lead. The line marked, he eased off the crowbar and grabbed it to utilize as a weapon against the concrete.

All along the mark, Joe hacked with the tipped edge. Flecks of concrete flew like sparks away from the wall. He only hoped they wouldn't cut into his eyes. After the mark was clearly scored he took up the mallet and screwdriver and pounded until his arms were sore. His face felt caked with sweat and grime but he kept at it.

An edge increased in visibility just above his head. A few helpers and better equipment would speed things along. His legs were soaked and icy from the cold fall air, the concrete dust probably not good for him to breathe either. But no amount of excuses or mental reasoning decreased his efforts.

The undertaking found pay dirt when the screwdriver broke through. Again there seemed to be nothing but air behind the concrete. Joe took up the crowbar again and slid it through the notch created from the screwdriver. He wedged his weight against it. The edge sliced into his hand as he slipped and fell into the water. The gash burned like hell but he couldn't give up now, so he slid his wet gloves back on to cover the sticky mess.

Joe didn't need them. As he picked the crowbar back up and prepared to try again, he found the wall had swung outward with his last effort. So it was a doorway. A tunnel. Leading where?

Joe snatched up the flashlight and shined it around the passageway. He forgot about the cold. He forgot about the pain in his hand. Concrete lined a tunnel angling downward. About fifty feet in Joe stopped.

Dirt and rubble blocked further progress.

CHAPTER 20 - A GLIMPSE

No explanation of the dead bodies piling up. None offered nor given.

Samantha fumed. "When am I to know what's going on around here? What happened to all those men shot to hell recently? Did they die for some *noble* cause or just for the sake of Debrille's sick and twisted pleasure? Then how is all this body building stuff getting back at Warner?" she asked in rapid fire as she followed Marcus down the hallway like an obedient doggie.

She'd become nothing more than their little bitch, always doing as told and asking no questions. Well at least not very often.

Marcus' stride didn't change. "Do you even know the meaning of the word patience? It will all come together in good time. For now, the gym."

The smelly He-Man hole again. As they entered the blue matted arena, the stench of sweat assailed her nostrils and joined the scent of blood floating around her sinuses of late. The moment they'd finished surgery for the day, Dr. Marcus had dragged her butt from the medical unit to change into her black Lycra workout gear. The catsuit fit like a glove, showing every curve and flaw of her body. She hated it because Marcus' eyes roamed every square inch as if he were preparing to give her a proverbial gloved exam.

"Today I am going to teach you the fine art of kickboxing," Marcus proclaimed.

Surprise stayed concealed beneath her furrowed brows. Things were certainly going to get interesting real quick. Could it possibly be that they didn't know or was this just another test?

Instead Samantha played along and whined, "I'm exhausted. Can I get some sleep first after last night?" At least it was true. Her limbs felt like lead weights hanging from her torso.

"I'm in no mood for your mouth today, so zip it."

After guiding her through limbering and stretching exercises then hand and foot positions, Marcus showed off a series of kicks and punches against the matted walls. She feigned ignorance, enjoying the feeling of having precious knowledge to herself. For a moment she got in touch with her sense of dignity again.

Hours ground on and exhaustion wore on her like a wilted blanket. Marcus' voice droned on in the recesses of her mind, his cocky attitude grating on her last nerve as they finally faced off against each other. Samantha didn't expect him to actually strike her but his heel connected with her temple, her reflexes sluggish as she slammed against the mat.

"Get your sorry ass up and be ready next time." Marcus smiled.

Fine. Time to grind that smile into the mats. The blow had warmed her blood as it raced hot through her veins. Her head throbbed, but her mind focused for the next blow.

His eyes registered shock as Samantha face-kicked him before smacking him back in the temple with a spinning sweep kick. A sense of power rose as the mighty Dr. Marcus fell to the mat, his lip swelling and bleeding at the unexpected attack.

As she bent to stare into his glazed eyes, she touched her nose to his. "Turn about's fair play, don't you think?"

To drive the point home she pressed her foot on his chest, enjoying his grunt, as she stepped over him and strode toward the exit. They were done for the day.

Marcus spat blood and sputtered. "Where the hell did that come from?"

Glancing over her shoulder, Samantha stared innocently at his pathetic form. "Didn't you know? Well then you should do your homework a little more thoroughly next time. My college roommate won the state kickboxing championship our junior and senior years." She smiled. "I was practice."

Samantha turned to leave as Marcus yelled after her. "Hey – hey, get back here. We're not finished yet!"

Let him shoot her in the back if he wanted. She called back without stopping. "Looks to me like we *are* finished. I'm going to bed."

His silence surprised her. But as Samantha plowed through the gym's double doors she heard following the low rumble of Marcus' laughter.

***

Marcus leaned on his elbow as he watched the sway of Samantha's retreating form. So she had it in her after all. For months they'd waited for a glimpse of the real Samantha, a haughty confidence Debrille had referenced in her mother. But this he hadn't expected. Her leg had flashed like lightning against his head – swift and to the point. Rising respect erupted as laughter.

The time had come.

CHAPTER 21 - SOMETHING'S UP

Joe stormed into the chief's office. "Who authorized the demolition?" The glass rattled as he slammed the office door.

Chief Snowe raised his heavy brows at the uncharacteristic outburst. "Gotta problem, Roberts?"

Joe plunked down in a chair and took a deep breath to calm the force of his frustration. It wouldn't be a good time to get fired. Snowe leaned forward as much as his paunch would allow. Sitting behind a desk for a decade hadn't done much for his figure.

"I just went out to the explosion site – the one in College Hill several months back. Castor's been there sometime in the last couple of days, demolished the site and spread fresh dirt. I never signed off on the demolition notice. Did you?"

"The Bartlett file? You know I'd have told you if I was going to pull rank on your case. You still had a few weeks left until I made good on my last threat."

Even though they'd had their differences over the years and had butted heads, Chief Snowe was a good man and one smart investigator. The plug in the leg was the only thing that had ever slowed him down. If nothing else, the man was trustworthy.

Joe paced the room. "I'm screwed. The tunnel would have come out somewhere eventually, but now I can't get back in there."

"Keep your voice down, Roberts. It's not good to let too many people around here in on that tunnel. Let me see if I can find out who gave Castor the authorization without consulting me."

Joe stewed, his mind roaming through all manner of possibilities while the chief scrolled through his cell records. In all the years they'd known each other, Sam had never mentioned a tunnel connected to the storm cellar. What purpose did the tunnel serve? Had Sam even been aware of it? If so, could she have been buried beneath the rubble? That would explain why they'd never found her body. Now what chance did he have to close this case? What chance did he have to close the hole she'd left in his heart?

Snowe dialed the number on his phone and propped his feet on his desk. Pity the poor person who answered the call. It never bode well for anyone to cross him.

"Sherie, Chief Snowe here. Is McMillan in? Well in that case, would you be available for a moment to look something up for me? Little city demolition job earlier this week in connection with one of our cases. Yes ma'am –

Castor Construction. No problem." He glanced back at Joe and winked. "You get further with most females when you're pleasant. I sure could do without this elevator music though."

"I'd listen to anything right now if I could just find out who's responsible for setting my investigation back."

"It's just a good thing I got Sherie on the phone instead of Donna. Now *that* woman is nothing but an impenetrable and unbending icicle. Strictly by the book." Snowe propped the phone back up to his mouth. "Yes – Bartlett. Tuesday? He did? I'd love a copy for the file if you could just fax it on over. Sure, email's fine. Thanks for checking, Sherie."

Joe could hardly contain himself. "Who?"

Snowe lit a cigar and blew out slowly, disregarding the city's smoke-free policy. One thing Joe loved about the guy – some rules were just made to be broken. But you always had to know which ones to break, and you better have one hell of a reason for doing so.

"Now it gets interesting."

"Who?"

"Mayor Spencer."

***

"Meet me tonight. There's a whole slew of shit here."

Joe tucked his hand around his other ear to hear Bill Proctor over the precinct chaos. The cell phone connection crackled. If Bill had called his personal cell instead of his office land line or work cell, things didn't bode well. He must have found a load of dirt.

"Where? When?" Joe asked.

"You know that coffee café down in Riverside?"

"The Percolator?"

"That's the place. Meet me there at five-fifteen."

"What'd you find?"

"It's gonna hit the fan with this one, and you-know-who is going to fight it all the way."

The excitement in Bill's voice sent his mind reeling. That old familiar sense of dread sat like a rock in his stomach, but nothing he'd said gave any reason for triggering it. Only thing he knew for certain – he didn't like feeling this way one bit.

"Bill, you okay?"

"Gotta go. Just meet me."

"You got it."

***

Five-fifteen. Joe fiddled with his watch and took a bite of his beef tenderloin sandwich. The place was an eclectic dive, but the food was homemade and usually melted in his mouth. But he only went through the motions, hardly tasting the food as it went down. The music wouldn't start until seven so the crowd was thin thus far. The place always drew an interesting cross-section of the community later at night.

Five-twenty-five. The large windows allowed clear sights for Bill's white SUV down all quadrants of the intersection. The cheese peeled off the last edge of the sandwich as Joe absentmindedly munched a fry before sucking down more strong coffee. The stuff was going to rot a hole in his gut if Bill didn't arrive soon – that and thinking too much about what had happened to Sam.

Two-plus-two usually equaled four. Why not this time? Logic said Sam had died in the explosion. She'd not surfaced since. Still they'd found no DNA traces in the ash, and they'd taken more than thirty samples. Chief Snowe about came unglued when he'd seen the lab costs for the case. Then he kept coming back to that crazy tunnel under the house – and the lady at the cemetery. If he'd only realized before the limo disappeared, he could've at least questioned her.

Five-thirty-five. Something felt wrong. Bill had found out something about Castor. Was it connected to Sam's house? About why Mayor Spencer had usurped the department's role in the investigation? Bill had tried to temper what he'd said on his end of the conversation as if he were afraid of someone overhearing and catching onto the drift of their discussion. Maybe it'd be best to get Bill to quit sniffing around for awhile, lay low and stay cool to avoid suspicion.

At five-forty-six, Bill's Explorer came careening through the intersection and slid into a parking space along the opposite side of the road. Joe breathed an audible sigh of relief as Bill hopped from the vehicle carrying a bulging manila envelope close to his leather bomber jacket.

"You're late."

Bill folded his lanky frame into the booth opposite Joe and waved down the waiter for a works burger and a straight coffee – black. If not for the knee injury during his second year of college hoops, the guy could've had a shot at the pros.

"I had to wait for some people to leave the office. Didn't want to be seen taking this out of the building." He slid the packet over to Joe.

"I usually tuck them inside my shirt."

"Well I'd meant to take it out to my car under my jacket earlier, but the more I searched the more information I came across until it got too big to hide. And this isn't all of it, I'm sure. Doubt if I've done more than scratched the surface."

Joe lowered his voice when another patron entered the café. "Today we learned there's a possibility of some connection between Castor and the mayor. Lay low on the searching for awhile, okay?"

"It's no secret Castor's been a huge contributor to the mayor's elections, but the info I've put together alone has made me really nervous. Buddy, you're onto something with this Castor thing. There's something really weird going through their hands."

"Through?"

"Had our friend at IRS email me a few choice items from back in the sixties and seventies. Wish now I would've run over there on my lunch break instead. Castor's cost of goods sold continued to rise steadily until they were more than sales."

"Bill, you're talking to a guy who passed Accounting 101 by the skin of his teeth. Speak English."

"Slacker." Bill smiled. "Okay, when you have a product to sell it costs you so much money to make it or have it made or whatever. So when you sell it you need to recover your costs of manufacture and then to cover your overhead and finally have something to put back in your pocket. It's called a profit. Got it?"

"I'm with you so far."

"Castor's cost of goods began to exceed their sales quite heavily in the sixties and it went on for decades."

"So logic says they should have gone out of business," Joe stated.

"Businesses eventually do if they don't adjust their pricing to recoup some of those costs. Others have sales under the table and don't report them. If this goes on for more than a couple of years, it usually triggers an audit."

"So what about Castor?"

"That's just it. No audits. No nothing in more than four decades. Plus the company continues to grow by leaps and bounds. Odd. So I went digging further and found this." Bill pulled a page from his jacket pocket, unfolded it and handed it to Joe.

"Looks like another page from Castor's tax return."

Bill whispered, "Lists all affiliations – ownership in other businesses."

"Thirteen? Is that normal?" Joe responded in kind.

"Most times it's legit with larger companies. Stock ownership options, passive dummy corporations set up to own the assets, others to run funds through for philanthropic causes, etc. Look at number seven."

"Oleander Enterprises?"

"I've just started looking into them. Hard to find more than just the usual puff stuff through normal channels. Company shows up out of Belgium dealing in art and antiques. From what I can tell, it's been around for more than a hundred years – Egyptian antiquities markets before the previous turn of the century. They made a killing after World War Two, probably dealing in works Hitler stole from the Jews and every other country he ravaged."

"Why would Castor get involved with that kind of company? How would they even develop such relationships?"

Bill shrugged. "Search me. Funny thing is Oleander only appears on this tax return. No other years reflect it."

"Might they have divested their interest?"

"Now you're talking my language."

Joe smiled. "I caught a few points in some classes, only things that might do me some good in my profession."

The waiter slunk over and slid Bill's platter on the table. It'd hardly stopped, before Bill ripped an enormous bite from the burger and stuffed a few fries into his mouth. The poor guy really needed his wife to lead him from the barn and teach him some table manners. Guess that's what you get without a mother around to domesticate the male species. Bill eyed the waiter as he walked away then continued.

"On the surface it appears they did just that, but I have a distinct impression there's still a connection between Oleander and Castor. Oleander suddenly shows up about the same time these anomalies hit Castor's finances. All connections seem to vanish on paper but the financial anomalies continue. Then there's this connection."

Another paper appeared from Bill's pockets, and he glanced around at the growing crowd before sliding the grease-encrusted slip across the table. He didn't release it until he'd tucked it along the edge of Joe's empty plate.

"What's this?" Joe asked as he laid his napkin across the paper.

"That, my friend, is the real shit in your pants. Our IRS buddy called me up late this afternoon. Not only was Castor linked in the past to her grandparents, but Sam's student loans were paid off a couple of months ago."

The mention of her name still jarred his nerves, but Joe kept his calm by nursing his coffee. "Mr. Eddis probably took care of that after settling with the insurance company."

Bill shook his head. "I already checked with the attorney on my way over to make sure. Mr. Eddis knew nothing about it. Payment was made through a maze of corporate and philanthropic interests. Tracking it completely will be a nightmare, but one entity showed up that immediately grabbed my attention."

A glance at the paper was the only signal needed. Joe slid the paper into the napkin's fold as he picked it up and dabbed at his mouth. Refolding the napkin as he returned it to the table allowed him to see the name Bill had written on the note. It sent a shockwave down his spine.

Oleander Enterprises

CHAPTER 22 - PHOTO OP

Fall leaves blew along the South Lawn, but President Warner paid no mind. He stared angrily from the Blue Room window before turning back to Benjamin Forsdale.

"Where is the old bitch?" Warner muttered. "That bill is waiting for my signature. The first important thing to hit my desk in months, and I'm sure as hell not sticking around here any longer than necessary because *she* decided to be late for this infernal photo op."

Photographers rustled around, making adjustments and trying to look busy while everyone waited – endlessly waited. The Blue Room was decorated like the end of December instead of the beginning of November. Christmas garland draped the fireplace mantle where a fire blazed while an enormous and gaudily decorated tree stood at attention like a whitewashed fence post. The missus had no design sense whatsoever, and she insisted on having too much say with the decorators. White House Christmas pictures would look even more tacky this year than last.

Warner grabbed Forsdale's arm. "If she isn't here in five minutes she can have *her* photo taken for the Christmas card."

Forsdale leaned over and whispered, "There is a possible advantage to that option, Mr. President. One might deduce you were too busy with the nation's business to attend a simple photo session."

Warner thought about the possibility and smiled. "Ah, Forsdale. You have saved me from worse situations."

Forsdale smiled in return. "I serve at my President's pleasure."

It was the first time Warner had laughed – really laughed – in a month. He slapped Forsdale on the back.

"Take care of the details and explain the way things work around here to the First Lady, my good man."

"Consider it done, Mr. President."

Warner plowed down the hall to the bewilderment and exclamations of the photography crew. He couldn't be bothered with this Christmas business. Hell, he'd never liked the stuffy and pompous holiday anyway. Glaring lights, sappy music, and gifts nobody really wanted – who needed it?

"Frederick! Where on earth are you going?"

Great. Abbie only waited around the corner for him to get fed up before making her appearance. He hated it when she called him that – sounded just like his mother.

Warner turned to face the sour-puss glare of the First Bitch, standing all high and mighty in her green suit accented by taut pasty skin, the result of too many face lifts. Forsdale had indeed saved him from worse situations – and there she stood. It'd been his good fortune when Ben had taken over the task of helping the woman with her diabetes injections. The reactions she'd have to the medication would have her in a stupor for hours and he didn't have the patience for it or her anymore. Why Ben had gone from a medical background into politics was his own stroke of luck.

Warner responded to her pinched stare with one of his own and a growl in his voice. "Abbie, I've been waiting for over an hour. I have a vital bill in my office awaiting my signature. You may not consider my time and position significant, but the nation does."

"Pish – you're a mere figurehead, a puppet for special interests. In my lifetime, I've known truly powerful men."

Her gray eyes narrowed. Warner refused to give her the pleasure of a scene concocted for the photographers and staff and continued down the hall. The continual glare pierced between his ribs like a knife. He no longer cared.

The Oval Office was silent, drear. No pretty young thing waited for him to take his mind off his troubles. Even so, he'd sworn off the dalliances, no more bulging tits and tightness between their legs to soothe his daily frustrations.

Warner slipped into Forsdale's office through the side door, silently poured himself a brandy and stared at the painting of the old ship – the HMS Resolute – before returning to the Oval Office. The Resolute desk glistened under the soft light. Interesting how a grand, old workhorse of a ship could be reduced to nothing more than a stodgy piece of furniture. The thought brought back memories of that awful day in Santa Fe – Jim's lifeless eyes, blood everywhere. Just like the great ship, a great man had been cut down in his prime, and for what?

A month had passed but it still felt like yesterday. Warner sat at the desk and massaged his temples. The sound of shots fired, bullets whizzing past, all swirled in his mind as he opened the file to sign the new bill. No big ceremonies in the Rose Garden for this one. It was too personal – too raw.

The fight over the bill had dragged on forever in the Senate, languishing in Committee with the threat of a filibuster if it reached the floor for a vote. But after Warner lost his best friend to the smoking barrel of automatic gunfire, party loyalty and sympathy quickly revived the bill with a unanimous Committee vote and overwhelming support on the Senate floor. Only five idiots dared vote against the ban to manufacture automatic weapons for public consumption. The military might need them, but no reason existed any longer for the public to garner access to such weaponry.

Legal challenges already loomed. Most likely the bill wouldn't make it past Supreme Court scrutiny before being struck down as unconstitutional. Days, weeks, or months – it didn't matter. He'd accomplished something for a cause greater than his own selfish existence.

With a flourish of ink, Warner scribbled his signature on the document, making it law for the time being. As he rose, the pen clattered to his desk. He lifted the snifter of brandy toward the heavens.

"For you, Jim."

CHAPTER 23 - ROAD MAP

Samantha wanted to die.

Humiliation set in the moment they stripped her of the soft robe and paraded her to a platform in front of a gilded three-way mirror. Debrille's sharp voice rang out as she hunched her shoulders to conceal her body and hide her flushed face. Any moment she expected to stare down the barrel of Marcus' gun or feel his hand smack her across the butt.

Gramm's voice echoed in her head – *chin up, young lady*.

Naked save for the tiny pink thong Debrille so *graciously* allowed, Samantha raised her chin and focused on the lazily twirling brass fan hanging from the ceiling. They'd made her wear pink – of all colors.

Her body became a roadmap as Marcus and Debrille discussed their game plan and drew the dotted lines, marked the V's, and swiped the arrows with the blue marker. No, not a roadmap but a map of war. No longer a woman standing in front of a mirror, Samantha had become nothing but an object to them. She had become a weapon of war, and the generals were plotting out how best to use her.

General Debrille, I say we take this northern path through the mountains here. No General Marcus, we should follow the southern route through the bush.

Cold hands gripped and lifted her breasts, probed her butt and prodded her nearly concave stomach. Perhaps instead of a weapon she was merely going to be the horse ridden into war by the cavalry, as they lifted her feet and inspected them as if they were hooves. A horse – she'd always wanted a horse when she was young, but that was before…

"Lift your arms," Marcus commanded.

Samantha felt like saluting but obeyed mechanically and stole a quick glance at their task. The man was all work, not even seeing her body as a woman but as the tool they planned to make of her. Leering eyes from one of the creepy goons in black drew her attention. She glared at him, but all he did was smile and let the hint of his tongue glide over his lip like a snake tasting the air. How she wished to drop-kick the beast. When was practice?

Hide the emotion, Samantha. Bury it deep.

Debrille had drilled the statement into her since day one just like her instructors back in medical school. No rage, no anger, no pain, no embarrassment. Just stone coldness, see actions as only a means to an end and nothing more. In other words, Debrille wanted her to be nothing less than a robot.

Thus far, through all the sweat and study, that concept had been the hardest part of her training to grasp. Forget happy or sad, but what was her motivation if not her rage toward Warner for all he had done to her family? It gave her reason for breath upon awakening to another day. But Debrille wanted even this pushed aside.

Samantha was rudely awakened from her deliberations by a stinging slap to her ass.

"I said stop moving!" Marcus yelled, and he jerked her arm nearly from her socket.

Stumbling from the platform, Samantha's free hand came whistling through the air as if it had a mind of its own. A red welt in the shape of her hand swelled across Marcus' cheek. Her hand burned.

The guards pounced on her and groped her flesh as if they were lions in a feasting frenzy. They took turns grasping at her breasts and sliding their hands over her sweating body. The greater the number of goons it took, the more strangely powerful Samantha felt, until they finally succeeded in subduing her.

"Get your grubby paws off me!"

Debrille gripped her chin and surmised. "Well, well, well. So the cat is in there after all."

With all her fury and humiliation, Samantha glared back. "Do you have no sense of decency, parading me around naked like a piece of flesh in front of this testosterone filled horde?"

"Don't worry, Sam. No one here sees you as a woman," Marcus offered. "You will be merely a weapon of destruction when we are finished with you."

Samantha stared questioningly at Debrille. "I've been driven to inhuman lengths physically, strained whatever brain cells I still possessed learning all you required these last months. When are you going to include me in this grand plan of yours?"

She received a raised brow from Debrille in response. "Did you not agree to do all you were told when I picked you up out of your pit of despair and brought you here? No questions asked?"

The fight drained from Samantha's limbs. The goons released her as Debrille tossed her the last shred of her dignity. The robe merely drooped at her side.

"Will you not at least explain this?" Samantha gestured to the map drawn across her body before shielding it with the robe.

"Ah, Dr. Marcus please do the honors."

With medical coldness Marcus related, "You are scheduled this morning for breast augmentation. We've also decided it would be wise to add lift to your buttocks and round them out." He smiled slightly then, but it didn't reach his eyes – it never reached his eyes. "That will give more leverage."

The room swam. Samantha stared incredulously first at Marcus then Debrille, then back to Marcus again. "Surgery?"

She'd wielded a scalpel numerous times, but to go under one herself? For what purpose? Again her gaze redirected to Debrille. "And when were you planning to inform me that I would be undergoing this plastic Barbie transformation?"

Debrille motioned for his henchmen to follow as he strolled from the room, calling over his shoulder, "Enough questions for today. Get to it, doctor."

Samantha shuddered and searched for escape. Never had she thought joining the Elite would require undergoing the knife. "I don't understand. How does this play into my getting to Warner? What am I to become, some stylized sex goddess?"

Marcus grabbed her arm, pricked it with a hypodermic and picked up her sagging form to usher her to the medical unit. "Very well put, Sam."

CHAPTER 24 – AT DEATH'S DOOR

The Wichita skyline lit-up like the Fourth of July as the downtown Christmas lights flashed on into the night. The Thanksgiving turkey had hardly digested before Christmas celebrations started, the holiday more of a leaping point to the main event these days. Few people seemed to slow down and appreciate the simple things in life anymore, such as the importance of family and friends.

Emeril Eddis sighed and turned his chair from the sixteenth floor Epic Center view back to his desk and sealed the letter. The legal documents needed his attention, but more and more he found himself drawn to the enigma of Samantha Bartlett and her family. Somewhere, somehow he'd missed something vital with them, and as the family attorney he should've known everything. First Detective Roberts asking about the house blueprints. Then Mr. Proctor asking about Samantha's student loans. How those enormous bills were paid was a complete mystery.

Insurance payoff for the house and even the forthcoming sale of the property wouldn't have been enough to cover her loans. Just to make sure, he'd called the bank president and reviewed the payoff through the Department of Education to ensure the government guarantee to the bank hadn't been written off after filing her death certificate. No such luck.

As an attorney, he should've questioned more instead of accepting the premise of a gas leak in the house. Detective Roberts probably still had this as an open case file, for more than just his personal connection to the family. But why? Perhaps after court Monday morning, he'd drop by the precinct and ask a few questions of his own. As a family friend, he owed them that much.

Maybe he really was getting too old to be doing this, his instincts slowing with creeping age. Maybe retirement wouldn't be so bad since he and the missus still had their health. They could do a bit of traveling. Just as Samantha's death taught him – you never knew when your time was up.

A figure stepped from the shadows near the office doorway, eyes molten with a look of death he'd come to recognize. A weapon raised and squared between his eyes.

"How did you get in here?"

The man's voice sounded calm, smooth – a practiced assassin. "We have our ways."

"What do you want? Who is 'we'?"

"You should have left well enough alone."

The rapid spit of fire silenced the questions.

***

Their calculations had gotten way off.

The high-speed train hardly stopped before Marcus disembarked and raced through the facility, past the greenhouse and to the research lab. After clearing through all of the biometric security points, he plucked two syringes from the refrigeration unit and tucked them into the portable dry ice module before heading to Debrille's suite. The shakes had likely begun.

The man would still blame him, even though he'd had to make another run to clean up loose ends. He couldn't keep taking care of researching, training, *and* ops. Others were brought in long ago to take care of that particular issue. Debrille probably just enjoyed knowing he had the authority to make such unnecessary demands. Well this was his own fault. Let the asshole suffer for a little while.

Marcus found Debrille hugging the toilet, his retching so severe it had the guards turning green. The sight of such a powerful man performing a common human ritual made him laugh on the inside – but he dare not show it if he hoped to live.

Debrille had enough state of mind to berate him between heaves the moment he opened the door. "You've nearly...killed me...this time."

Marcus ignored him and directed two of the guards to assist Debrille into his bed, while another hooked him up to the cardiac monitor and pulled out the defibrillator. The equipment had long ceased to be necessary, but it didn't hurt to keep it handy in the event of an emergency. They were, after all, dealing with a potentially lethal substance – that is if the dosages weren't one hundred percent accurate in each lot.

With practiced care, he slipped on gloves and drew the first syringe from the container, ice having begun to form around the plunger from the extreme temperature. The contents had to remain stabilized in a near frozen state at injection, though it made the liquid entering tissues at body temperature excruciating for the patient. He couldn't even begin to imagine the horror those first test subjects endured under the crude Soviet serums. At least they'd provided a base substance model from which he'd perfected a viable formula.

Foam flecked around Debrille's lips like a rabid dog as the liquid entered his veins. The man made no attempt to conceal his agony as he retched amid convulsions. The reactions continued in close succession while Marcus watched the clock and waited to administer the second vial. Their timing had to be dead on.

The whine of the monitor echoed around the chamber as Debrille flatlined. His eyes bulged from his skull. His breathing stilled. Marcus counted to ten then plunged in the second needle.

Then waited.

The beep of the monitor started erratic then smoothed into a slow, steady rhythm. Debrille's chest heaved. His face relaxed and eyelids drooped.

Once Marcus was certain of Debrille's sleep pattern, he

excused the guards and packed away the syringes to refuel later. He pulled a thick medical file from Debrille's nightstand, made notes and reviewed its history. The reactions concerned him. They were growing more severe, the requirement of injections occurring more often than even a year ago. Debrille was developing a tolerance to the drug. They'd have to take development all the way back to square one if Debrille wanted to keep his proverbial fountain of youth.

Otherwise they'd all have to eventually give it up to the natural progression of time.

CHAPTER 25 - GODDESS OF THE NIGHT

The thin scar along her jaw line had disappeared. The familiar reminder of that horrible day of loss had marked her for so long, but now the identification had been stripped from her. Samantha ran her fingers along the empty space almost as a farewell to a lost friend.

Five weeks – Samantha still felt sore over her entire body. Again she opened the emerald silk robe and stared at her new body in the cheval mirror. Marcus should've saved himself the trouble and just completed a brain transplant into a new body. The medical technology the Elite had exposed her to thus far was still unbelievable. The voluptuous curves, enormous and perky breasts – well, those were kind of interesting. But the iris transplant looked just bizarre. Emerald green eyes stared back where before she'd had brown. She didn't even want to know where the plugs had come from for the long auburn hair.

Yep, certified Barbie doll.

Marcus had said he would go easy on her, be careful

with her healing incisions which were amazingly miniscule. She didn't feel up to this yet, but Debrille insisted. Maybe she never would. Best to get it done and over with, especially considering she had no choice.

The goons came around eight. Debrille had to make such a demonstration of the whole affair. Two guards walked before her and two behind as if she were royalty or something, probably afraid she might try to run away. Where on earth could she even run away to in this maze of tunnels? Hell, even if she tried they'd just activate the ear chip and splatter her remains across some unknown area, that is if she were able to make her way to the surface somehow.

The door to Marcus' suite creaked as she entered the empty living quarters alone. The lights were subdued, a fire crackling in the marble hearth. The guy lived pretty sweet in his suite. Ebony velvet draped along the walls as if there were actual windows behind them. A white suede sectional took up the center of the room with a huge polar bear rug in the middle, its jaws gaping wide as if it would swallow her in one bite. A rustic mahogany table sat to one side surrounded by several chairs as if the doctor did a lot of entertaining. A bottle of wine nestled in a bucket of ice. Maybe it would be a good idea to get drunk first.

Samantha hugged her robe closer. Her legs trembled, as she perused the selection of books along the wall. Anything to get her mind off of the inevitable.

At the clink of glass, Samantha glanced over her shoulder to see Marcus. The black silk robe hung open on his muscled frame as he popped the cork from the wine bottle and poured two glasses. His hands were irritatingly steady as he held a glass out to her. Samantha grabbed it gratefully and downed the contents in one gulp.

Samantha averted her eyes and felt heat rising to her face. "Tie your robe, please."

"I guess I've become rather accustomed to this. I've trained a lot of women over the years."

And she would be only one more in the mix. Samantha stormed over to the table and poured herself another glass of wine, sloshing almost as much on the table as what ended up in her glass. Marcus took the glass from her before she even had a chance to steal a sip. Instead of his usual roughness, his hands were gentle as her turned her toward himself and raised her chin.

"Careful, you are still under doctor's care, and the doctor says to limit your alcohol intake." His lips curled into a seductive smile.

No smile would erase everything he'd done to her and forced on her these last months. She snatched her glass back and sloshed the contents onto the floor. "I need all the help I can get tonight. Don't expect me to do this sober."

"Relax, it's just like riding the proverbial bicycle – you never forget."

"Well, it helps if you've at least ridden the bicycle in the first place."

The fire crackled. The silence palpable. She felt rather than saw Marcus' stunned countenance. The robe felt entirely too small as she hugged its silken fabric closer, willed its length to the floor. She'd never felt more exposed.

Wasn't like she hadn't had the rare opportunity for sex. In college and especially medical school, most of her classmates were going at it wherever and whenever they could to relieve stress. Hell, many times they never even got a name. But she'd been focused on school and surviving as a Midwesterner in New York City. She'd wanted more than just to have a guy treat her vagina like a pit-stop on his way to the next race. She had Joe to thank for that.

"I had no idea. I just assumed..."

"Yeah, well I never found the time."

For a moment Marcus grew thoughtful, his mouth set in a hard line when she glanced his way. He took her glass and set the stemware on the table before grasping Samantha's hands.

"You're trembling."

What could she say? *Well duh, doctor.*

He draped a hand across the small of her back and drew her closer, the thin silk doing little to mask his manhood as he pressed against her hip. The rush of his heartbeat gave away his desire as Marcus cradled her head to his chest and stroked her new-found hair. He didn't rush her.

Samantha stared at the flames in the fireplace, willing

her mind to focus on the job that must be done. When Marcus brushed his lips against her forehead, she closed her eyes and imagined they were Joe's. As his fingertips lightly traced her spine and glanced off her skin below the robe, she shivered and remembered Joe's touch. Warm lips pressed against her neck. She leaned into him as slowly he traced the wet trail of his lips with his fingers. Samantha's heart beat faster.

Marcus whispered as his lips rose to her ear. "Tonight I want you to let yourself feel. Feel the hush of every breath – the spark of every touch. The thundering of your heart."

How this act played into the grand scheme of things she still didn't understand, but as their lips brushed she tried not to care. Marcus' lips probed hers, parting as their breath met in between. Hadn't she hated this guy once? Why then did his touch send such shivers up her spine?

Instead of a glance, Marcus' hands slid down her back and up the robe to stroke bare skin. The pressure against her hip grew. An ache developed deep in her groin.

Just as her body melted in his arms, Marcus drew back and stared into her eyes, his like a deep blue ocean wave crashing around her. Samantha felt off-kilter, unstable. The wine must have done something to her. Her legs felt unsteady as he led her into the inner room.

His gaze continued to hold hers as they lay upon the black velvet comforter. The robe skewed, exposing his taut skin down to his abs. The rush of her heartbeat pounded in her ears as Samantha traced the exposed muscles with her fingertips until reaching the belt. Marcus smiled, removing his robe as he settled his mouth to hers. His kisses were again gentle, soothing before growing into a passionate breath.

Before Samantha realized what she was doing, she draped her leg over his. As if on cue, Marcus reached around to the knot of her robe. In one deft motion, she lay exposed until he pulled her to his own form.

A flash of fire tore through Samantha's mind as their mouths probed deeper, their tongues dancing in rhythm as their naked bodies pressed harder against one another. Marcus' hands ran down the skin of her back and slid over her newly rounded buttocks. Samantha responded in kind, running her hands down his muscled torso and gripping hard flesh. Her heart raced. Their sweat mingled.

Then his mouth left hers and latched gently onto her breast, lolling her nipple with his tongue. When Samantha winced, Marcus seemed immediately aware of the pain he'd caused. His gaze again drew hers.

"You okay?"

Samantha responded by pressing her lips once again to his, yearning for more. She no longer cared that this had all come about against her will. Now she embraced it with a passion burning deep inside.

He came over her. Samantha opened her legs to him and entwined her ankles over his buttocks. She opened her eyes with a gasp as he entered. Their gaze connected as they rocked the bed, pressing her pelvis to his in synchronized rhythm, matching his increasing pace. A tingling began in the base of her spine and traveled all the way up before exploding in her head as Marcus exploded into her body.

They lay entangled, wrapped together among the sheets as their breathing gradually returned to normal. Samantha couldn't believe what she'd missed all these years. Then again, she was in the hands of a pro.

Marcus took a deep cleansing breath. "How do you feel?"

Samantha smiled at him. "A little lightheaded."

"Do you hurt at any of your incision sites?"

Samantha got in touch with that warm feeling again, but didn't sense any pain. "Nope, all seems well."

"Good."

Without any warning Samantha thudded to the floor, swept from the bed in one swift kick.

"What the hell was that for?"

Marcus rose from the bed and slid into his black silk robe. Samantha remained on the floor – stunned. He picked up her emerald robe and threw it at her face, his eyes appearing coal black.

"We are done here. Now get out – whore."

CHAPTER 26 - THE PLAN

Samantha didn't know how she could face Marcus the next morning. How mortifying. How could he have held her like he did, kissed her with such passion only to toss her out of his bed like so much garbage? Was it to toughen her up for the job? Did everything around here have to do with the job – the plan?

Sleep had eluded her all night long as she alternated between rage at his kicking her out so unceremoniously and…she didn't know how to characterize the other feeling. All she knew was when her mind drifted back to the manner in which he'd held her, caressed her body, pressed his lips to hers, she couldn't help but feel utterly confused. How many other women had he *trained*?

Debrille insisted on their sharing breakfast with him, probably to explore and discuss every disgusting detail of what had transpired last night. She'd considered refusing to attend, had even stayed cooped up in the bathroom to escape the degradation when the guards arrived. In the end, what little life she had with the Elite she still valued, but

Samantha had her fighting gloves ready.

Debrille set his coffee cup aside and smiled as the goons escorted her into his presence. He looked insignificant sitting at the end of the long formal table surrounded by the Tuscan marble room. A fire blazed in the gigantic hearth behind him like the very fires of hell itself – with Debrille taking on the embodiment of the devil.

"Ah, my dear, you are looking well this morning. I'm sure you could use a hearty breakfast." He cut into his Eggs Benedict and held up the morsel as yolk slowly oozed down the Canadian bacon. "At one time in my life I professed vegetarianism, but circumstances sometimes force us to leave behind our ideals, hmm?"

Marcus shoveled poached eggs and strawberry crepes into his mouth without acknowledging her presence. Yeah, he'd worked up a good appetite all right – at her expense. As he slowly gulped a glass of milk, he glanced over the rim in her direction. The usual cold eyes and demeanor were back. If only last night were a bad dream.

"I have very little appetite this morning." Her glare bored through Marcus before addressing the butler. "I'll just have a glass of orange juice."

"Nonsense," Debrille stated. "Prepare Miss Bartlett a full course."

Samantha gripped the arms of the chair until her juice and a plate were set before her. She willed her hands to remain calm, but her knuckles turned white as she gripped the glass.

Pick your fights carefully, girlie.

Debrille continued, "Did you sleep well last night, my dear?"

Gee, the man seemed like Hitler reborn sometimes, loving every minute of making her squirm before going in for the kill.

"No I didn't. As a matter of fact, I was rather uncomfortable – a bit sore still, I suppose."

"Well probably to be expected. It's been awhile, has it?"

Marcus interjected into the conversation without missing a bite. "She was a virgin."

Samantha's jaw almost hit the floor along with her chair as she stood and knocked it over, her juice glass shattering against the wall behind Marcus. Nails ready like claws, she started over the table at him before being held back by Debrille's goons.

"I'm talking about the rough treatment of the doctor here so soon after my surgeries." Samantha glowered at Marcus. "Your penis is too small to be felt anyway. It's a limp noodle!"

Debrille's brow furrowed with Marcus' revelation. The guards unceremoniously plunked her back into the recovered chair and hovered nearby.

Debrille continued addressing Marcus as if she weren't even in the room. "This could complicate things a bit, put the plan off schedule."

"No, she's a quick study. Leave it to me, and we'll keep things right on target." Marcus glanced her way and for the first time that morning he smiled. "We'll just have to work overtime."

Samantha remained in her chair, but in her heart she was standing, pummeling the doctor in her mind. "If you think there'll be anymore of last night, you aren't as smart as Debrille thinks." She couldn't believe they were arguing over her sex life as if she were a still life painting on the wall.

Debrille sighed and spoke to her as if she were a doe-eyed child. "Now Samantha, dear, you know right where that's going to lead you, yes? You always put up such a fight but the only person it hurts is you. I really don't want to ask Dr. Marcus to draw his gun over breakfast."

"Why not? It's never stopped him before."

The report of the gun stopped Samantha cold. Strands of her hair fluttered as the bullet whizzed past her ear and splintered the edge of the chair. The smoking barrel of Marcus' gun moved ever so slight to square between her eyes. If required, the next shot would not be purposefully missed.

Debrille shook his head and rubbed his temple. "Now see what you've done? You've gone and made Dr. Marcus ruin a perfectly good Louis the Sixteenth – and it isn't even noon yet." Beady eyes reflected flames like those in the hearth.

It would only take one tiny incident to put Debrille over the edge. The man placed the value of his treasures much higher than the dregs of human life. The Hippocratic Oath meant nothing unless saving a life bode well for his plan. Always the plan.

Breathe deep, girlie. Breathe.

Samantha willed her racing heart to slow. It took all the feigned humility she could muster. "I'm sorry for my outburst." Samantha hung her head.

When would the nightmare end? Would it always be this way with them? Using her, tormenting her in whatever way they chose? Could she never have a life of her own again? Might she claim she was under the influence of painkillers when she agreed to join this wayward group of control-freaks?

Oh, Momma, what did they do to you?

Immediately Debrille's voice sounded as if his perfect morning had not been so sorely interrupted. "Now that we have that little tiff out of the way, it is time we discuss how you and your new found talents are to fit into the plan."

Samantha's head shot up in anticipation. They were actually going to let her in on what the last six months had been all about. She had to be dreaming.

Marcus stated, "First, we have chosen an operative name for you of Alexandra Shuvinovsky, since he is fond of all things Russian. That should immediately pique his interest."

"Alexandra – I like it. Sounds appropriate and goes with the hair." She had no choice but to go along but couldn't hold back the sarcastic jab. They had her playing a part in their little spy game.

"Alexandra needs to be sexy, confident," continued Marcus. "She will be capable of drawing a man in with her eyes as well as her mind, making him desire her above all, opening up to him in many ways while staying in complete control. Then she will crush him."

Samantha nodded. "Sounds interesting. I kinda like this chic. Who will be her target? Someone close to the President? Does she do the whole Cabinet and work her way up to the Chief of Staff?"

Marcus narrowed his eyes. Debrille lit a stogie and drew on it. Their silence was deafening. Samantha glanced back to Marcus then Debrille again. Something didn't feel right. Breakfast churned in her stomach.

Finally Debrille broke the silence. "We go straight to the top."

The realization hit her like a truck. The room spun. "You can't mean…."

"Alexandra's target is Frederick Douglas Warner, President of the United States." A smile curled the edges of Debrille's lips.

Samantha lost her breakfast all over Debrille's smooth marble floor. The orange juice burned like fire coming up. Funny, it didn't do that going down.

"But he's my – he's, uh…." Samantha didn't know how

to categorize the man without losing another round of juice. They were well aware of the *connection*.

"Your father," Debrille offered.

"Don't ever call him that to me again."

Cigar smoke stung her eyes as Debrille blew into her face. "But he has no relation to Alexandra. She has no one – no ties whatsoever."

"But Alexandra is me. I'm supposed to be Alexandra. You're asking me to willingly commit incest here."

Marcus interrupted. "No, Alexandra is completely separate. She resides in you, yes, but you will learn to find her and let her have free reign as need and situation demands."

Any moment she expected someone to break into a smile and yell *just kidding*, to let the poker faces slide. But they were serious. She stared at them. Incredulous. They actually thought what they were asking her to do seemed perfectly reasonable.

"So what you're proposing is that I'm supposed to be some sort of schizo – multiple personalities and the whole gamut?"

"Alexandra is your power, your confidence," Marcus began. "She does not feel but analyzes. You will harness these qualities and allow Alexandra to take shape. Don't worry, I will train you in this process."

This was crazy. How could they expect her to do such an

abominable thing? Had this been her part in the plan all along? She should have asked more questions. The sound of the splintered chair echoed in her memory, the zing as the bullet had whizzed past. Now the questions were too late. No turning back.

"But how can I separate what I feel about what you are asking me to do from the act itself – the revulsion, disgust?"

"Your feelings will always be as Samantha and as such you will make them disappear when needed for Alexandra to be prominent."

"I just don't understand."

Debrille interjected. "Remember when I told you Samantha Bartlett is dead?"

"Yeah."

"Now is the time to put it into action. In the coming months you will see to that before returning topside. At that time you will be no one else but Alexandra Schuvinovsky, because Alexandra must be your strength to endure what you must face."

CHAPTER 27 - THE CONNECTION

The snow had settled in, the sky a leaden December gray. If the ice and snow didn't force him into a slide, the sideswipe of the wind might. Joe tried to focus on the road through the blowing snow but his mind continued steering him toward Mr. Eddis' death – and the letter. Sam's grandmother had lived off payments from Castor after her husband's death. Large payments. From what he'd gathered, the man had subcontracted on a project with Castor only once – and gave his life for it. After his death, his widow had funds to live well and never work: never drove a fancy car, stayed in the same house, and never gave to any organizations except her church. Gramm wasn't the type to accept a payoff – or was she?

Then there were those enormous energy bills to consider. It went on for years and then suddenly stopped without ever starting up again. If Castor funneled money to them, maybe they'd also somehow tapped into their utilities for several years. If so, for what purpose?

The cell phone jarred his thoughts back to the present.

"Roberts."

"Chief Snowe here. Glad I got you. What's your position?"

"East on four hundred and heading back. What's up?"

"I need you to get in as soon as possible."

"ETA in thirty if I can stay out of the ditch." Something about the tone in the chief's voice got the gut churning again. "What's happened now?"

The chief hesitated. "Your friend, Bill Proctor. His Explorer rolled on the ice."

Joe swallowed hard and gripped the phone harder as he stared through the blizzard conditions – white like Bill's vehicle.

"What hospital?"

"I'm sorry, Joe. He didn't make it."

***

The hole in Joe's heart kept growing. People who'd meant something to him were being fast cut out of his life – too fast. He hadn't even had much of a chance to get to know Sam again after her absence all those years, but he'd never stopped thinking about her. First Gramm, Sam, then Mr. Eddis.

Now Bill.

It ate away at his soul, and there remained no one to

blame but himself.

An accident – yeah right. Instinct said Bill hadn't laid low like he'd told him to. Someone at Castor had gotten wise to his snooping, yet he still didn't have a single piece of direct evidence to link Castor to the murders – but his gut told him their hands were covered in blood. Bill had been digging around for his investigation. Who was next? Better they come straight for him than anyone who'd assisted him. He'd have to do better covering his own tracks. Forget it. They already had him in their sights. Better to hit them head-on than hide like a frightened animal.

Then came the connection between Castor and that strange company – Oleander Enterprises. Why would an international antiques dealer be interested in a Midwestern construction conglomerate? Normal channels hadn't turned up anything further there, and nothing in the letter from Mr. Eddis mentioned Oleander. They were still the unknown fly in the soup. Maybe if he focused his attentions there for a little while, the trigger-happy Nazis at Castor might lay off.

Maybe he'd just pay Manny Castor another little visit.

Chief Snowe stuck his head around the corner during the mental deliberations. "Mind if I join you?"

"Always a pleasure, Chief."

Joe rearranged the stacks piled on his desk so the chief would have someplace to prop his feet. They sat staring at each other for several minutes, the noise of the precinct dying down in the background. The concern in the chief's eyes was palpable.

"It's been a rough year for you."

"That it has, Chief."

"How's his wife holding up?"

"Rebecca? It's tough this time of year, especially with the kids, but she's always been a strong woman. Given time, she'll pull through."

"And you?"

"I'll manage."

Manage – it's what detectives did best. At least he did. Nothing to hold him back. No family to tie him down. He could work from sunup to sunup and no one would think the less of him for it. Besides, it was what kept him sane. If he had too much time on his hands, he might actually stop long enough to consider what he'd missed out on in life thus far. At least he'd never leave a Rebecca and two kids waiting on a doorstep for him never to return.

"Would a change in routine and scenery help?"

"I think I've got enough here to keep me busy through next year and then some. A vacation is out of the question at the moment."

"Wasn't talking about a vacation. A spot has opened up at Quantico."

Joe's ears perked up at the statement. "The FBI training facility?"

"You still interested?"

169

"But I put my last application in over a year ago. Figured they'd weeded me out for more qualified candidates again."

"They just sent over the forms and a letter of acceptance. You ready to throw away twenty weeks of your life?"

Chief Snowe plopped the documents on the desk, the acceptance letter practically staring him down, daring him to make the leap. His dream job. It finally lay in his grasp. But he couldn't leave his current investigations on Castor and Oleander. Who knew what additional information was waiting to be scrounged up.

Then again, where else could he glean the most intricate of investigative databases? If he got into the FBI, he'd have those databases at his fingertips. It would take some time to earn the necessary security clearances, but then he would blow the investigation wide open and tie up the loose ends between Castor and Oleander. Perhaps it wasn't even Castor, but someone at Oleander who pulled the strings.

The timing was perfect. Yes, he needed to get away where he could clear his head and start the investigation afresh. He owed it to Bill…and Sam.

"Where do I sign?"

CHAPTER 28 - SCARS

The technology the Elite utilized continued to amaze her. Surgical scars were sped along in their healing by daily ultraviolet therapy to lesson appearances. The scars gradually turned a silver gray before miraculously blending into the fabric of Samantha's skin as if she'd never undergone the knife. Debrille would not have it known that her body had been enhanced. Would be a dead giveaway and endanger the plan.

They had Samantha up and running again – stairs in the gym to add natural contour to the buttock enhancements. Martial arts focus moved from power to sleek movement, limbering and stretching the muscles and tendons of her body until she felt like a contortionist. The arduous pace of study increased, with the Russian language added to the mix. Then began the strangest thing of all – ballroom dancing, not her strongest subject.

The physical scars healed as the emotional scars built. Each night as Marcus utilized his *training* techniques, Samantha's heart ached with the knowledge that she'd never have love behind the deed. As Marcus drilled his member into her body, he drilled her thoughts to see everything clinically, calculated, as if they were in surgical care together merely prepping a nude body.

The Elite had her. She'd never escape the destiny they had planned. The realization forced her to focus on learning everything possible so she'd be ready – so she could become Alexandra.

Marcus flipped her over the mahogany headboard and thrust into her, gripping her breasts and tugging as if he were milking a heifer. At least they weren't sore anymore. Samantha gripped the carved wood and stared as if thru the wall, Marcus whispering directives in her ear as his hands slid over her supple body. But just as Marcus had taught, she ignored his hands and focused her thoughts inward to her studies: White House history, D.C. monuments, the archives, internal workings of the State Department, the Department of Defense. She dredged up all the minute details of the latest White House briefing transcripts. Then her mind turned to *him*.

Frederick Warner had graduated Harvard Law, summa cum laude. Served in the Navy, but failed the Seals. He'd married a debutante from a respectable Virginia family. Why then had he eventually returned with her to Kansas when living in Virginia presented greater political opportunities? That had probably gone over well with the wife. History showed him to be a driven man, as if he'd always planned to become President as he moved up the political ranks. But something in the equation seemed to be missing.

An image of her mother flashed in Samantha's mind. She imagined her on the campaign bus, still wearing her pure white hat. Then Warner had coaxed her into his private room and defiled her. The bus swayed as Warner thrust into her, her mother helpless to stop it. Anger boiled to the surface.

In a sudden burst, Samantha spun around, gripped Marcus' shoulders and threw him onto the mattress before straddling him. He didn't fight her, but pressed upward with each downward stoke of her pelvis. With her muscles, she pressed herself tighter around his penis as if she would rip it from his body. Her rhythm increased. His breathing kept pace until red crept into his chest and neck and Samantha drew the semen from his body.

She slid off the bed and slipped the robe around her shoulders in a huff. Anger burned in her veins, but Marcus grabbed her arm before she could escape.

"That was good to see – you took control of the situation."

Samantha silently stared at the door but yielded to his touch. With uncharacteristic gentleness, Marcus sat her on the bed in attempt to look her in the eye.

"But Samantha took control out of anger – emotion. What were you thinking of in that moment?"

Samantha seethed. She didn't want to talk to him or anyone about it. Marcus would never understand, the man remained a cube of ice with no heart or feeling. But if she didn't speak up, he'd get it out of her one way or other. It was the 'other' that always unnerved her.

"What *he* did to my mother."

Marcus sighed. "You can't be thinking of him that way during sex. It always leads to emotional responses – reactions. Alexandra has to stay in absolute control when she is using her body. No emotion whatsoever. She doesn't react but initiates, calculates. After all this time, what is it you don't understand here?"

The attitude set her off. They treated her like a child one moment and expected her to be a robot the next. First Samantha then Alexandra. Marcus had the audacity to be upset with her, and after she'd agreed to go along with this lunacy. Warm tears cascaded down her face. The words just spilled from her mouth in a torrent.

"What is it you don't understand? That monster raped my mother, and I live as the product of that act. What do you expect me to do, be able to just walk up to him someday, rip off my clothes and tell the man to have at it? Then somehow I have to pretend that I'm not the by-product of his past indiscretion? That I'm not committing incest? At least he would be an unwitting party in that regard."

In medical school she'd never been able to cast aside emotion. She couldn't do it then. She couldn't do it now. All this downplaying of emotions and feelings, never able to give acknowledgement to her disgust over what she had to do, wore her thin to near hysterics. Be Alexandra. Be

Alexandra. The mantra swam in her weary mind to the point that even when they allowed her time to sleep by herself she just stared at the ceiling or walls. How in the world could one separate oneself from it all? From reality?

The dead eyes of the prostitutes in the New York emergency rooms, on the subways and street corners, came back to haunt her. She had become just like them.

A hand flew at her from out of nowhere and connected across her cheek. It stung. It burned. It rattled her mind. Marcus stared at her with dark blue eyes before his image blurred. Samantha slid from the bed and dissolved in a heap on the floor. Sobs wracked her body. The ache had seeped through to the core of her being, more stark and overwhelming in its force.

Arms lifted her and lay her in the soft folds of the bed. Marcus stretched out beside her and wrapped her with the same unusual gentleness he'd displayed moments before. Eventually Samantha's tears subsided. She slept.

The darkness clawed at the edge of her dreams.

***

The release of pent-up emotions set Samantha along the path the Elite needed her to walk. Her mind focused, sharpened, and absorbed every morsel of study, whether by book, body, or bed. As Debrille grew more pleased with her progress, he rewarded her with increasing autonomy and welcomed sleep. The security of her position increased, her life holding greater value in the circle of the Elite. She saw it also in the way the guards approached or handled her –

more so in the way they avoided her. This confidence she exercised with Marcus during their nightly excursions.

Their sex grew meticulous, and with Samantha's increasing sense of Alexandra's power it sizzled hot and intense. They broke in the beautiful mahogany dining table, the countertop, and the enormous bear rug near the fire one night. Her mind worked constantly during the act, noticing the obvious and then ever so slight changes Marcus made around his rooms – the mirror on the west wall instead of the north, a red candle on the mantle in place of the white, the lampshade, a Cabernet instead of the Merlot on top of the wine rack. But never did she lose track of exactly what to perform with Marcus' mouth suckling her breasts, the muscles between her legs pulsating rhythmically around his rock hard member. She felt without feeling.

Marcus swept her up in ballroom dancing, the two left feet of Samantha replaced with the elegant and exacting steps of Alexandra. Samantha's body became Alexandra's the night she'd seductively slid from the black, silk dress and danced around Marcus in nothing but the diamond necklace and black patent stilettos. It was Alexandra's hands that assisted Marcus from his shirt and pants and led him by his willing penis.

No space existed between their sweating bodies as they danced the waltz, the tango, and the sultry rumba. Marcus' hands slid over Alexandra's hips, up Alexandra's back, as their naked and unencumbered bodies melted into fluid movement across the floor. They ended by writhing together on the parquet floor, uncaring if anyone should stop by to watch their escapade as Alexandra drew the semen from his body like sucking poison from his veins.

Alexandra knew she had Marcus the night he visited her chamber.

Throughout the months of training as Alexandra increased in prominence, Samantha's heart calloused over, never allowed involvement in the actions – only the mind of Alexandra, calculating, memorizing every movement and visualizing every document and schematic read that day. Samantha by day but Alexandra by night, a cunning seductress…

…and murderer.

CHAPTER 29 - A HOLIDAY

The sun warmed Samantha's face as she lounged on the soft, manicured park lawn. Tears streamed from her eyes behind the dark sunglasses, but she didn't mind dabbing them dry with the tissue as needed. For too long she'd not experienced the sunlight's embrace, felt the whisper of a breeze through her hair. Nearly a year they'd kept her practically bound and chained in the dungeon of the Elite. She felt like a parolee just released from a maximum security prison, the spring grass pure heaven as she ran her fingers through the tender strands.

Marcus too seemed to enjoy the rays from where he sat on the patchwork blanket, his eyes closed as if in sleep. Debrille's goons took up positions here and there around the park, a few even held up newspapers. Yeah, right – like any of those thugs could possibly read. They were good for bulk and brawn only, never for brains.

Thoughts of escaping the Elite were fleeting. Even if she could get away from these idiots, where would she go? How would she live? It'd only be a matter of time before they found her anyway, what with the little GPS chip embedded in her ear lobe, giving away her position twenty-four hours a day and threatening to blow her up at any second. Still, with all of her training Samantha couldn't help calculating any numerous possibility of flight – no matter how elusive. That was one part of the Alexandra puzzle she had gotten down very quickly. Probably something to do with her medical mindset of always trying to figure out every possible solution to a problem.

Several women ran by on the path, their faces reflecting the focus of a workout instead of enjoyment of the beauty around them. Sad how humanity took so much for granted. If she never saw another jogging path again it wouldn't bother her one bit. Anything but the daily grind of running.

A group of small children ran about playing catch with a big red ball. A strange longing arose – something she'd not allowed herself to think about since her surgeries. The Elite had severed all chances of having children with the removal of her fallopian tubes. Couldn't risk the possibility of pregnancy and production of a genetically deformed child.

Samantha hugged her knees to still the thoughts. "Tell me again why we're here."

Marcus rolled his head toward her and peeked out of the slit of one eye. "You need to be re-acclimated to the real world, see the sights, familiarize yourself with the D.C. area the next couple of weeks."

"So I'm a tourist now, am I?"

"More or less, but a tourist with a purpose."

Samantha swiped again at the dribbles running down her cheeks. It'd probably take said weeks before her eyes got used to the bright sunlight again.

"Wish you would have brought me above ground on a more overcast day. Why today?"

"No specific reason, just seemed like the time was right."

Rolling her eyes, Samantha responded, "Oh, puh-leeze. Don't give me that crap. I can't even relieve myself unless it fits into the grand plan of the Elite."

Gripping her arm, Marcus sat up slowly, his eyes burning through the darkness of his sunglasses. Caution seethed through his voice. "Never mention that name while on the surface. It doesn't exist here. You got that?"

Just like he'd taught her, Samantha kept her cool even though his grip nearly cut off her circulation. She stared off after the kids again, but inside her heart pounded as she fought to keep automatic reactions under control.

"I understand, your highness."

"Enough with the theatrics. Just remember who you are up here."

Marcus let go of her arm. It felt like hundreds of needles jabbed it for a few moments after he released his stranglehold. She didn't even bother to rub it because it would only make him mad. Debrille would be angry with Marcus if bruises surfaced, and she could almost hear Alexandra's laughter in her mind at what Marcus would endure should bruising occur. Samantha shivered.

Several food vendors had set up their carts at the bottom of the hill. "I'm hungry. Are you allowed any cash?"

Marcus got up and stretched. "It might be a good idea to walk around a little bit, be seen and noticed." He wrinkled his nose as he stared at the vendors. "Corn dogs? That isn't part of your diet."

Samantha leapt off the blanket and crumpled it up before smiling at the good doctor. "But you see I'm a vacationing tourist today. Make it two, please." She nudged him in the ribs. "I'll take a soda to wash it down."

Mr. Grumpy complained all the way down the hill, the luscious scent wafting in her nostrils. After securing her snack, they strolled along the sidewalk toward the Washington Monument, two corn dogs in hand while Marcus held and occasionally sipped her soda. To the casual observer they might appear like any other couple on holiday, touring the numerous sights, tasting the local fare, and soaking up the beautiful day. When Samantha finished the first corn dog, Marcus casually held her free hand as she offered him a bite of the second.

"For appearances," he told her as he sampled a nibble.

A cavalcade of black SUV's tore past with lights flashing, two limousines sandwiched between and followed by additional black vehicles flying by down the street. Samantha stopped. She gripped Marcus' hand tighter until the rapid processional ended. The corn dogs sat like rocks in her stomach. It took all of her will to swallow the bite she held in her mouth, and she stared at the remainder before tossing it in the nearby trash can.

Her father had just passed.

CHAPTER 30 - HOLES

After each day's excursion, they had to descend into the dreaded hell-hole again. But when Marcus finally put a gun in her hand, all she could see was the President's face. Target practice encompassed the evenings below ground while her tourist experience continued above ground. Seemed an interesting combination: catch a glimpse of the President during the day and pretend to shoot him at night.

Something didn't fit. Why force her into being intimate with the President if they intended for her merely to shoot him? Marcus could shoot him in his sleep. They had a myriad of guards among the Elite with extensive weapons training. What about the Secret Service detail always running about? They were taught to take a bullet for the President without hesitation. No, shooting him didn't add up at all. She missed something in the equation.

However Samantha didn't mind learning her way with a weapon, well besides the weapon of sex. She'd readily pick up both with ease. Maybe if riding him to death didn't work she could throw a pillow over his head and suffocate him.

Or maybe she was supposed to use the pillow to muffle the shot.

That's what silencers are for, stupid.

Alexandra's thoughts frequently broke through Samantha's, the line between the two sides of her life no longer distinct. Made her think of in a marriage ceremony when the preacher would read that part about the *two becoming one* or some such blather. Samantha only hoped she could be one mind again someday. Hell, at this point she could almost have a conversation between the two factions warring inside her head. She longed for her life before the Elite. But there had been no life there either. Everything was a mess.

The cold Glock warmed in her hands as she repeatedly took aim at the paper target. Bam – right through the heart. Bam – right through the hole in the heart again. It went on and on, the shots muffled by the ear muffs.

One for Warner – bam.

Two for Debrille – bam, bam.

Three for Marcus – bam, bam, bam.

Bam.

Bam.

After emptying the clip she inserted another and continued until tears blinded the shattered target where Marcus' face stared back in her mind. With a frustrated thrust, Samantha lobbed the empty handgun at the mocking smile.

"Damn, damn, damn you all to hell!"

The entire thing left a gaping hole in her wounded heart, but Marcus had crossed a line. As she slumped to the floor the shameful day's events flooded back and sliced through it like a dull scalpel. The way he'd held her, kissed her – to know it all meant nothing.

Nearly every day they traipsed about D.C. as if they were a happy couple, lounging here, exploring there...finding shelter from the rain in a covered bus-stop. The various exhibits at the Smithsonian complex had drawn their attention that morning. The chill of the overcast day did little to disturb the pleasure of being above ground even if it meant she might run into Warner again.

Marcus had held her hand, his grip warm as he talked attentively to her about various artifacts, and stole aside to show her how their ear chips would display various escape transport tunnels around the complex if needed. They had a labyrinth of options all over D.C., the breadth of Debrille's vast undertakings shocking.

Late in the afternoon the clouds thickened over the area and caught them in a torrential downpour. The enclosed bus-stop offered the only sanctuary to wait out the rain but not before they were soaked to the skin. A small group of parochial school girls followed them into the enclosure and stared in wide-eyed fascination.

She hadn't expected Marcus' tender kiss, sliding his hands up her wet arms to her face as his blue eyes poured into hers. Then he'd pulled her closer. For a moment Samantha had felt sheltered from the cold spray, the cooling day, the darkness warring in her mind. But as always, it was only for appearances. The innocent girls broke her trance with their stifled giggling.

The mad sex she could handle. The tender kiss she could not. It wormed its way into her soul – her mind.

Her heart.

She had to escape before she went mad, but futility always invaded those thoughts. All exits recognized only the signal of the implants in Marcus, Debrille, or the guard leaders. The elevators to the surface were locked down without their biological component. Then, of course, they tracked her everywhere she went. Damn the microchip.

Samantha had to walk. She refused to pull up the holographic display and didn't care if she got lost somewhere within the cavernous tunnel system. The glass wall of the greenhouse drew her attention, the entrance secured by more of Debrille's goons. They weren't growing marijuana or anything that she could tell just some sort of flowers, so the need for the security had to be because of the research lab on the other side. Thus far they'd not allowed her access to the lab where Marcus concocted only God knew what.

Over the tops of the plants, Samantha watched Marcus at work in the lab. What made the man stay? Better yet, what was the catalyst that made him join the Elite in the first place? If anyone could figure out a way around the ear chip conundrum it was Marcus. Regardless of how much she hated the man, she also respected his obvious genius. Without him, Debrille basically had no one to carry out ongoing research – at least no one she knew. Then again, Marcus probably liked all the training he got to do. Perhaps Marcus was the heir apparent to their little hell.

And you're nothing more than his whore.

Angry tears gathered in her eyes again, and she stormed away from the scene. Soon the familiar station where she'd disembarked so long ago loomed. The train happened to be docked and the doors swished open to admit her to the lush world. Dim lights and the faint hum of the air system were the only signs of power, no direct control system on board. She made a mental note to check down track for an operating system or control conning. Something had to power the slithering snake.

It had been so long since the day she'd first boarded the luxury liner. She didn't even remember half of the rich burgundy and mustard colored décor – probably had slept most of the way since she'd still been recovering from the explosion. Everything from her old life had disappeared, even her appearance. No more home to go to, no car, no job – no Gramm.

The old ache rushed back. Did anyone miss her? Joe? Was he sad when he'd thought she'd died in the explosion? Mr. Eddis? Were they safe?

What do you care? It'd be your own fault if something happened to them anyway.

Alexandra again broke through her thoughts, but Samantha didn't want to listen. Not tonight. She wanted to feel comforted by the past. There was something good in it at least, not like what she had become and what she soon had to do.

The columned walkway led back to her quarters. She was tired. She wouldn't go to Marcus tonight. He'd see right through her and sense her struggle – and that wouldn't bode well for the *Plan*.

After jamming a chair under the doorknob, she undressed and crawled beneath the billowing white down comforter, snuggling into its warmth and imagining Momma's arms around her. Tonight she was only Samantha, a little girl without cares.

For a moment, the darkness lifted from her dreams.

CHAPTER 31 - ON DISPLAY

"Cease fidgeting, my dear. Let her check the hem one last time."

Being Debrille's Barbie doll should've become second nature by this point. But Samantha's nerves wouldn't be stilled.

The seamstress checked and rechecked every detail of the white silk dress made for the occasion. The ruffled edge of the plunging V-neckline lay gently over her breasts, accentuating every curve and nuance to the most exacting detail. The recent weeks in the sun and time under the sun lamp had bronzed her skin to perfection. Every eye in the crowd would be drawn to her.

The stylist had pinned up her auburn hair and let curling tendrils escape from the nape to fall into the valley of cleavage. They may as well have pointed a blinking neon arrow to say *big boobs on display*. If she got even slightly chilled, her nipples would protrude from the thin silk to entice any man nearby.

Samantha had to swallow her surprise when they placed on her head a wide-brimmed white hat – just like Momma's. She felt weak in the knees as she stared at herself in the mirror, still unable to get used to the green irises gazing back at her. Momma would never recognize her little girl now.

Marcus looked comfortable and relaxed in his white linen slacks and jacket, like something straight off of a Florida beach. A quick tuck of her arm into his, and they entered one of the surface air lock elevators. The ride up always felt like it would never end, but this time Samantha hoped it wouldn't. The past weeks she had looked forward to the top-side excursions in the sun, the wind, the rain. But now her job began, her part in the Plan. Alexandra would make her grand appearance.

Breathe deep, girlie. Be Alexandra. Be Alexandra.

The cold steel of the tube doors reflected her image as fear melted into confidence. Power flowed into her legs. Strength straightened her back. She lifted her head and looked square into Alexandra's eyes – and smiled at what she saw.

The elevator opened into another glaring white shaft. They chose the next doorway and climbed a few additional floors. After jogging through several high-speed rides, they finally opened onto an elegant hallway, different than the other apartment floor she'd seen on previous trips to the surface.

The lush golden carpet was riddled with faint swirls of emerald and red. Marcus didn't explain where they were and Alexandra didn't ask. She allowed herself to be escorted, keeping watch on everything as they passed by and down the flight of stairs into the lobby of the Melrose. The doorman hailed a taxi that whisked them down Pennsylvania Avenue.

To the White House.

***

The Easter Egg Roll took place on the White House South Lawn every year. Scores of families lined up early to earn their children a place of prominence to sport with the President and First Lady. The First Dog kept the children entertained as he disrupted the festivities with his antics, running after the eggs and entangling the legs of the children.

Alexandra waited, hidden beneath the hat and sheltered by a tree at the edge of the milling parents. The President chased down the dog and laughed with the children. The First Lady gazed adoringly at him as the President nestled the naughty Schnauzer in her arms. They played the image of a happy couple quite convincingly.

From beneath the hat, Alexandra carefully scanned the faces of the crowd and peeked at the Secret Service detail stationed at the ready. Every aspect of the grounds and the building deserved scrutiny, mentally matching every blade and stone with the data she'd spent months only reading about. As the time grew near, Marcus gently nudged her, the festivities drawing to a close.

The media cameras picked her up as soon as she stepped

into the sunlight and the breeze fluttered the ruffle at her breast. For a moment, Alexandra separated herself from Marcus and the throng and glided across the South Lawn, the white of her dress contrasting against the green. She sensed all eyes upon her, felt the hush of the crowd for but a breath. The breeze fluttered and pressed the silk against her legs, outlining every curve. Alexandra paused for effect and glanced up demurely from her hiding place beneath the hat.

The tiny white purse slid off her shoulder in one fluid motion and dropped to the grass. Slowly she bent to retrieve it, giving ample view of the sculpted cleavage between the ruffle. Shutters snapped at such a rapid pace, if the photographers weren't careful their cameras might explode. Alexandra chuckled.

She didn't even have to look in the direction of the President to know she'd captured his eye. For a split second revulsion arose at the thought.

Be Alexandra, girlie.

Marcus glided up next to her and tucked her arm in his as they blended again into the crowd. He steered them to a conveniently waiting taxi beyond the Ellipse.

Her hands shook. Her knees felt weak. But she had to hold it together and play the part at all times on the surface. Alexandra closed her eyes and leaned back against the cool seat.

Marcus leaned in close and brushed her cheek with his lips. "Perfection," he whispered.

It was enough to allow her to breathe again. She snuggled into his arms and relaxed against his solid frame. For just a moment she let down her guard and became Samantha, imagining the arms were Joe's.

Tears pooled in her eyes as she touched the hat brim and thought again of Momma – and the atrocity she would be forced to perform.

***

President Warner could barely contain himself among the innocence of the crowd as he watched Vice President Durksen assist a little girl with her dropped eggs. The younger man would make a good father if he ever took the time to relax and settle down – unlike himself.

"Who was that incredible creature?" Warner whispered to his Chief of Staff as he pulled him aside.

Forsdale kept his composure, so solemn and serious. The breeze didn't dare to muss even a single hair on his head. He always played his part well.

"I've never seen her, Mr. President."

But Warner had – once – just a glance, but it had been enough. The motorcade had buzzed down the street a few weeks ago. She'd been arm in arm with the same man, her gaze alluring, disarming, the red hair caressing her face. Immediately he'd been enraptured and tossed aside last year's resolve to temper his dalliances, even dreamed one night about her wrapping those long legs around him and burying his face among those tits. He'd awoke with an aching hard on that had to be tamed.

How long had she been part of the crowd today? How could he have missed noticing her voluptuous body until the opportunity had passed through his fingers like sand?

"Damn it, then find out who she is and make sure she is invited to the next State Dinner."

Forsdale arched his brow ever so slightly. "Sir, the next State Dinner is a full three months away."

Warner groaned inwardly and waved to a passing family – couldn't wait that long. "Do we have any pressing business with the Russian President?"

"Nothing's on the books, but I'm sure we could *create* a reason. President Viscinskiev is always willing to clear his schedule to toss down a few bottles of vodka with you."

Forsdale never missed a beat. But tossing down vodka was not what he wanted. "Devise a premise and get him here as quickly as you can. Find a reason to arrange the dinner in his honor."

The First Bitch had noticed them and strolled in their direction with a fake smile plastered on her face. Her eyes smoldered with scorn.

Warner continued, "In the meantime, find out who that woman is and make sure she's there. She can even bring that man if she wants."

"What if *that man* is her husband?"

Warner smiled. "I'm sure he won't mind if the President of the United States has urgent business with his wife, hmm?"

Abbie strolled up to him and slid her arm into his for one more photo opportunity. Then he could get away from the woman for the rest of the day and consider his next conquest.

Just thinking about it threatened to give Warner a hard on in front of the cameras. His smile grew. What would the children think of that?

CHAPTER 32 – LOOSE ENDS

The murky alley stunk of rotting produce, stale beer, and fresh vomit. Hiding out in the dark alcove between the dumpsters allowed a sheltered view of either end behind the Off-Broadway bar strip, but the aroma left little to be desired. Of all the places in New York City, someone should be shot to suggest such a meeting place.

Eric lit another cigarette more for scent disguise than for personal need, careful to hide the glowing embers from watchful eyes. Tremors in his hands increased before the moment passed. He'd need a fix soon.

Glass rattled along the far end of the alley. A drunken panhandler swayed into a trash can, picked himself up, then sorted through the spilled contents. The shadows enveloped him as Eric slunk deeper into the alcove and crushed out the cigarette. The bum might or might not be his contact – he couldn't take chances.

After slowly picking his way along the alley, the vagrant made his way to the dumpsters. Eric heard a low mumble.

"Marco."

"Polo," Eric grunted, and rolled his eyes at the juvenile secret code.

The man squeezed into the alcove and nearly overcame him with the accompanying stench. Eric lit another cigarette. How informants managed living in such squalor he'd never understand. He wasn't nearly as dedicated to his job to endure such filth.

The vagrant studied him through strands of grime encrusted hair. "Where's Harry?"

Eric drew on the cigarette and blew smoke into the informant's face to staunch the foul breath. "Reassigned. Name's Eric."

"Tom."

He half expected Tom to teach him a secret handshake in order to be ordained into his club. Instead Tom snatched the cigarette out of his mouth and drew hard on it before relaxing against the brick. The lines in his face eased. Time to get this circus over with.

Eric lit another cigarette. "You have something for us?"

Tom stuck out his greasy palm, and Eric dropped the remainder of the pack and the lighter in it with an accompanying wad of hundred dollar bills. Tom's hand disappeared into the frayed trench and pulled out a smeared envelope.

The contents were startling.

Tom continued, "The Russian connection isn't even the half of it. You know all those prostitute murders lately – the redheads?"

"I'm aware," Eric stated as he rustled through the documents.

"I don't have anything definitive to give you yet, but my sources are telling me it goes all the way up to someone at the White House."

Shit!

In one fluid motion, Eric pulled the Glock and shoved it into Tom's chest. The close proximity diffused the shot and kept it from echoing along the corridor. The lighter he'd given Tom clattered to the ground, the cigarettes scattering around his inert form. Eric picked up the lighter and held it under the envelope until the flames caught and raced up the edge.

After dumping the smoldering evidence in the trash, Eric fished the cigarette pack out of Tom's coat, lit it and laid it near the dead man's outstretched hand. The frayed edge of the trench caught before Eric made his way to the end of the alley and out of sight around the corner.

CHAPTER 33 - THE MEETING

While Marcus stayed in his suite to slip into his tux and clip on cufflinks, Samantha stroked on liner and lipstick, slid into silk stockings, and had the auburn curls coifed. With everything in place, the seamstress eased her body into the dress. The body condom left little to the imagination.

The nude silk had appliqués in just the right places coated with silver threaded embroidery, small sequins and creamy pearls. If she sat, walked, or bent the wrong way she would be exposed to the world from head to toe, that is if she didn't pop the seams of the glove-like fabric first. The ride in the limo was going to be sheer torture. It'd be a miracle if they arrived with her dress in one piece and still clinging to her curves. With everything else she had to think about, it irritated Samantha that Debrille had arranged for the design of such a delicate piece.

The dress moved with fluid grace as Samantha glided down the corridor to meet Marcus and Debrille for the final briefing. There remained little else to be said, however Debrille had one final decoration for Samantha to juggle. A lovely sapphire jeweled and enameled comb was tucked into the folds of her curls, peeking just above her crowning glory.

Debrille stated, "This piece you will not have to bother with. It will function on its own – only make certain it remains in place for the full of the evening. Once you have completed your mission allow him to take it as a token. Then and only then may you remove the comb from your hair – gently."

"What is it for?" Samantha asked.

"That is not your concern."

"I'm going to be toting it around all night – damn straight it's of my concern."

"You are already damned to hell, my dear. Don't make Dr. Marcus send you there tonight before you complete your task."

Marcus slithered up to her side and extended his elbow for her arm. "Focus your mind, Alexandra."

Samantha slipped her arm through his and closed her eyes. A shiver passed down her spine. Breathing deeply, she willed Samantha's thoughts and mind into a dark small corner before easing into Alexandra just as she'd eased into the dress. The click of her heels on the tile floor matched the cadence of her breathing. Her back straightened. She lifted her chin. When she opened her eyes, her purpose drew to a sharp focus.

***

The limousine snaked through the gates of the Ellipse. Media came out full-tilt as cameras flashed non-stop each time a limousine pulled up to the entrance and vomited its passengers onto the carpeted walkway. Butterflies momentarily erupted in Alexandra's stomach, but she pushed them back down where they belonged. Nothing would stop her tonight. She would have her way with him and then spit him out like the garbage he was.

Emotion – swallow the emotion.

Their turn came. The attendant opened the door and Marcus stepped first into the fray and held his hand out to her. Alexandra slid her legs demurely out the door and laid her hand in his before she stood. A chorus of lights flashed in her eyes. Murmuring among the crowd rose in intensity as the pair glided down the carpet and up the steps of the North Portico into the White House.

The Entrance and Cross Halls were brightly adorned with two elegant cut-crystal chandeliers from 1775 London. The marble floors swept to the red-carpeted colonnade of Cross Hall where portraits of previous Presidents stared back. Pink lilies graced the 1817 Monroe pier table, while occupants interred on the suite of early 19th century gilded Italian settees. The Marine Orchestra strummed out a smooth rendition of Tchaikovsky in the corner near the Grand Staircase. Everything of which she'd previously only read appeared to be in place.

"Tell me again how you managed this," Alexandra asked Marcus.

Marcus stared off toward the Blue Room and steered them toward the doorway. "We have friends."

Marcus' chiseled features twitched when he clenched his teeth. What did he think about what she had to do? How did it make him feel? Alexandra drove Samantha's thoughts from her head. None of them could feel anything. There was only the job to do – follow the plan.

The line curled through the doorway of the oval-shaped Blue Room to greet the President, First Lady, the Vice President, and the Russian President. So there he stood – live and in the flesh, the bastard who had raped her mother and murdered her family.

Samantha's, not Alexandra's.

Warner had a distinguished bearing, smiled, shook hands jovially as he introduced his Russian guest. The room seemed to shrink. The light filtered as Alexandra focused in on her prey. The hair appeared a finer gray in the light than in pictures, deeper creases around the eyes. Strong jaw line – eyes dark like…

A shiver passed down her spine, and Alexandra turned her focus from the President to the First Lady. The woman appeared elegant, regal with the lithe body of a dancer. Her face had seen too many plastic surgeries, her eyes drawn into slits. The slit gray eyes suddenly turned and stared in Alexandra's direction. They were cold, penetrating – knowing.

A man approached the President and whispered in his ear. Alexandra mentally sorted through photos of the White

House staff she'd memorized – Benjamin Forsdale, Chief of Staff. Warner excused himself and was immediately flocked by Secret Service agents as he exited, earning a momentary glare from the First Lady and a hushed utterance from Marcus.

"Damn."

"What's wrong," Alexandra whispered in kind.

"Change of plans."

Pressing bodies jostled to get past as butterflies crowded her stomach. They pushed through the horde and back out into Cross Hall, the silver head of the President rapidly disappearing down the red carpet of Cross Hall to the West Wing.

Alexandra grabbed a fluted glass of champagne from the tray as the server passed by and willed herself to nonchalantly sip as she scanned the room. It wouldn't do for her to get tipsy. The music seemed too loud. The crowd stared, and Alexandra suddenly felt conscious of the thinly protective condom caressing her curves. She couldn't do this – not with her…

Samantha's, not Alexandra's.

As she started to gulp the champagne, Marcus strolled up and stripped the glass from her grasp.

"Keep your wits about you, *Alexandra*. Breathe deep and focus before you draw attention to yourself."

A tinge of anger reflected through the thin veneer. Very

un-Marcus-like to allow emotion. Was it concern driving him or something more?

They were so close to accomplishing their goal – her goal. Did Marcus suspect her ongoing inner struggle between the factions of her mind? She'd worked so hard to hide it.

Don't screw this up, girlie.

Alexandra straightened her shoulders and faced Marcus. "I imagine the dress draws more attention than anything I could possibly do." She smiled and winked.

Marcus visibly relaxed. "Why don't you tell me a bit of history concerning some of the artifacts you see here. Dazzle me with your expertise."

For the next half hour, Alexandra strolled the rooms joined to Marcus' arm and recited the many artifacts and their history. She told him of the men behind the portraits in Cross Hall, the busts in the niches, the furnishings and artwork. All the while gazes were drawn to the artwork Marcus had created with her body. She immediately knew when *his* gaze caressed her form as the President again entered the room.

The First Lady slid her arm through the President's and directed him toward the State Dining Room as dinner was announced, but Alexandra could still feel the warmth of his stare, the heat of his lust. Even as Marcus pulled the chair from the round table for her, Alexandra sensed the passion of Warner's presence. During polite and guarded conversation with those seated at the table, through each course to the beef Wellington, Alexandra remained aware of what the night held. It gave her a heightened sense of herself – a heightened sense of power.

As the elegance of the evening moved again to the Entrance and Cross Halls, the Russian President escorted the First Lady to the marble floor while Warner took the Russian consort into his arms to begin the dance. They crossed the floor with fluidity through Mozart, but as the Marine Orchestra began the strains of Beethoven, Marcus glided with Alexandra to the floor. Every time Warner would dance near, Marcus would weave them out of reach.

Alexandra whispered in Marcus' ear. "I thought you wanted me to meet up with Warner tonight. When will I have the opportunity if you keep pulling me away from him?"

Marcus responded, "Have you never heard of the infamous cat and mouse game? The more the mouse tries to get away, the more the cat wants him – toys with him until the cat is delirious and goes in for the kill."

"So now we've moved down the food chain to cats and mice. I didn't know the two could mate."

Marcus shot her a glare to rival the First Lady's before it melted away behind his mask. "Just be patient. Play him along a bit. You've got all evening."

At that moment, Alexandra glanced up and stared across the room into Warner's eyes. The hall seemed to slow as Marcus spun her round and round in the waltz. Each time Marcus' head moved away Warner's gaze locked onto her.

205

Her heart rate increased. Sweat beads gathered along her brow. She smiled before lowering her eyes. Had him.

After spinning around the room to countless waltzes, Marcus steeped himself in conversation with a gentleman who'd sat at their table during dinner. Alexandra strolled the room, hypnotized by the pianist as his fingers tickled the ivories, flying up and down the keyboard in a blur. Gramm had always wanted her to take up piano, had urged music of any sort to calm the raging tornado inside her. *Ah, Gramm.*

Alexandra snapped from the reverie and pressed the thoughts back down – Samantha's thoughts. Dangerous thoughts. A server strolled by and again she snatched up and sipped from a champagne flute, willing her hands to stop trembling.

The droning voice of Marcus came up from behind and cut through the fog as she focused on who she was.

"And I'd like to also introduce you to my lovely escort this evening. Alexandra Shuvinovsky, may I present President Frederick Warner."

She turned to face the up-close and personal stare of President Warner. For a split second her stomach lurched, felt as if it caught in her throat. Then flashing a smile and handing off her glass to Marcus, Alexandra found her wits. As his hand found hers, she gripped it without hesitation.

"Mr. President, how delighted I am to finally meet you in person."

Warner's voice was smooth and controlled. "The

pleasure is all mine, Ms. Shuvinovsky."

"Your tax policies have been well received, I believe."

He waved away the praise. "Politics are on hold tonight. Shuvinovsky – Russian, Ukrainian or Lithuanian, I presume?"

"You presume correctly, sir. My great-grandparents were part of the nobility that escaped Mother Russia before the tide turned against them in the October Revolution of 1917."

"And did they teach you the mother tongue?"

Alexandra put on her best pout. "Sadly, I never knew my great-grandparents. But the tongue was passed on as part of my heritage." She slipped into fluent Russian.

Warner's face grew flushed as he moved her to the dance floor and carried on a conversation with her in Slavic. The warmth of his hands spread through the thin fabric. She steeled herself to his touch – fought to steady her voice and bury the thoughts that threatened to surface, smiling through his efforts to maintain a proper decorum among the watching crowd.

Warner steered the conversation. "I've heard you are quite the historian. Do you specialize in Russian history?"

"Knowing and understanding my heritage was always of importance to my family, but they were proud to assimilate into our American culture. It is fascinating how quickly we have come to dominate the world pecking order, is it not sir?"

"Ah, the power of American ingenuity. The great melting pot, as it were."

"And I am privileged to be dancing with the most powerful man in the world," Alexandra purred.

An otherworldly gleam leapt into Warner's dark eyes. She'd seen that sparkle in only one other eye – that of Debrille. It glinted sadistic, maniacal, of a man who knew he had the world at his feet, control his and his alone.

As they left the dance floor, Warner introduced Alexandra to Russian President Viscinskiev, and the three of them carried on a brief conversation in Slavic. The lies of a past never lived flowed from Alexandra's mouth as easily as the words she spoke. She'd always had an ear for languages in school. But that hadn't been Alexandra's school.

Warner eventually drew her again to the dance floor. They danced to Grieg and Tchaikovsky, eyes watching as the couple slid along the floor. All the while, Warner remained pleasant and admiring, but Alexandra knew he could little resist an occasional glance downward into his anticipated cup of pleasure.

Though he maintained an acceptable decorum to the studious watchers, he wanted her – from the heat of his hand pressed into the small of her back, the controlled passion in his voice and lust in his eyes, to the blatant brush of his thigh against hers. Yes, he desired her with all the fire in his belly, even half expected him to give into the passion and stroke her breasts for the entire crowd to see.

To all the attentions Alexandra responded with acceptance – a sultry smile, a smoldering glance. She succeeded in the first fruits of her assignment. Yet somewhere within the dormant recesses of her mind the thought threatened to make her lose the lovely dinner they'd recently consumed.

The introductions, the admirations, the façade all culminated to a slight crack in her performance. Her hands trembled. Her knees felt unsteady. After being introduced to and seduced by more than half the D.C. powerhouse in attendance, Alexandra's focus waned with the night. The evening wore on her like the deepening of a moonless sky – the darkness called.

She couldn't answer it – couldn't hold onto it all long enough to complete the task as the minutes rolled into hours. Urgency pressed a quick scan of the crowd for Marcus, who'd made himself scarce since introducing her to Warner. How odd to find him sitting on the Italian settee in conversation with the First Lady. The woman's attempt at a smile was as cold as her eyes.

The Elite had taught Alexandra to be constantly aware of her surroundings, to deduce more from every detail than mere appearances. The memory of the First Lady's gray slits turned on her in the Blue Room earlier in the evening gave her a moment's pause. Then it hit with stark clarity. The First Lady knew – knew why she was there. Not the whole of it perhaps, but she knew very well the reason for Alexandra's presence.

Benjamin Forsdale's second interruption of the evening

saved her from the night's fate. "Mr. President, your presence is needed again on that previous matter."

The regret stenciled evident on Warner's face, in his moment's hesitation. "My...Ms. Shuvinovsky, your presence this evening has been a rare pleasure," his glance darted to her breasts before settling again with a sly smile on Alexandra's face, "one that I hope may be soon repeated."

With a flick of her clutch, Alexandra extracted her card and slipped it into Warner's hand. "My card, Mr. President, and may I say the pleasure has been all mine."

As Warner disappeared down Cross Hall, it took all the effort Alexandra could muster to keep from melting on the spot. Marcus caught her urgent stare and extracted himself from the attentions of the First Lady.

"Get me out of here...please."

Without argument, Marcus slipped her arm into his and escorted her to the Portico. The cool night air penetrated the sleek dress, but no comfort remained in the cool breezes. Marcus handed off the valet card and their limousine pulled around. Alexandra fought to maintain a semblance of control as they entered the vehicle then collapsed against the dark interior as soon as they pulled away. Samantha emerged.

A slap across the face pulled her alert as Samantha stared into the rage of Debrille. His nostrils flared, his face almost purple.

"You did not complete your part in the plan!"

Instinctively she lashed out, but Marcus' rock-like arms were there to subdue her before her nails could dig into Debrille's face. The precious jeweled comb came flying out of her hair and caught Marcus across the face.

"Damn the plan!" Samantha yelled.

"Get your cat claws back where they belong."

"I'd rather use them to tear your eyes out and let you bleed to death."

Debrille didn't even flinch. His eyes stared wild, out-of-control.

"Shoot her."

Marcus released the gun from the limo case and pressed the cold hard steel to her temple. Samantha didn't care anymore – she welcomed the momentary report that would put her out of her misery. But the flash and fire never came. She peeked through a slit to find Debrille with his hand out to stop Marcus from completing his directive. The extreme color had faded from his face and a disconcerting serenity spread across his countenance.

"I have a better idea for the cat, Dr. Marcus."

Marcus offered, "An extended version of the cat and mouse game?"

Debrille smiled. "Precisely."

CHAPTER 34 - AN INVITATION

"Disturbing developments have come to my attention. I should be back from Peru within a week."

Marcus glanced up from the microscope at Debrille's revelation. The reformulation had him stumped, but some promise had shown in another possible application of the new substance.

"Now? Alexandra meets him again tonight."

"Then it is up to you to ensure the cat does not strike until my return. I have decided your original idea of drawing out this game to have merit."

Merit. The idea was damn brilliant and why he'd gone through the trouble of fully educating her in the first place instead of making her ready for nothing more than a brothel. Samantha was his masterpiece.

Once upon a time, Debrille had taken him on his South American jaunts to the meeting of the minds. No longer. Ever since Samantha had joined them, she'd become his prodigy, his complete responsibility. It kept him chained to the nearby underground instead of giving him the freedom of worldwide travel he'd previously enjoyed.

However, it also had allowed him greater time for research and development of new specimens, to develop new uses for the plants he'd germinated in the lab. Research had always been his first love – at least in another life.

"Understood."

"I'll bring back whatever Josef has concocted in our absence. Auf Wiedersehn."

"Auf Wiedersehn."

Marcus watched as Debrille left through the biometric compartment and headed toward the train before focusing back on the microscope. Disturbing developments. Wasn't like they hadn't faced such scrutiny before, so why the urgent meeting at the head? Everyone appeared well and in place above ground. Must have something to do with elsewhere in the world. All moved along swimmingly in their own backyard after recent updates.

Debrille had received the information of her health and well-being with eagerness, pleased she wasn't experiencing the extreme side-effects. The news must have made Debrille feel nostalgic for the old days.

Why else would he wax German?

***

Even through the packed Georgetown campus crowd,

Alexandra could make out Debrille's goons stationed throughout the nearby floor seating. They'd taught her well. The invitation to the President's televised speech had referenced one Alexandra Shuvinovsky, but somehow Debrille still managed to get his beefcake seating as well.

The stares of the nearby attendees wouldn't have disturbed her as much with Marcus close by. For so long all she'd wanted to do was get away from him, and now that he wasn't tailing along she sensed his absence. She hadn't realized how confident in her role he'd made her feel.

But Alexandra was a capable woman, confident in her ability to capture attention and keep it. The rest she'd have to improvise.

The tension electrified when President Warner and Vice President Durksen took to the stage. As the crowd erupted in thunderous applause, Alexandra plastered on a wide and seductive smile that immediately drew Warner's glance. In mere seconds his eyes canvassed the lavender chiffon clinging to her curves as if his stare might rip it from her body, before focusing his attention over the adulating throng.

In the back of her mind, Alexandra heard the speech, had already memorized the copy of it they'd received that morning. Only twelve Secret Service agents surrounded the stage, but though Alexandra kept her attentions focused on Warner, she still had in mind the likely placement of other agents throughout the arena from the floor plan she'd studied.

Other invited dignitaries sat nearby and fidgeted on occasion as the speech drove past the twenty minute mark. The flash of cameras dwindled to a sporadic dance until the end of the thirty-nine minute speech when they erupted like strobes as Warner and Durksen began making the rounds of the dignitaries.

As he neared, Alexandra's heart raced. What would Warner do? What signal would he give? Surely he hadn't invited her to just get some eye candy. There was a greater purpose to the invitation, otherwise Debrille wouldn't have been in such a frenzy to make arrangements.

Then he was in front of her, a twinkle in his eye as he took her hand in his. A jolt like an electric current passed over Alexandra as their cheeks grazed one another, and he whispered above the din.

"Go to the agent at the north floor exit."

Alexandra smiled with all the coy confidence she could muster and watched him make his way through those remaining down the line. At the first available opening, she picked up her purse and made her way toward the designated rendezvous. Her heart pounded. Was this the night? Were they going to have to do it here among the concrete and crowd?

Be Alexandra, girlie. Be Alexandra.

An arm curled firmly over her own before she was even aware of his presence. "Ms. Shuvinovsky, please come with me."

Though she allowed herself to be directed, inside Alexandra berated herself for not seeing the agent first. The goons had probably already phoned it in, Debrille unhappy and preparing her punishment. How could she have been so careless?

Nevertheless, she followed along through the labyrinth of concrete down beneath the arena. The events of her life these days always took her back underground. A black steel door greeted them as the agent directed her inside.

Warner had removed his jacket and tie and poured cocktails among a spread of gourmet finger foods. How had he beaten her to the room? Last she saw, he had continued stirring among the crowd.

No bed, not even a sofa, just a couple of leather chairs occupied the quarters. Perhaps they'd go at it on the floor like she and Marcus on occasion. The thought of Warner touching her like that momentarily repulsed her, but Alexandra never let it show on her face.

As he handed her a glass of champagne, Warner's blue eyes traveled to her ample cleavage. She could almost feel his desire to reach out and stroke them to see if they were real.

Nope. Plastic Barbie doll, Mr. President.

"Ms. Shuvinovsky, so good of you to accept my last minute invitation."

"So good of you to invite me, Mr. President." Alexandra flashed an engaging smile before taking a sip of the offered beverage.

"Too bad your gentleman friend could not join us."

"The invitation was only for one."

Warner's feigned regret could not contain the slight smile that curled the edges of his lips. "A terrible oversight on my part."

The seduction charged the atmosphere, and Alexandra forced herself to drink in the sensation, allowed it to pulse through her blood. She seated herself in one of the nearby chairs to offer him a better view. Warner's knuckles whitened as he stared.

"To what do I owe the honor, Mr. President?"

The other chair remained empty as he made the arm of her chair his perch. "It was unfortunate that I had to cut our delightful discussion short last week at the dinner. Of course, a historian such as yourself could never pass up the opportunity to research subject matter up close and personal."

"So you are appealing to my work ethic now?"

Though she expected it, Alexandra still shivered from the soft stroke of Warner's fingers on her arm – the night's true invitation. From where he sat, she could get a good bite out of his penis and stem the approaching madness. But she purged Samantha's rising rage, staunched the spread of emotion.

"I'm very interested in hearing more about your work

ethic."

"But wouldn't you rather see it?"

She took his hand in hers and slid his finger into her mouth, suckling it and stroking with her tongue, all the while watching Warner's face and eyes twitch with pleasure. Success radiated as she blasted past his thinly veiled attempts at seduction and took the upper hand. His guard melted at her feet. Alexandra gripped his hand tighter and held the finger fast in her mouth.

Red flushed Warner's face. "You are the little vixen."

For a moment, she removed his finger from her mouth. "I serve at my President's pleasure," she purred.

That was all he needed. She lost her grip on his hand as he pulled her to his lap and slid the hand up her leg, fondling the clips on the garter belt.

"Such a classic undergarment, Ms. Shuvinovsky." Warner's breathing paced far ahead of her own.

"Fits well for a historian, don't you think?" She felt his growing hardness against her thigh. Could she really go through with this?

Warner's next question surprised her. "What color is it?"

Ah yes, his weakness. Alexandra smiled and brought his face nearer her own. Breath fell hot against her cheek – the breath of hell.

"Red."

Before he could release the clasp, commotion outside the door stopped them cold. They leapt to their feet like two teenagers who'd been caught making out on the basement sofa, as the black steel door ground open.

The imposing presence of Vice President Durksen darted into the room, momentarily holding Alexandra's gaze before settling on Warner.

"Mr. President, my apologies, but we just received an urgent message from Forsdale. The Defense Secretary's call has been forwarded to the limousine."

The agony in Warner's eyes reflected clear as he kissed Alexandra's hand. "Ms. Shuvinovsky, it appears we must again cease our *discussion* to make way for service to the people. Until next time."

Alexandra's legs threatened to give way, a reprieve once again granted. After Warner bolted from the room, Durksen closed the door but not before his green eyes settled on her. His steely gaze remained in her mind even after the door clanged shut.

CHAPTER 35 - ROSE GARDEN TEA

The invitation to the Rose Garden Tea brought a sense of triumph. Even Debrille had to admit that her coy actions had only increased Warner's interest. If she played it right, she could have Warner completely subdued within a matter of weeks. Even so, Samantha had to fight the overwhelming revulsion when she thought of where the game must culminate.

Be Alexandra.

The robin-egg blue skirt covered her rear but little more, the squared neckline of the matching linen top accentuating her robust bosom. At least the wide-brim matching hat gave something to shield her from prying eyes.

The First Lady eyed her when she rose to welcome the guests. Ladies of many nationalities and status smiled like the good little debutantes they were, their hat brims saluting in unison as the First Lady offered her greeting. They all shared a similar reason for coming to the tea, but Alexandra had a purpose. Conveniently, her place at one of the many cast iron tables allowed a view near the Oval Office windows. No doubt Warner had so arranged it to ogle her body and salivate over the object of his *affections*.

Fine. She'd play her part – after all, she'd win in the end.

As a continuation from their previous seductions, Alexandra slipped off one pump and slid her foot along her other leg, long and languishing. Occasionally she reached down as if to scratch her ankle and slowly slid her fingertips up her calf and along her thigh. Though her skirt could get no shorter, she carefully raised the skirt's edge to momentarily flutter the red garter beneath and toy with the clasp.

When tea and cucumber sandwiches were served, Alexandra raised her eyes demurely to stare from beneath the edges of her hat toward the Oval Office. The heat of his gaze radiated from the windows. She sensed his heightened desire.

Thus it was no surprise when the waiter appeared again to offer her a torte and slipped a fragment of paper at the edge of the plate. *Excuse yourself*, the note commanded. Her stomach tightened.

Play the part, girlie. You are not Samantha but Alexandra.

As such, Alexandra would not go right away into his arms. Alexandra would make him work for it. Alexandra would taunt him further, increase his fervor.

The thoughts pleased her, so she remained seated and enjoyed the raspberry filled torte, taking slow, sensuous bites, letting her tongue curl the edges of desire. After touching her napkin to her lips, she let it drift to the ground and bent over to pick it up. Her ample breasts hugged the neckline of her top and threatened to spill over. Again she lifted her eyes to glance at the Oval Office windows, smiling as she shared her abundance to the man hidden in the shadows.

The waiter soon came again to her table.

Alexandra called him up short. "Excuse me, but could you direct me to the nearest powder room?"

The waiter's green eyes pierced. "Certainly, ma'am. Please follow me."

The tall waiter led her through a labyrinth of White House corridors, his dark hair cropped like military. Secret Service. This guy was no waiter and proved as much when he led her to the top of the Grand Staircase and told her to wait around the corner, his eyes ogling every inch of her perfectly formed body. He knew what she had come for. Slowly he descended the stairs and stood near the column on the ground floor.

"My dear Alexandra," Warner breathed into her ear.

Alexandra swallowed the knot in her throat and turned to stare into the face of the President.

"Why, Mr. President. It is my pleasure again to see you," Alexandra replied. "I want to thank you for the kind invitation." She rested her hand invitingly on his chest, felt the rapid pulsing of his heart. In time she would still it.

"The pleasure is all mine." Warner's eyes delved into her cleavage as he pressed his hand to hers. He raised Alexandra's hand to his lips and first kissed her fingertips, palm then wrist. "I enjoyed your little exhibition."

Alexandra's hand burned with his touch, the flecks of saliva. All she wished to do that moment was scratch his eyes from their sockets. Instead she removed her hat and tossed it onto a nearby chair. Could he see her trembling, feel it?

"I'm glad to be of service," Alexandra cooed.

Warner pressed her to the wall and leaned into her, his breath hot on her cheek. No preliminaries. No veiled seductions this time. His craving emanated from every pore.

If he knew, would he still proceed? Be Alexandra girlie. Be Alexandra!

"You set me on fire like the flame of your hair."

"Mr. President..," she began huskily, toying him with her eyes. "You speak so poetically."

Hunger and desire reflected in his stare as she played her fingertips along his sleeve in a welcoming gesture. He nuzzled her neck. Flesh seared as his hand traveled over her shoulder and down her arm. His breath came faster as Warner stroked the top of her breast, Alexandra's breast, and slowly ran his hand down the linen to squeeze the peak.

"I want you...need you now."

Stale tobacco wafted in the close confines as he pressed

in closer. Warner's body trembled with a passion he couldn't contain. Seemed everyone needed her. Alexandra smiled with the realization of power she had over men, then noticed her trembling hands.

Warner slipped his tongue in her ear and nibbled her lobe. Inwardly she cringed as he squeezed her breast. Nausea rose from the pit of her stomach, but she lifted her knee and audaciously ran it up the inside of Warner's thigh until contacting his swelling hardness. The idea of it inside her made her stomach lurch.

Hold it together girlie.

Incest. Adultery. It all flooded over her as an image of Samantha's mother flashed in her mind, replaced by a stare of Abbie Warner. The portrait of the First Lady hung on the far wall and glared back from the canvas.

Warner groaned with pleasure and swept his hand underneath her raised thigh and up her skirt, his slimy hand both cold and scorching. Gripping her ass, he pressed her knee harder into his groin before sliding his hand between her legs.

Alexandra nudged her head against the wall as reflexes took over. She dropped her leg and coyly slid from his grasp. If she didn't get things under control he'd do her here in the hallway.

"Only a taste of what is to come," Alexandra stated as she pressed her hat firmly back into place. She could hardly breathe as she glanced back at the portrait. "But not while *Mrs.* Warner is here."

Alexandra nearly flew down the staircase and met with the waiter again as he escorted her back to the festivities.

Speak of the devil.

Surrounded by her entourage, the First Lady strolled up the hallway in her sunshine yellow suit. Her icy glare threatened to crack Alexandra's already fragile veneer.

"Go easy on him," Mrs. Warner stated matter-of-factly as she swept past toward the East Wing.

Alexandra's heart pounded, her awareness heightened. She felt like going straight up to the old lady and having it out with her. What did she know and when did she know it? More importantly *who* did she know? But there were too many others surrounding the First Lady, and Alexandra would never get her say before they dragged her off the premises. In the meantime she couldn't get away from Pennsylvania Avenue fast enough.

Debrille had some questions to answer.

CHAPTER 36 - THE TURNING

When she reentered the hell hole, Samantha was ready to tear into whoever she ran into first. The greeting party just so happened to contain both Marcus and Debrille.

Good, two for one night.

The glass beads on the purse scattered as she slammed it against the tile. "Someone want to tell me what the hell is going on?"

The surrounding goons stiffened, but Debrille didn't appear ruffled by her outburst. "More questions, my dear?"

"You betcha, like why do all the cronies surrounding Warner seem to have this look in their eyes as if they know why I'm there. And that reminds me." Samantha turned her attention to Marcus. "What were you doing at the state dinner talking so intimately with the missus? Who else on the surface knows about the Elite and what do they know about me?"

Debrille interceded, but fire burned in his eyes. "*We* are

the Elite, my dear. We don't keep cronies, as you so eloquently put it, on the surface."

"Bullshit!"

They each stared the other down. Electricity crackled in the air. The vein in Debrille's neck throbbed, his eyes dark pits. She'd hit it right on the money. Fear no longer welled in Samantha's throat – confidence and knowing replaced it.

A smile pulled at the edges of her lips. "You've taught me too well to be able to pull the proverbial wool over my eyes. Your goons are too easy to pick out among a crowd of thousands. There were thirty there at Georgetown, yes? What about that waiter today? He's one too, isn't he?"

Debrille's response only solidified her knowledge. His voice was measured. "Be wary of cockiness, my dear."

"You can't play me anymore. It all hinges on me. I'm the ace of spades here, and it's now in *my* hands."

"We can still replace you, you know."

Samantha threw her head back and laughed, the sound more like Alexandra than herself as she became lost in the chasm between the two warring entities. "But you won't, Debrille. You're so close now you can taste it. It's in your eyes, the sound of your voice. Your reaction in the limousine after the state dinner spoke volumes. No, you can't replace me now – you *need* me."

Her heels clacked on the tile, echoing down the hallway as she made her exit for the evening. No response followed, but Samantha could feel Debrille's anger and frustration.

There had almost been a glance of pride in Marcus' eyes, the hint of a smile on his lips. The tide had turned. The knowledge made their confrontation all the more sweet.

CHAPTER 37 - THE ROOKIE

The SAC's voice boomed. "Rookie, get me a coffee – black."

"Sir." Agent Joe Roberts started toward the break room to see to the Special Agent-in-Charge's request, but before he'd even left his desk he was inundated with additional demands from other senior agents.

"I'll take a soda, rookie."

"Coffee here, one sugar."

"Make mine two – and add a little creamer but not too much."

"I like mine light, no sugar."

"Scotch on the rocks."

Joe rolled his eyes. "Funny, Laturno."

Special Agent Laturno's green eyes sparkled with mischief as he propped his legs up on his desk and slicked back his black hair – just like Chief Snowe in Wichita. He sure missed the guy.

Laturno continued, "Coffee – black."

"Coming right up."

The good natured harassment transpired as part of the overall initiation into the FBI. Joe had been none too happy when his assignment had come down after completion of training at Quantico. Why the D.C. Bureau wanted a good old boy from Kansas puzzled him. Yeah, he was a good detective, had been tops at Quantico, but the D.C. climate seemed a bit beyond his expertise. Thus far they treated him more like a gopher-boy than an agent, but he knew it all came as part of the routine.

If Joe were honest with himself, he had to admit the real reason for resenting his placement. It took him away from his important investigation back home, of finding out what had really happened to Samantha Bartlett. Haunted dreams had him hacking away at that underground doorway only to open it and see Sam fall down the shaft and disappear into blackness. The possibilities of what he'd have found if Castor hadn't completed demolition ate away at his brain day and night. Finding out what had happened to Sam drove him.

The one good thing about being in D.C. was the proximity of readily available information – espionage, international intrigue and speculation of events before they even happened. So much knowledge at the fingertips, it made his head spin. Thousands of tips of crimes, mob connections, and terrorism had to be sorted through and catalogued every single day. After getting settled, he'd waited a few weeks before sporting through files from the Midwest and discovered a very interesting file on Castor in the process. They even had copies of his reports from Wichita.

It took everything he had to keep his time in the computer files to five minutes on each occasion. No need to bring about undue suspicion so early on the job. One thing he'd learned at Quantico was that there were potential turncoats in the Bureau, and if you didn't play your cards right you could end up kissing the pavement with a slug implanted in the skull. If he could get into the document archives instead of having his searches tracked on the computer, maybe he'd have more luck. No way they'd let a probie in that place.

They hardly let him do anything except catalogue speculations, a little research for other agents, and tag-along on basic assignments. In Wichita, Joe had been used to being his own boss in a way – questioned by the chief but not in that irritating, patronizing manner as if he didn't know his nose from his butt. Then the connections he'd had there – felt like he was starting over from scratch, the last ten years a virtual nothing.

The day dwindled until only the SAC and a couple of other agents remained. Most of those with families usually left by six. The hour hand pushed eight before he decided to wrap it up to go grab a beer and burger with Laturno. No doubt they'd meet up with a couple of other agents carousing the night.

Still Special Agent-in-Charge Denver Hitchens remained – no telling what his wife had to say about the late nights, always the last to leave and the first to arrive. Did the guy even sleep? The man was impossible to read. Joe had always prided himself on being pretty accurate in his immediate estimation of suspects and people, but the atmosphere of the D.C. scene made him paranoid about everyone.

The raucous laughter and loud music trampled their ears when Joe and Laturno stepped into the bar. Laturno seemed to know every face in the crowd and immediately blended into the surroundings. Joe lifted his chin in acknowledgement to the few agents he recognized. Lately he'd felt on edge when they were out and about, as if he were being sized up by unknowns. He hated the fact that he couldn't fully trust his cohorts yet, might not ever trust them. Not a pleasant thought when you had to place your life in their hands. The D.C. life hardened the average soul. In just a few weeks it'd affected him too.

After greetings all around, Joe and Laturno found a table and managed to confiscate a couple of chairs.

Laturno started in. "So what's eatin' at you lately, kid?"

Joe nursed his beer. "What conspiracy theories do you have swirling around in that brain of yours now?"

"Hey, if I'm gonna play nursemaid to a probie, I need to know what's going on with you twenty-four-seven. Haven't known you long, but long enough to tell you've got some thoughts on the mind this past month."

"Nothing any other fish out of water wouldn't have."

"The D.C. life gettin' you down?"

"Just trying to adapt, that's all."

Laturno's green eyes bored into Joe's before he broke into a wide grin. "You need a woman, that's what."

Laughter erupted. "Now there's a complication I can well do without right now."

"I'm not talking strings and commitments – just a great stress reliever. See that sweet thing over by the door? She's just looking for a one-nighter."

The blonde sat at the edge of the bar near the door, short skirt showing off long legs and a revealing silk blouse. Otherwise, she was the picture of a political powerhouse aide. She sipped a white wine as she scanned the crowd and occasionally spoke to a few people she apparently knew as they passed by.

Joe shook his head. "Sorry, man. I don't work that way."

Laturno leaned in closer and lowered his voice. "But she's one of the top of the line. Only works government haunts. Hell, she probably works for the government during the day too. Expensive, but at least you're not getting some common street-walker. Who knows what kind of diseases those other girls carry."

Joe's blood ran cold. "Wait a minute, are you saying that girl is a prostitute?"

Laturno cocked an eyebrow. "You really are a greenhorn, aren't you?"

The beer soured in Joe's stomach. "In Kansas, we'd arrest her."

"Don't get your bloomers in a wad, kid. This isn't Kansas, if you haven't noticed. No fairy godmothers and ruby slippers. Around here, you gotta find stress relievers wherever you can get them. Hell, most of these high-class kind are better than government operatives. You've no idea the information you can glean from them if you're smart about it. Get a little between the legs and you can get a wealth of data between the ears."

"You're serious?"

"Hell yeah. Matter of fact, I could use me a couple of legs wrapped real tight tonight. Mmm-hmm."

Before disgust overwhelmed him, Joe changed the subject. For another hour he listened to the senior agent's blather before he excused himself to return to his tiny apartment. What had he gotten into? Those who were hired to police corruption were themselves corrupt. How long could he hold out until his soul was sucked in as well?

CHAPTER 38 - A WICKED WEB WE WEAVE

Joe took in everything Laturno said, all the while being careful not to say too much himself to conceal his distrust. Interactions around the office helped him peg who he likely could and couldn't bank on. He'd even given thought to asking Hitchens to reassign him to another senior agent, but that would cast suspicion in his direction. No wonder he'd always hated politics.

"Hey, rookie," Laturno called. "It's pushing eight. Time to get some grub."

"Go ahead, and I'll catch up with you after a bit. We had a crap load of tips today on the Peruvian money laundering scam, and I'm still trying to sort through them."

"I can wait."

"That's okay, shouldn't be more than thirty minutes. Crab night tonight, right?"

"I'm getting a hard-on just thinking about it."

"Order me a pound of legs, couple of crab cakes, and a side of slaw. Keep someone from stealing my chair, and I'll be right over."

"You can pick up the tab then."

"On a probationary agent's salary?"

"Hey, if I'm gonna have to fight for your chair until you can get your sorry ass down there, then you owe me."

"Fine," Joe grumbled.

One of the perks of living close to the ocean was the incredible array of readily available seafood. Had to find the occasional good in being stuck in D.C. – the only way to maintain one's sanity.

After Laturno left, Joe dug back in, sorting and cataloguing all the various tips, dividing them into credible information and crackpots merely looking for attention or a reward. The SAC would have the final say, but thus far his gut had been pretty on target. Some tips were more easily dissectible while others required a bit more discernment.

Joe could almost taste the crab melting in his mouth as he pondered the last tip. He glanced at the clock and realized he'd need to hustle before Laturno gave away his chair *and* his meal. The SAC's voice resonated behind him.

"Agent Roberts. Burning the candle at both ends, I see."

Joe glanced up to see Special Agent-In-Charge Denver Hitchens propped against the corner of his desk, picking up his award. The bushy, salt and pepper eyebrows made it difficult to see into his eyes unless his interviewee stared up at him. Joe enjoyed the rare luxury. Maybe that was why it always seemed so difficult to read the man.

Hitchens read the inscription. *"Director's Leadership Award.* Pretty impressive."

"Wish I could put it away, sir. You've no idea the flack I get for having to keep that on my desk."

A smile danced in Hitchens' dark eyes before his lips pressed together – back to business. "You're analyzing the Peruvian scam?"

"Yes, sir."

"There's a case I worked in the past that may have some relevance in this instance."

"Sir?"

"In your short time here, kid, you've shown an incredible ability to separate the wheat from the chaff. According to Laturno, you've also proven to be a man of integrity, and that's the kind of man we need more of around here."

Joe smiled. The girl at the bar the other night – now it made sense. They'd set him up to see how far he'd stretch the limits of the law. Several other conversations and *opportunities* resurrected in his memory, probably also set up to test his mettle. So Laturno was a good guy after all.

Hitchens continued, "There's more than one reason why I requested assignment of the top Quantico graduate to this office. This case has been ongoing for many years and the longer it has been around the more strands connect to the web."

"I'm interested."

The SAC lowered his voice. "I need you to do some research in the caverns for me. I want no written reports on this. Anything you discover you commit to memory, all kept between you and me. Don't even be talking to Laturno about it, got it?"

"Yes, sir. But I don't have proper security clearance to access the caverns without a senior agent."

"You'll have a temporary, high-level clearance in your desk first thing tomorrow morning. There will also be a signed form designating what division you'll be assigned to research in, but your verbal assigned division will also be nearby. Make nice with the bookworms and stiffs who oversee the caverns, at least for the first week. They'll tire of watching you and get lazy. That's when you work your way down the aisle to where I need you to dig."

"And where's that?"

Hitchens leaned closer and whispered, "What do you already know about Oleander Enterprises?"

CHAPTER 39 – THE DEED

Her worst dread was about to culminate as Warner's hot breath steamed against her neck.

Alexandra's neck. Alexandra's body. Be Alexandra.

The Lincoln bedroom beckoned, the curtains on the canopied bed swaying in welcome to the lovers embrace. Samantha's stomach turned as Warner tore her blouse open and suckled her breasts like a newborn calf. If he only knew.

Samantha fought to gain control of her mind and disappear into Alexandra. Alexandra would welcome the advance, the warm mouth sliding over her supple body, the cold hands expelling her clothing as fast as possible.

How did Debrille expect her to accomplish the deed? He hadn't provided a weapon, no poison to extract the final breath from Warner's lungs. The jeweled comb had disappeared after that first night. Was she to ride him to death? Did he think she would find a tool of destruction in the room and bludgeon him senseless? Why did she actually have to perform the sex act with him if all Debrille wanted was the man's death? Why had the question never occurred to her until now?

The hour had come and she couldn't back out now. With everything she possessed, Samantha fought to allow Alexandra prominence. Only Alexandra could do what must be done. There was no stopping it.

As Warner tossed her onto the bed, Alexandra rolled to straddle him from above. She unzipped her skirt and slid it over her head to join the growing pile of clothes on the floor. Warner's hardness rose beneath her, his desire urgent. She stopped the action by climbing to her knees and allowed him to ravage her glistening body with his gaze. Shame disappeared as his hands traced sweat rivulets down her curves. Touch electrified Alexandra's mind, her purpose, her moans encouraging exploration of her perfectly formed frame.

His voice panted need. "You are such a glorious specimen."

Alexandra pressed against him and stared into his eyes. "My body is yours."

With a flick of her tongue, Alexandra licked the sweat from his chest then drove down onto his ramrod member. His eyes narrowed and he threw his head back with a gasp. No more thought. No more questions. Alexandra hurled herself into the deed with full frenzy, drawing his seed as if drawing blood from his veins, raking her nails into his flesh to join the pleasure with pain. Again and again.

Alexandra extracted every last ounce of strength from his body before she rose triumphantly from the bed, leaving his spent casing gasping for breath. The power she'd drawn from him fed her hunger, her need for control. She needed him to want her again. Killing him had to come later.

As Warner lay in a stupor, she dressed before leaning over to whisper in his ear. "I'll let myself out, Mr. President."

"Yes, my dear. Tell the agents outside the door…that I am not to be disturbed." He smiled weakly. "First time anyone's outlasted me."

"To a night of firsts then. May there be many more."

The door creaked as Alexandra excused herself. The Secret Service agents stopped her as they realized she was leaving alone.

"The President said he is not to be disturbed."

One agent held her in her tracks as the other agent called into the darkened room. "Mr. President, are you alright?"

"Didn't you hear her?" Warner yelled back. "Leave me be."

"Yes, Mr. President."

As they released her, Alexandra smiled when their gazes settled into her cleavage. "I'm sure you'll get used to seeing me around for awhile, gentleman."

As she sauntered down the hallway, Alexandra gave an

exaggerated shimmy to her strut. Perhaps they'd enjoy another view of what they missed.

CHAPTER 40 – UNBIDDEN EMOTION

Samantha leaned against the wall and let the steaming rivulets of the shower flow over her head and onto her shoulders, streaming hot down her back. The water left red streaks on her skin, scalding like Warner's hot breath. Her hands clenched, arms and legs shook as she fought to keep raw emotion in check, little feeling the water that seared her skin.

Only feeling the horror that seared her soul. Damned her to hell.

Over and over she repeated to herself: *He's not your father. It was Alexandra, not you. He's not your father.*

An hour later as the water grew frigid, her skin changed to mottled blue and purple. Goose pimples covered her flesh. Samantha's legs no longer supported her, and she slid down the wall to where the water puddled in the stall. Her teeth chattered. She no longer felt the cold.

The darkness enveloped her.

***

In the dark of night, Marcus crept into Samantha's suite. Something nagged at him as he'd settled in for the night. He couldn't fall asleep. Thus he found himself in her suite, but no one lay in the perfectly-made bed.

Samantha had been noticeably quiet after their debriefing, giving short yet focused answers to Debrille's incessant questions. This first experience with Warner couldn't have been easy, but she had flashed him a brilliant smile upon her return, obviously satisfied with her performance. He had taught her well.

The faint sound of running water perked his ears, the sight greeted him upon entering her bathroom. Samantha lay huddled and shivering violently in a stream of ice-cold water, her skin mottled and lips purple. How long had the crazy girl laid here like this?

Marcus shut off the water and patted Samantha's cheek. "Hey, are you trying to invent a new shade of blue?"

His joke fell flat as she stared blankly at the wall, never acknowledging his presence with any false modesty or other nonsense. Marcus half dragged the little statue toward him to get a better grip, all the while getting soaking wet as he stepped into the tub. The water was freezing. Brusquely he toweled her off as best he could while she lay shivering against him. He really needed to get her warmed up soon.

Lifting her in his arms, Marcus carried Samantha into the bedroom and laid her on the bed. After tucking her among the covers, he turned the temperature down slightly on the radiant heating. It'd be just as harmful to warm her up too fast.

As Marcus watched her shiver violently among the covers, the slightest twinge of emotion tugged at his heart, something he hadn't felt since...

He closed his mind to them.

Debrille would want a situational report in the morning. Even though he'd been instructed to leave her alone tonight, Marcus struggled out of his clinging pants and crawled in behind Samantha, drawing his arms and legs around her chilled form. Gradually her shivering lessened, and her breathing relaxed as she drifted into legitimate sleep.

The rising emotion disturbed him, to realize it could come up so unbidden. The circumstances of Samantha's evening must have been much harder than any of them had realized. So many years he'd spent numb to true feeling, it had not registered when she'd returned. But he felt it now.

A concern for someone other than himself.

CHAPTER 41 – THE SEARCH BEGINS

A headache followed him incessantly in the beginning, but after spending weeks in the caverns Joe had adjusted to the musty odor emanating from acre after acre of documents, photographs, and texts. The outdated lighting hadn't helped either but perhaps it had become an ally of sorts. The stiffs at the front desk rarely bothered him in the murky light.

Joe pulled another box from the shelf and sat down on the cold concrete floor. In case anyone happened by, he again turned the label toward himself to avoid advertising his quest. The idea of getting caught digging through unauthorized boxes didn't sit too well. They'd toss him from the Bureau for sure, and Hitchens would deny instructing him to search in unauthorized territory.

More yellowed sales slips from Oleander. The Belgian-based company made a killing after World War Two, selling off confiscated art from throughout Europe. Before that they'd dealt in Egyptian antiquities. They'd found many a willing buyer in America – too many. If only Bill were still alive, he'd have found muddling through the numbers fascinating, though deplorable to see how the Nazis had profited from their thievery.

The sales slips were getting him nowhere. How soon did the chief expect some real results to his special clearance? At this point, Hitchens probably suspected he spent his days sleeping in the caverns instead of investigating.

When Joe surfaced toward the end of every day, Laturno would chide him. Even though he knew Laturno had to be itching to ask where he'd been every day, he never did. Sometimes agents spent time in the office while others disappeared for weeks on end. All worked hard, long hours regardless of assignments.

A green file appeared as Joe neared the bottom of the yellowed stacks. The sight gave him goosebumps. Perhaps this oddity offered something more tangible, but as he perused it, his heart sank in frustration. He slapped it shut, sending receipts fluttering across the floor – just a file on the death of Adolf Hitler and his mistress, Eva Braun. Who knew how long since it had gotten crammed into the wrong box.

Joe shoved the box aside and pulled out his lunch. The questions tumbled about as he munched on the chicken sandwich. How was a Belgian art seller connected to a little Kansas based company like Castor? Then why was Castor connected with Samantha Bartlett and her family? Some of the art through Oleander had come to a few wealthy Wichita families, but Sam's family was never wealthy, even with those large payouts from Castor. That money had gone initially to pay those ridiculous utility bills then support Gramm.

Joe stopped chewing in mid-thought.

The art.

Nazis overran Belgium in 1940, an early casualty in the European conflict of World War Two. Oleander was based in Belgium and had sold pieces the Nazis had stolen from Jewish families during the course of the Holocaust. However, Oleander existed long before the Nazis came to power in Germany. Oleander had to be more than just a front. Who ran the company? What did the name mean?

Joe stuffed the remainder of his sandwich in his mouth and grabbed the green file again. Hitler's death file in a box with information about Oleander. It seemed ludicrous, but one thing he'd learned over his career was never to immediately discount any possible connections no matter how ridiculous.

Oleander was European — Hitler was European.

Oleander sold Nazi confiscated art — Hitler was the supreme Nazi.

As he scanned through the file, Joe read of the suicide of Adolf Hitler and Eva Braun in an underground bunker in Berlin. The Soviet Red Army were the first upon the scene of the bombed out area. The Soviets interviewed and documented witnesses saying two wrapped bodies were removed from the bunker and burned.

The handwritten notes in the margins moved into the realm of speculation. *Hitler and Braun bodies. Soviet cover-up. Tunnel underground bunker.*

Joe's mind froze. A tunnel from the underground bunker.

Samantha and the concrete storm shelter – with a tunnel.

South American drug cartels and human traffickers used tunnels.

Nazis were found throughout South America after the war.

Middle Eastern terrorists used underground bunker systems.

Nazis were connected to Middle Eastern terrorists in the past.

The chicken sandwich churned in his stomach as his mind grasped a horrifying thought. Was Sam's family somehow connected to terrorism?

The file had an identifier written on the back. Carefully he wormed his way through the aisles until he found the proper section and pulled the box. Instead of putting the file back where it belonged, Joe glanced through the contained files of former Soviet communiqués from the forties, the translations notated below the Cyrillic script. The facts pieced together before his eyes.

He needed a computer, but he couldn't use a government issue. Not his home computer either. Joe scanned the contents again then chucked the files back in the box and tucked it where he'd found it. A quick sign-out of the facility then he hit the road south to Alexandria. No way he'd use an internet café in downtown Washington D.C. Couldn't have some agent or God knew who else peeking over his shoulder.

***

As he sped down I-395, Joe's mind whirled from the crazed thoughts. The file would have sure come in handy. Why hadn't he hidden it in his jacket? The act was beyond his normal character – the thought alone sent a shiver down his spine. He'd done it before in Wichita, but now the consequences of such actions could land him in jail…or worse.

Even though Hitchens commanded he commit everything to memory, Joe exited the interstate just outside of Alexandria and pulled into a drugstore. They only had four packages of 3x5 cards, so Joe grabbed them all and took them to the cashier.

"Is there a cyber café nearby?" Joe asked the plump woman behind the counter.

"Yeah, go east through this intersection and two stoplights down take a right and it's down the sidewalk, second door on the left." She smiled through her bright lipstick and handed him the bag. "Have fun researching."

The paranoia level thickened. Was he that obvious? It reminded him of Samantha's paranoia over her grandmother's death. Now he realized she was likely onto something — and gave her life in the pursuit. He truly needed to keep his head about him. No telling who they were dealing with.

The café seemed surprisingly devoid of human life. Unable to risk using his personal information, Joe obtained a temporary log-in and settled at a corner computer. The espresso helped to settle his nerves as he sipped the steaming brew.

After unwrapping a package of cards, Joe wrote at the top of one 'O. E.'. On the second card he wrote 'A.H.' and 'E.B.'. He'd worry about Sam's connection after he deduced any between Oleander and the reported deaths of Adolf Hitler and Eva Braun. Which one should he start with? Might as well start at the beginning.

He glanced over his shoulder before typing into the search engine the name *oleander*. An online encyclopedia popped up first, and he read all about and made notes on the oleander shrub native to Mediterranean and Asian regions, its ancient medicinal uses, and its dangerous and almost immediate toxicity as a poison. It sounded like very scary stuff — a medicine and a poison from the same plant. Hopefully doctors knew which to administer in ancient times.

Years in Sunday School class tickled his mind – something in the Bible about people being bitten by snakes and drinking poison without dying. Did the poison mentioned there perhaps apply to the oleander plant?

A click on another link took him to an ancient Egyptian

myth, a recipe of sorts reportedly utilized by the Egyptians in the time of the pharaohs to prolong his life – something to do with his god-like status to the people. Perhaps that's where the fountain of youth mythology arose. Oleander Enterprises had gotten their start selling Egyptian antiquities. Had they come across this so-called recipe along the way?

Numerous reports referenced modern day attempts at replicating the recipe – with disastrous results. A doctor in France had received a life sentence for killing five patients, even with signed authorization and hold-harmless forms from said patients. Ditto in Italy and Austria. After the fall of the Soviet Union, rumors swirled about deaths from experiments authorized by Stalin to develop a formula from the oleander plant.

As Joe scanned through all the documentation on the plant, he came across something that seemed almost too coincidental. Another name for the oleander shrub screamed out from the screen of the computer — Adelfa. The track he was on seemed almost logical in his present state of mind. Could the name of the plant perhaps have a tie to Adolf Hitler himself? And thus through this plant a tie to Oleander Enterprises?

Just for the heck of it, Joe typed *Oleander Enterprises* in the search engine. Information on the company popped unexpectedly onto the computer. It seemed too easy. If this was a secret underground company, why did they even have a public website? For the next forty minutes, he perused well known material on the company, its origins, operations, and reported history. They even had a site with information about the officers, board members and worldwide partner auction houses. If they were trying to keep the organization shrouded in mystery, they were doing a piss poor job of it.

Anticipation deflated. The last dregs of the coffee were cold as he tossed it down. Maybe this whole train of thought was an enormous waste of time.

The door chimed as a new patron entered, a voluptuous redhead. She reminded him of the world of high-class prostitutes Laturno had introduced him to. The muscles in his neck tensed as she glanced his way and smiled before she ordered an espresso from the clerk. Not the same girl, but something about her seemed odd – calculated. As he continued pecking his way through various websites and information about Oleander, Joe kept his senses trained on the woman. She wanted to be noticed.

Of course, if she was a prostitute then being noticed was an important part of her job – the hike of the skirt to scratch her leg, the high dollar clothes accentuating key curves. Something about her presence nagged at him – her actions, or lack thereof.

She expected to find him there.

After flirting with the clerk and giving him ample cleavage views while she drank her coffee, she excused herself to the restroom. Her smoldering eyes invited him to look as she passed by. Joe clenched his teeth and focused on the computer screen to slow the uptick in his heart rate.

These girls were well trained in the subtle art of seduction.

After exiting the restroom and with a final glance his way, she walked out of the café. Joe gathered up his note cards and stuffed them in the bag, careful to ensure none had floated to the floor, then signed off the ID. The clerk had other things on his mind, still gazing out the glass after the departed woman. Joe thanked him before clashing again with the busy realm of humanity in the bustling city. The woman had disappeared.

Glass acted as shrapnel with the explosion. The blast tossed Joe behind a parked car along the sidewalk, shielding him from further damage. The stun fogged him for a second before he recovered his wits. He'd have to dig a little glass out of his skin, but otherwise he felt relatively unharmed. The shop smoldered but the blast was fortunately minor – not so lucky for the clerk.

A screech of tires alerted him to the oncoming car. It sped up onto the sidewalk and mowed down three people before coming straight at him. Joe leapt and rolled across the hood of the car before landing in the street to stare after the speeding car — but not before he'd had a chance to stare into the eyes of the redhead from the cafe. He dialed emergency services on his cell as he tended to the injured littered along the sidewalk.

No doubts remained – his investigation was apparently on the right track.

CHAPTER 42 – THE RESOLUTE

The June sun beat down all afternoon on the Little Leaguers playing on the South Lawn. Alexandra had occasion to glance toward Warner and the First Lady as they worked the crowd and cheered the teams, but she maintained her distance. She rather enjoyed observing him, catching his occasional heated stare. Then Abbie Warner would ruin the moment.

The Missus looped her arm through Warner's and steered him among the crowd. He hardly had time to enjoy watching the game. If Abbie knew and cared less about her purpose in screwing the President, why did the woman cling so protectively to her man? It only made the fire in Alexandra's belly burn the hotter. The Missus wasn't woman enough to satisfy her husband.

Yet it still remained – Abbie Warner knew her husband was unfaithful. So why did she stay beside him? What did she have to gain, save for face? Hell, she had lost the face too many years ago even. No love remained between the two. The way Warner talked, there hadn't been almost since the beginning. So why did *he* stay with *her* then?

Their dalliance had thus far lasted two months. She'd never imagined in the beginning that she'd keep his attentions for so long. From all points and purposes, Warner's liaisons usually lasted a few weeks before his interest waned and he found a new skirt. Then he'd dump her off on that smarmy Chief of Staff. At least she wouldn't be forced to endure his hands and mouth on her body. Or would she?

Debrille seemed ecstatic and in no rush for her to carry out the final purpose with Warner. However, once completed, what were the Elite's plans for her? Would they force her to tolerate a man like Ben Forsdale or perhaps endure another surgery and get to Durksen? The man seemed to be cut from a completely different cloth. Even though Warner spoke in frustration at times about the Vice President, secretly Alexandra suspected he respected Durksen's focused work ethic.

Alexandra's musings were cut short as the familiar green-eyed staffer strolled nearby – her cue.

"Excuse me, sir. Would you direct me to the nearest powder room?" Alexandra called.

"Follow me, madam."

***

"Well, what do you think?" Warner asked as he snapped shut the door of the Oval Office.

Alexandra slowly walked around the striped sofa and stared up at the presidential seal gracing the coffered ceiling. The power. Here she stood in the office that had housed presidents – the power of the United States since 1934. She shivered with awe.

"Are you chilled, my dear?" Warner asked as he settled his clammy hands on her bare shoulders.

She knew what he was thinking – what he wanted.

"I was thinking of the power this room holds," Alexandra whispered. "The power you hold."

"Yes, the power. Can you not feel it?" His hands burned with desire as he slid them down her arms and around to her breasts. "Doesn't it excite you?"

Alexandra glanced at him seductively as she pried from his grasp and strolled over to the massive desk. The aged wood glistened in the sunlight streaming through the drapes.

"The Resolute or Kennedy?" Alexandra purred. She stroked the polished surface as she held his gaze with her own.

Warner smiled, the creases of his face deepening – his eyes hungry. "I see you know your Oval Office history. It is the Resolute".

Slowly Alexandra walked around the desk as she one-by-one unclasped the unending line of pearl buttons down the front of her coral-hued dress.

"The Resolute," she began, "from the oak of the H.M.S. Resolute, a British navy ship retrieved from the Arctic ice by the United States in eighteen-fifty-five, restored and presented to Her Majesty, Queen Victoria, as a gift of goodwill and friendship."

Alexandra let her dress slip to the floor and unclasped her bra, releasing her pent-up breasts and exposing her naked body save for the red garter belt. Warner's eyes bulged from their sockets, the throbbing vein in his neck pulsing with each rapid beat of his heart.

"Decommissioned in eighteen-seventy-nine," she continued, "the Queen presented to President Rutherford B. Hayes this desk made from the ship's hull." On hands and knees Alexandra crawled onto the desk and flared her legs. She stared over her shoulder, her eyes narrowing – welcoming. "It's time we break it in."

Warner scarce could get out of his clothes fast enough, seeming to care little for the open drapes. He pressed his face between her legs as he let his slacks fall to the floor and struggled to unbutton his shirt. Alexandra arched her back and moaned to urge him on, beginning a slow rhythmic dance with her hips as he lapped up the heat of lust.

The aroma of desire swelled as Warner climbed atop her back and gripped her breasts hard, searching for their peaks. When Alexandra dropped her head forward, he pressed his mouth into her neck, biting as a male subduing its female. He growled softly just before plunging into her.

Alexandra pressed her buttocks upward to match his

forward thrusts, their sweat mingling and dripping onto the historic desk. He swirled her nipples faster as their intensity grew. Instead of weakening over the months, Warner's desire for her had grown beyond anything she could have hoped. He had fallen completely within her power. He was totally hers.

Alexandra smiled with the thought. It spurred her on with each thrust. No longer did she think of the biological connection he held with Samantha nor the revulsion she had fought to hide with his first touches. Samantha had completely transformed into Alexandra with him.

And *she* enjoyed it.

CHAPTER 43 – THE PAST

A left. Another left. Turn right. The light changed red as Joe floored it through the intersection and onto the interstate. At last it seemed as if he could safely make his way without threat of a tail. Even so he weaved his way in and out of traffic for several miles. The neon sign of a seedy motel flashed in the rising dusk as he exited the interstate near the edge of the city. Lightning flashed in the distance.

His stomach rumbled in reply. After a quick run through the drive-thru of a burger joint Joe considered his options. Going home was out of the question at present. They'd probably traced his vehicle to the Bureau and thus assignment to him. He needed time to think, to sort through the information floating through his mind and plan his next moves. The motel offered a needed respite for the night. Just to be cautious, Joe parked his car in the lot of a new high rise three blocks down and skirted the lengthening shadows. Yet all the while he remained watchful of the few faces passing along the walkway.

No one ever smiled in the city, not a glance or eye

contact ever passed from one human to the next in the day-to-day passage. In the D.C. area everyone bred suspicion of everyone else. His heart ached for the friendliness and camaraderie of those he'd left behind in Wichita, but he stuffed the thought down inside. Right now he couldn't afford to think of what was in the past – he had to keep his wits about him just to have a future.

The cell phone vibrated against his hip. He let it be – no need to draw attention. What if it was Hitchens? Guilt washed over him. He hadn't checked in with the SAC all day – the man had to be a tad worried, especially if he'd already heard about the impromptu dance with a car hood earlier.

The simple room appeared surprisingly clean compared to the rough exterior. After devouring the contents of his bag, Joe pulled the packages of note cards from the bottom of the sack where he'd hid them and spread them across the table.

His hip vibrated again – the SAC. "Roberts."

Hitchens' voice boomed over the line. "We have a cardinal rule when you're out in the field, and you've broken it, Roberts."

He should have called from the car when his tail cleared. "Yes, sir."

The relief in the SAC's voice was palpable. "Heard about the wrestling match with the Chrysler. Glad to know you came out on top."

Joe smiled. "It's always the outcome I prefer, sir."

"Not going to keep the line open, and I don't want to know where you are. I had your low-jack signal turned off until you get a chance to brief me. Just glad to know you're safe. You got a lead?"

"I do, sir."

"Glad to hear it. Check in from now on like a good soldier but never from the same place."

"Sir?"

A serious tone replaced the gruffness. "You're targeted now, Roberts. They've got ways of tracking you even without GPS signals. If you're not careful, you'll be pushing up dirt real soon, so watch your back and keep your nose clean, you got it?"

"Yes, sir." A chill passed down his spine as the line went silent.

The note cards glared at him from the table – evidence. Hitchens' caution echoed in his head: *I want no written reports on this. Anything you discover you commit to memory.* Agent Roberts set about to do just that.

***

Marcus woke in a cold sweat, the dream from his subconscious clawing its way into his consciousness. They wouldn't stay away.

Quietly he slipped on his trousers and padded through

the hallways to her suite. Most nights he stayed up and tracked her whereabouts above ground until she made her way back to the cover apartment. Then he'd transport her below and debrief with Debrille.

These days Alexandra rebuffed him, and Debrille allowed her concession. But tonight he didn't want Alexandra – he needed Samantha.

The closet light glowed behind the closed door, Samantha's contrived nightlight casting a comforting serenity in the otherwise darkened bedroom. Why she chose to sleep with the light never made sense to him, but perhaps he'd find solace in it as well.

Samantha started as he climbed into the bed and nuzzled up behind her. Marcus reassured, "It's just me – Marcus."

She growled, "Leave me alone. I'm too tired to be Alexandra tonight."

The warmth of her skin drew the dream back to the surface. His body ached with longing for the past.

"That's okay. Samantha is who I need."

Her body stiffened as if she was ready to launch out of the bed or into a tirade, but she didn't move or speak. Slowly she turned to face him. The light's glimmer shined into his eyes, and it took a few moments for his vision to readjust before he noticed her studying his face. The hardness of Alexandra's distrust gave way to Samantha.

Marcus embraced her softness and brushed his lips against her forehead. Damn – he didn't want to need her. She was supposed to need him, not this crazy messed up shit. After all of these years, all of the women, why now? Why her?

His lips caressed hers. Still she continued watching him, her gaze connected to his.

Questioning.

Searching.

Yearning.

Yielding.

Their bodies knit together. Marcus made love to Samantha.

As he'd once made love to his wife.

CHAPTER 44 – A VACATION

The security gate swung wide to allow the convoy of SUV's into the compound. Relief washed over Samantha as the road trip into the mountains finally came to an end. Camp David loomed before her, the tall trees flashing by in a green blur. The presidential motorcade remained in a perpetual rush no matter where the road led.

The expeditious trip had been offered, but breaking away from the D.C. area to some place new made it difficult to hold onto Alexandra's persona. Getting stuck in the staff car wasn't what she'd envisioned either when Warner asked her to accompany him on the jaunt. The stares and half-hearted attempts at conversation from the regulars spoke volumes and threatened to break her façade. She was grateful the First Lady chose not to accompany them.

Truth be told, the vacation offer had come at a judicious moment. Anytime she wasn't with Warner she now had Marcus to deal with. Marcus. The man confused her – had her in knots. He'd changed in a way she couldn't identify. Around Debrille he treated her with the same indifference, but at night when he'd come to her bed?

Just as she'd come to the height of Alexandra's power, at the time when she felt it pulse through her being, Marcus had to go and screw with her mind again. The questions brought Samantha back to the forefront. The struggle between the two commenced as at the beginning. Was this all another test?

The vehicles vomited their contents en masse at the main lodge. Ben Forsdale herded the group into the building to set up shop. Even though she knew he was aware of her service to Warner, Samantha always felt like taking a steaming hot shower whenever Forsdale passed her way. His eyes ogled her in a way Warner's never did. The man was as slimy as they came.

The thought made her ponder Debrille's hold over her. Did Debrille have access to the Camp David compound? If she could get into the compound, could she also get out? Would the guards let her freely leave? No doubt she could lift a set of keys to one of the vehicles and play it cool through security at the gates.

The ear chip – the damned ear chip. The Elite would track her like a hound in a fox hunt before she could get more than a mile from the compound. Then they'd just have to decide when to hit the trigger to blow her head into a million pieces like a suicide bomber.

The thought froze in her mind. Samantha stared out the lodge window to avoid scrutiny as her brain processed the new realization. If they'd really wanted to kill Warner,

Debrille could have detonated the ear chip while she was in his presence. That would have been the easiest way to rid the world of the man. It might also provide the logical way to dispose of her and any evidence she carried to point toward the work of the Elite.

Samantha resisted the urge to rub her ear. So why hadn't they done it? What were they waiting for? Why require her to sacrifice her body on the altar of man all these months? Was it possible that Debrille had lied about that particular function of the ear chip? No, that didn't make sense because he had to have a way to keep her actions in check – keep his subjects from escaping his grasp. Could she perhaps detonate it and solve two problems at the same time? The next question surprised her. Did she even want to?

Ruminations ceased as Warner and his entourage swept inside from their walk around the grounds. He had an uncanny way of almost ignoring her while at the same time acknowledging her presence among the crowd. The cabinet members flocked to Warner, and the group adjourned to the conference room. Samantha caught the attention of the assistant.

"Could you please show me to the ladies room?"

He smiled. "Follow me, madam."

***

Moonlight streamed through the slit in the curtains. Samantha lay in Warner's arms and listened to him draw breath, a slight rattle deep in his chest. She could do it now – get the job over with – but then how would she get away? They'd discover Warner dead before she had any chance of leaving. Debrille probably didn't have access to get her out from the Camp David compound, a fact that gave her an odd measure of comfort.

A strange voice whispered in her mind. *Once the job is done you have no value to the Elite.*

Chills chased up and down her spine. She pried herself from Warner's grasp, careful not to wake him, wrapped herself in a blanket and stared through the slit into the wilderness beyond the pane. Secret Service agents probably stared back at her; she couldn't see them but knew they were there somewhere in the shadows of the trees.

The unbidden thought tumbled around her mind as if caught in a clothes dryer. *Once the job is done…once the job is done.* She hadn't done much thinking beyond getting to the final page of this chapter with Warner. Hell, she hadn't done much thinking beyond Alexandra in so long she'd almost lost her grasp on reality. But being Samantha was too hard. It at first felt warm, like running into an old friend, then painful as the memories surfaced of what had transpired to separate them in the first place. What did life hold beyond this chapter?

"The bed is getting cold, my dear."

Warner's groggy voice broke through her thoughts. She struggled to put back on the Alexandra mantle – and failed. What did it matter anymore? Samantha remained at the window.

Warner continued. "Is something troubling you?"

Though the water was already at a breaking point, Samantha treaded in with both feet. "Why did you marry Abbie?"

She could feel rather than see Warner's questioning countenance. They were in very dangerous territory, territory upon which they'd never dared.

Moonlight fell softly across his face as Samantha turned to watch him. Had he looked at her mother that way? Had he touched her the way he touched *Alexandra*?

She continued, "It's obvious you don't love each other."

A smile played on Warner's lips as he rolled to his side and propped up his head. "This is an unusual line of discussion coming from you, Alexandra. Are you feeling a bit romantic and nostalgic tonight?"

The playful attitude set Samantha's blood boiling. "Have you *never* really loved a woman?"

"Are you feeling alright?" Concern played across Warner's face. "Why don't you come sit with me here on the bed? Your face is swathed in shadows over there."

Get yourself under control, girlie.

Samantha gritted her teeth, her body shook, but she couldn't draw back from the precipice now. "Love – have you ever felt that for someone or do you just use them for what you can get?"

"You're serious?"

"Yes."

Warner pondered her question. Would he get angry? Would he toss her out on her ass like he'd done her mother? Or would he actually answer?

Finally he opened his mouth to speak. "There was one woman." Pain drooped his shoulders. "But we met too late."

The open revelation softened Samantha's response. The bed gave as she sat on the edge. "What happened?"

The question shook her. She should've never asked it. The answer Debrille had already given her about her own mother – she'd also read something about it in her letter so long ago. Could she handle hearing his confession? Would it change what he did to her mother? To her?

With a shrug, Warner continued. "I was married – she was married. My political career had already escalated. It would've been suicide to have attempted to start over then."

Disgust knotted her stomach. "Your career over her?"

"A decision that has haunted me my entire life."

"Why?"

The bed jiggled as Warner squirmed with discomfort. He finally sat up and looked her square in the face. His words caused Samantha's heart to skip a beat.

"Because I never knew our daughter."

CHAPTER 45 – A CONFESSION

"So why did you and Abbie never have children?"

Samantha linked her arm through Warner's and walked beside him along the mountain path. The overcast sky threatened rain and cast a chill pallor over the morning that matched the chill in her gut. She'd never intended to pick up the shocking vein of conversation from the night before, but once the floodgates were breached Warner seemed to desire the opportunity to bare his soul – needed to even, as if he were giving a deathbed confession.

Warner answered, "She never wanted them, couldn't have them – take your pick. Abbie's a few years older than I am. Hell, after the second year it was never really a possibility anyway."

"What happened after the second year?"

Warner laughed bitterly. "It would've had to occur by immaculate conception then."

"She rebuffed you after only two years?"

"From then on." He tossed a wry smile her way. "A man like me cannot function for long without release."

If she'd have felt up to it, Samantha would have flashed him a spectacular Alexandra smile. He looked as if he almost expected it. But try as she might, she couldn't muster the heart behind the effort.

"So why did you marry if you didn't love her?" Samantha asked.

"At one time she was a striking woman. She came from good family, had good connections. That sounds trite, I know, but my focus has always been toward the White House, and she was just as ambitious. We clicked well together in the early years – looked good together. I had her father's blessing. It all just naturally progressed us toward the altar."

"I'll bet she wasn't too keen on moving to Kansas."

"That took some convincing," Warner laughed, "but in the end she saw my logic. Middle America produces some of the finest presidents."

Samantha forced a chuckle, but her mind already drifted in another direction. "So what was different about…?"

How could she ask a question that involved her own mother and pretend she knew nothing? His professed love for her mother and the letter she'd read years ago speaking of the rape didn't mesh. Could it possibly have been a different woman and daughter? It seemed quite plausible, considering the number of dalliances he'd had throughout his years.

Warner completed her question. "The woman I fell in love with?"

Samantha only nodded.

The trees drew Warner's gaze as they walked along in silence. A muscle in his cheek twitched. The silence followed them until Warner spoke again.

"Her eyes – they were dark yet full of light, her hair a chestnut brown. There seemed an almost reserved sadness about her, as if she had a deep understanding of grief."

He breathed deeply as if remembering her scent. But his next words only solidified what deep down Samantha already suspected.

"She worked for one of my campaigns in Kansas. That was for governor because…well, that's when we conducted the bus tour."

The stomach churning almost came to a full boil. Samantha gripped Warner's arm tighter to stem the shudder that passed through her body. There could be no doubt now. Even though she'd hoped for someone else, she knew he was speaking of her mother – and her. She didn't dare trust her voice.

Warner continued, "She was a good listener. You rather have that in common with her."

The strangest sensation passed through Samantha's heart and lodged there. His statement, so simple and so heartfelt bore up an emotion she'd rarely experienced for anyone else. Pity – pity at living a life without love. Pity at living a life with little of any real value to show for it. Pity at being stripped of an opportunity for a family.

Pity at *knowing* her, but never as a daughter.

What she'd done with him as Alexandra fell away into the abyss of darkness. There was more to this story than what he'd told her – what Debrille had told her. What untold truths remained?

A knot formed in her throat and nearly choked off her next question. "What happened to the other woman and your...daughter?"

The pallor of the day swept over his face and deepened the shadows under his eyes. "They died."

CHAPTER 46 – A NEW TRUTH

The three days at Camp David ground to a halt, and all too soon Samantha descended the shaft into the hell-hole again. It was all Samantha could do to get through the debriefing with Debrille. All the while Marcus alternately scrutinized her face then glanced away, an odd gleam in his eyes. Could he read the questions on her face? For once she was glad for the Alexandra persona. Seemed easier to play that part now below ground to protect the growing doubts.

After escaping Debrille's grasp, Samantha quickly changed into workout gear and headed for the underground park. She had to smile as she huffed around the pathway, remembering her frustration at being run near to death in the beginning. But now it offered a respite from prying eyes, helped to clear her head to get in a good run.

After the fourth lap, Samantha pulled up at the waterfall pond and splashed her face with the cold water. The crash of tumbling water helped block out troubled thoughts as she closed her eyes. She jolted from the tranquil moment when an image of her mother flashed in her mind.

The letter – if only she still had the letter she'd found from her mother describing the inability to conceive, the campaign tour, the rape. The look on Warner's face when he'd spoken of loving her mother didn't compute. If he'd loved her, why would he rape her?

No matter how much Samantha still wanted to hate him, she couldn't deny that from Warner's perspective the feeling between he and her mother had been mutual. A misunderstanding wrung out of control? No. According to Warner's remembrances, it sounded as if the liaison was consensual.

A new question nagged her. Was the letter from the tombstone really from her mother? She strained to see it again in memory. She'd just assumed it was her mother's writing at the time she read it, but she was very young when they'd died. Was the letter forged? But why? More importantly, was it possible her mother had actually had an affair of her own free will? Her mother? There were too many sides to her mother now, she wasn't sure if she'd ever really known her in those short years.

All manner of emotion welled up and swept over her like a truck. Tears streamed down her face against her will. She splashed more cold water on her face to stem the heat of anger, frustration, confusion, and sorrow.

"Am I disturbing something?"

Marcus' question jolted Samantha from her dark reverie. She glared. "I'm not in the mood for anymore questions right now."

"Obviously."

Samantha saw a myriad of questions in his eyes, and there was no way she could voice the questions tumbling around her own mind.

"What do you want?"

"You seemed in a hurry to complete the debriefing today."

"Well after more than two hours, can you blame me?"

He started to retort then perhaps thought the better of it. "Maybe not. Will you be coming to my room tonight?"

They could zap her with the ear chip all they wanted, even to the point of frying her brain. Her emotions were too raw. There was no way she would give him any part of her mind, body, or soul tonight.

Samantha stood and stretched her legs, then she sprinted off again along the pathway.

"Go to hell."

She meant every word.

***

Marcus watched Samantha's retreating form and sighed. They were losing her. If he didn't watch it she'd end up taking him down with her. The time had come for her to carry out the purpose of her mission – that is if she could still perform. He shook his head when he thought of what would happen to her after the deed was done.

If only he had the courage to tell her the truth.

CHAPTER 47 – THINGS HEAT UP

Third hotel in four days. Joe parked the car and dragged his meager belongings into the shabby lobby to check into the room. He had to get some sleep.

"That'll be one hundred thirteen dollars and eighty-seven cents," the clerk stated.

His cash supply dwindled. They didn't want him using the ATM's anymore. The SAC had tried to arrange a meeting, but he'd missed the drop point in time. Got a good butt-chewing later on the phone. There had to be a way to connect with Hitchens or even Laturno without compromising them in his investigation. Just a few hours sleep. No way could they trace him that soon. Joe passed his card to the clerk and grabbed the key.

The investigation grew deeper and more bizarre by the moment. After depositing his stash in the room, Joe once again reviewed the latest bit of information with what he'd already committed to memory. Coupled with the lack of sleep, the insanity magnified ten times over.

Was it possible? Had he finally gone off the deep end?

Hitler alive?

There was no denying how the obscure references he'd found all seemed to fit together to form a carefully designed pattern.

Oleander sells off billions in stolen goods from Nazi Germany. Then those completely whacked sites talking about Hitler's Jewish roots through a man that his grandmother worked for as a domestic: Franken-something or other. That line of family had immigrated to Austria a generation before from Belgium. They had made a fortune as art dealers. Then Hitler an Austrian not a German – go figure. If he ever extricated himself from this, he'd have a field day with companies that sold textbooks to schools.

Then the oleander plant itself used for medicinal purposes but poisonous if ingested. For hundreds of years people had poisoned themselves trying to replicate the Egyptian recipe. Believers were feverish in their support of such fantasy. Could it be possible the fantasy had become reality?

During the Third Reich, Hitler was known for surrounding himself with the greatest scientists in all known and developing fields at that time. Countless lives were sacrificed during his experiments all in the name of perfecting the human race. With those lives at their disposal, was it possible that the Nazis had perfected the recipe?

Joe couldn't escape the memory of that piece of tunnel he'd seen in the remains of the bunker back in Wichita either. Nazi records revealed countless bunkers and an elaborate tunneling system all over Germany. Throughout Europe and the Mediterranean there were ancient caves, catacombs, and tunnels bored out of rock centuries before the Nazis. The Egyptians were famous for their elaborate crypt systems.

Perhaps they'd finally perfected the tunneling systems too and had brought it to America after the war. Far too many war criminals had escaped punishment after the end of World War Two. Many were traced to South America. With the southern U.S. border as porous as a sieve, it wouldn't take much to smuggle them into the States. Border agents had discovered numerous elaborate tunnels between Mexico and the United States.

Joe yawned. The weaving of the details in his mind had to stop for a few hours at least. He needed rest in an awful way. After kicking off his shoes, Joe slid between the sheets and closed his eyes.

The dream kicked in almost immediately.

***

The concrete chipped and splattered against his face as Joe hacked away at the bunker wall. His arms ached, the effort like moving through sludge. Each blow made hardly a dent, but still Joe kept at it. The flying pieces sliced through his arms and flayed his cheeks. If he weren't careful he'd lose an eye.

Days seemed to pass with little advance until the hammer broke through. Light glimmered beyond the wall.

He could hear her cries for help. With renewed effort, he dug with his bare hands until they were bloodied and raw.

When the hole was big enough for his head, Joe leaned in to see Samantha fall into a bottomless chasm.

"Samantha!"

His voice echoed down the crater after her rapidly descending form. Once again, he was too late to save her. The concrete wall swelled and wrapped itself around his neck, entrapping him forever in its grasp. Always he could hear Samantha's continual cries for help.

***

Joe awoke barely able to breathe. The cell phone jammed into his hip as he rolled on his side and swung his legs over the edge of the bed. The dream haunted him more and more. If Hitler were still alive was it possible Samantha lived also? He remembered her scent, the way her hair blew across her face in the wind. She seemed more real every time he woke from the dream. How would he even begin to find her if she really was alive?

Stay the course.

When he found Oleander's lair, would he find Samantha too? Was she wrapped up in her family's connections to this web? Had they kidnapped her, or did she go willingly?

Stay the course.

Samantha's image faded from his mind as the inner voice pulled him further from the dream. He had to focus on piecing the clues together on his investigation without letting it become personal.

A knock sounded and a muffled voice called out. "Room service."

Joe glanced at his watch – almost three A.M. What did room service want at that hour? He'd never even ordered dinner in the first place. Could this old place even have a kitchen?

His mind snapped fully awake. Like a cat, Joe crept across the floor and glanced through the peephole. A small metal cart sat right outside his door. No attendant.

Joe popped the Glock from its holster and unlocked the door. Just as he peered through the slit of the opening, a slight click drew his attention toward the floor.

Damn!

In one motion, Joe leapt toward the bathroom, slammed the bathroom door and pulled the shower curtain down as he landed in the tub.

The explosion rang through his ears and knocked the air from his lungs. The heat almost melted the plastic shower curtain to his clothes. A weight crushed down on him. As his senses adjusted from the fog back to reality, Joe realized the heavy bathroom door had landed over the tub in virtually one piece. The tomb had miraculously spared his life.

With his feet, Joe tossed back the door, grabbed his gun, and climbed gingerly from the tub. Acrid smoke and fire smoldered around the edge where the door used to be, the remainder of the wall tattered and flaming. The tub faucet still worked so he soaked several towels, wrapped them around his socked feet, and covered his head and mouth. He felt like a tiger jumping through a flaming loop at a circus as he forced his way through the blown out area.

The room lay in shambles. Smoke coated the air. Joe only wanted to escape and breathe freely again. Little time remained. He grabbed the chair and slammed it into the shattered window. With the second blow, the glass gave way and rained down two stories below along the sidewalk.

His shoes were nowhere to be found. This was going to hurt no matter how he handled it. Then an idea hit him – Joe grabbed the mattress from against the wall and with effort shoved it out the window. With a leap, he followed suit.

As he made contact with the mattress, Joe bent his knees and rolled to help absorb the impact. The cell phone would leave a nasty bruise, but besides being sore for a few days he'd made it. Or so he thought.

A bullet zinged past his ear. Joe jumped into the bushes and hugged the ground as he searched the darkness for the source. These guys weren't leaving any stone unturned. They were determined to take him out – and for what? They couldn't know what he was thinking, where the web of investigation was leading him unless each piece led exactly where his mind had traipsed.

They knew.

He'd painted a big bulls-eye on his chest by using that

blasted credit card. If he got out of this, he could teach the Idiot Agent 101 course at Quantico. Laturno would make a mockery of him to the others, but he didn't care as long as he made it out alive.

No more shots. He couldn't just pretend to be a bush for the next few hours and wait for whoever hid out to sneak up on him. As he slowly stirred from the garden, a barrage of shots sliced the air. Joe's feet hardly touched the pavement as he dodged the bullets and sought safe haven in the dark at the corner of the building, where he proceeded to take out as many lights as possible around the parking lot.

His car. This group probably located it and had it under surveillance or planted full of explosives to shoot up as if it were Independence Day. He slipped between cars and tried doors, hoping all the while that he didn't come face to face with his attempted killer. Finally a car door unlatched, an older model. The passenger seat covered him as he leaned under the driver's side dash. He'd never had to hot-wire in the dark, but Joe didn't have time to mess around. The pierce of the engine was a welcomed noise.

As Joe sat up and slammed the car into reverse, another series of shots rang out and shattered the rear window. Hopefully the owners had good insurance coverage. Rubber burned as he laid it down in the parking lot and the car leapt toward the highway. The explosion of his parked car nearly blocked his escape, but he careened by before the impact hit. The fireball lit up the night and allowed a glimpse in the rearview mirror of his assailant.

He could have sworn it was the redhead who'd tried to

run over him several days ago.

CHAPTER 48 – THE DIRECTIVE

"And when you put it on, the fabric bleeds into your own skin so that it is virtually indistinguishable," Marcus continued.

Debrille took up the reins with a smile. "Then when you must act, you press this area here that connects to the nerve impulses near your navel and you disappear in the blink of an eye."

"You've got to be kidding," Samantha chided. "I'm supposed to believe that you've been able to capture atomic energy in the molecules of this simple hosiery and *whoosh*, I disappear?"

Marcus spoke up. "Actually it is a lightweight fabric, not hosiery."

Samantha rolled her eyes at Marcus as if to intimidate him. Sad attempt, but it made her feel better. Seemed almost as if they were trying to talk her into putting on a body condom. At this stage, what was the point?

"We've used a combination of atomic energies and nano-technology and taken it further than anyone on the surface will ever discern."

Debrille certainly was proud of the accomplishments of his scientists – crowed like a blind rooster at midnight. She could almost see his South American sweatshop workers sewing the *fabric*. It still felt like hosiery – a little thicker, perhaps, but it certainly wouldn't leave much to the imagination when she put it on. A nauseous churning ensued. Why did she need to put it on?

"So what is the point with this high-tech hosiery?" She couldn't resist tossing a smirk toward Marcus.

"To assist in leaving the scene, if needed," Marcus deadpanned.

"The scene of what?" She didn't want to know, but deep inside, she already knew Marcus' response. The time had arrived.

"The scene of the murder."

It felt almost as if hands gripped her throat and held it tight. Her voice sounded small in her ears.

"Whose?"

"Warner's, of course."

The cavern spun with confusion. The Elite told her Warner had killed her parents, her grandmother, attempted her life. But after the months with Warner, the discussions, his frank openness about his relationships, her mother –

could it be they were wrong? Had the Elite misled her and Warner been honest? Who had lied? Who was really responsible?

Her stare shot straight to Debrille. "I won't do it."

She'd expected Debrille to turn beet red with rage, tell Marcus to draw his gun, maybe even shoot her. Fear coursed through her veins. Instead he stared back until a smile toyed at the edges of his mouth.

"Oh, but you will, my dear."

"Debrille, you can kill me and start over again with someone else. But that will still leave Warner alive and in power...a place where you will never be."

"I still have power over you."

"Only in your twisted mind."

Hot breath steamed against her neck as Marcus drew close behind. Debrille walked slowly to her, that sick smirk permanently etched on his face.

"You *will* kill Warner."

"What is this, some sort of Jedi mind trick? It isn't going to work."

"Or we will kill an old friend," Debrille stated.

Cold fingers of terror gripped Samantha's mind. A friend? She didn't have the luxury of friends. Who could they...?

"I don't have friends."

The pout on Debrille just didn't fit. "Are you so quickly forgetting the love of your life, Detective...I mean, *Agent* Joe Roberts?"

"Agent?"

"Yes – he's realized his dream of joining the FBI. Agent Roberts was at the top of his class at Quantico, and he's now stationed just above us."

Samantha's mouth went dry. "He's here? He's in D.C.?"

Debrille winked and motioned for Marcus to follow him as he walked away. "You always did catch on quick, just like your mother."

His words rang hollow in the air as the door slammed.

***

Marcus strolled down the hallway alongside Debrille, dejected, deflated, but he kept the mask in place. So Samantha still had feelings for this Roberts character. Too bad for him.

Debrille's words slid through his teeth in a whisper. "Is there still no word on relocating Roberts?"

"Sasha is working on it. Records show he entered the archives again early yesterday morning."

"Then tell that bitch to find him today or she's going back to that Peruvian brothel. Better yet, tell her I'm sending over some help. Contact Eric."

"Is that wise to pull him from cover?"

"We've got to find this guy quickly, or all our work will be for naught. Just tell him to be discreet about being seen with her. He'll know what to do."

"Yes, sir."

"And Marcus."

"Yes?"

"Don't ever question me again."

***

Tears dampened the bodysuit as she slipped it on. Would saline cause it to explode? Debrille was too smart for that – he was too smart for everything. Every time she thought she'd gained the upper hand, Debrille brought it all crashing in around her. He could kill her and it wouldn't even matter anymore. But Joe?

Joe Roberts. Even after all those years apart, he'd still set her heart pounding when she'd stormed into his office in Wichita. Yet she'd still pushed him away with her anger. How long had he been in D.C.? So close, yet forever out of reach. Her voice might sound the same, but he'd never recognize her after all the cosmetic work they'd done to her body.

How had she gotten in so deeply? Stupid question, she knew how, but she was no longer sure of the why. That had all been based on a total and complete fabrication. Warner wasn't all they'd led her to believe. Sure there were elements of corruption, philandering, lying, but he'd also shown her a side of himself that was tired of it all – a man who regretted some of what he'd done with the hand that life had dealt. The missus had some guilt in that too. Cast aside a guy's manhood and it was pretty scary what could happen.

Samantha stared in the mirror, straightened her shoulders and arched her back. Alexandra had to be in there somewhere, otherwise she'd never carry it off. Warner was the target. Warner deserved to die.

Corruption. Samantha whittled off the elements in which Warner had played the odds without getting caught. Philandering. All the different women he'd wronged and how he'd tossed his marriage vows aside. Importance lay in reminding herself of his bad character traits.

No matter what, she could never let Joe die because of her.

CHAPTER 49 – CATCHING UP

This was ridiculous – insane – but Joe had to risk it. They'd probably never expect him to show up at work anyway. Hitchens might just have arrived already, since he practically lived there.

The guards at the security checkpoint eyed him warily, checked then rechecked his credentials and badge. They let him through without too much questioning, but their eyes spoke a different story as he limped toward the elevators. He had to admit – he would be suspicious of him too if in their shoes. Ah, shoes.

"Good God, man!" Hitchens exclaimed. "Why didn't you call? I've been pacing the floor since three a.m.

Joe collapsed into a chair. "News traveled fast then?"

"Of course it did. You don't get to my position without a proper network." The SAC glanced down the hall before closing and locking his office door. He drew the blinds as he picked up the phone. "You've got one minute to get my hallway and staff office cleaned up."

After slamming down the phone and rummaging in his desk, Hitchens knelt beside Joe. "Let's see those feet of yours."

The numbness left as the SAC touched a moistened cloth to first one foot, then the other. Throbbing replaced it. Joe sucked in his breath and clenched his teeth.

"Had to...ditch the...car I took. Mine's gone."

"I know. Lit up like the Fourth of July, or so I heard. You've got some nasty burns here."

Joe winced and groaned. "Third explosion in four days."

"And some glass."

The extracted pieces rattled around the candy dish on top of his desk. "Ditched the car about a mile back and hoofed it here."

"Better not stick around here too long."

Exhaustion threatened to draw Joe down like the undertow of the ocean. "I know, but I broke my cell when I dove out the window. Hell, the damned explosion may have knocked it out first – who knows. Anyway, I couldn't call."

After bandaging the patient's feet, Hitchens walked back through the office and glanced down the hallway. "Good – all cleaned up."

"What?" Gingerly Joe stood.

"Your bloody footprints, that's what."

Stark realization flashed through his head like a cold shower. "They probably know I'm here then."

"Most likely. Come with me."

The SAC pressed a button on his key ring and the back wall moved aside to reveal another room. Speculation had surrounded Hitchens since the day he'd arrived. Everyone in their entire division theorized how their leader came and went. Hitchens *always* seemed to be in his office, which left no opportunity for anyone to snoop. Most of the other guys would be jealous if they knew.

Then why show it to *him*? Why now? He was just a probie agent, for crying out loud.

The room darkened after the panel slid shut and a screen rose to reveal a large situation room. As his eyes adjusted, he noticed diffused light came from the mass of screens lining the far wall. Blue lights lit pathways around the room like an airport runway. Amber lamps flicked on and off as people moved from one area to another like researchers at a library. The room bustled with energy.

"Did we just step into Mission Control at NASA?" Joe asked.

"Ours is more sophisticated," explained Hitchens. "Welcome to the Special Units Division of the FBI, Agent Roberts. Now follow me. We need to get you some fresh clothes and comfortable shoes."

As Joe waddled behind, the massive screens drew his attention. One was marked *Paris*, another *Berlin*, still another *Brussels*, and others with various locales around North and South America.

"What is all this?"

"Satellite imagery – part of a very long and involved investigation. Some of it may tie in with your recent work."

"Like what?"

"You tell me."

Caution seemed appropriate. What did these people running around here know about what he'd found? If they already knew, then the SAC had basically sent him on a wild goose chase. What for? Was the man sadistic or did he truly not know of the information Joe had found? How would that play into this other investigation?

"Brussels as in Belgium? Berlin as in Germany?"

"The same."

They came to a large glassed-in office. Hitchens flicked on a dim light before he scrounged around in a closet and pulled out a blue shirt and tan corduroy slacks.

"These should fit you alright. I thought I had a pair of tennis shoes in here too, but someone must have borrowed them. I'd give you mine, but you'd probably have a hard time squeezing into them."

"That's alright, sir. I'm sure I can find something before I go."

"Speaking of which, give me a rough and dirty on what you've got from your end."

Joe gave him the rundown on Oleander Enterprises and the strange oleander plant recipes. When he started in on his crazed idea about Hitler and the Nazis, the possible cover-up by the Soviets of the burned bodies at the bunker near the end of World War Two, he cringed. It all sounded so ludicrous coming out of his mouth, but the SAC's concentration never wavered. He soaked in every word as if it were gospel.

"I was pretty distraught at the time, so I don't know if any of this makes sense or not. Strangely enough, the pieces all started falling into place the further along I let my brain meander down this path," Joe said.

Hitchens nodded. "Good work, Roberts. This confirms pieces of several other investigators and brings the puzzle a little closer to completion in other areas. We've sat at a dead-end for some time."

So he wasn't crazy. Joe couldn't hold back a deep sigh of relief.

Before the SAC could get out another word, the office door flew open. They stared into the astonished eyes of Agent Laturno.

CHAPTER 50 – THE PIECES COME TOGETHER

"Rookie! You're alive."

Agent Laturno gripped Joe in a bear hug and practically snatched him out of the chair as if he were a rag doll. Then he held him at arms length. His green eyes flashed.

"Where the hell have you been, kid? You look like shit."

"Feel like it too."

"What kind of mess have you gotten yourself into?"

Hitchens intervened and handed Joe a new phone. "He's working a back alley for me, and he's obviously on the right track."

Laturno asked, "Does it have anything to do with…"

"Yes."

"Then you're going to like what I've found." Laturno slipped a picture from his jacket and slapped it on the desk.

"Marcus Stinson, MIT graduate, medical degree from Stanford in '57 – top of his class. Brilliant man. Showed great promise in research. Supposedly killed with his wife and kid five years later in a fiery car crash. Sighting reported two years after the accident by his mother."

Joe butt in. "Couldn't that have been a mere coincidence? Someone who just looked like him?"

"If you ran straight into your son coming out of a gas station, don't you think you would recognize him?" Laturno laid another more recent picture down on the desk beside the older one. "This one was taken within the last few months."

The recent shot was somewhat grainy, as if the image had been magnified several times. A bit of gray dotted the man's temples, and the face appeared more chiseled and hard. But the eyes – comparison between the two pictures, giving allowance for slight aging, was truly remarkable. The blue eyes were so similar.

The SAC stated, "A relative. That would account for the similarities, but there is no way this is the same man. The man in this recent picture appears too young to be Stinson."

A cold chill passed through Joe's mind. "Not if he'd found a way to slow the aging process – slow it like maybe with an oleander recipe?"

Hitchens eyes flew wide open. Joe could almost see the puzzle pieces falling together into place. He grabbed Laturno's arm.

"What does this Stinson guy have to do with your investigation?"

Laturno glanced at the SAC, who nodded consent. "I believe he may be the leader of an underground organization that is infiltrating every major player on the world stage, from Russia to England.

"And I'm convinced they've infiltrated the United States."

***

Samantha fought to keep Alexandra at the forefront as Warner suckled her breasts. Images of Joe tramped through her mind like a movie in rewind, his penetrating brown eyes, ready smile, tender touch. How had things spiraled so out of control? How had she been brought to make such a horrible choice between two lives? As her grip on reality drifted, she knew no other choice remained.

It was time.

While Warner remained occupied, Samantha opened her mouth and lifted her tongue to extract the tiny needle. Marcus had warned her – one miscalculation and she'd die. He'd stated it with caution, no glee. However, if she died instead, could she save both men? If she died, would they send someone else to kill Warner? If she died, would they attempt to pull Joe into the group? If she survived, could she somehow turn the tables on Debrille and the Elite and save others from her fate? A resounding *no* echoed in her mind.

No other choice remained. She wrapped her arms

around his back and slipped the needle from the thin rubber sleeve, careful to avoid pricking her finger. As he raised himself to enter, Samantha thrust the needle into his neck.

Warner's eyes widened in stark horror. His mouth opened as if to yell for the Secret Service outside the door, but foam sputtered out instead. Eyes rolled into the back of his head. Convulsions rocked the bed as Samantha struggled to drag herself out from under him, but he gripped her hair and left her hanging halfway off the bed.

With a sigh of *why*, the President of the United States expired.

One by one, Samantha pulled back his stiffened fingers to release her hair. Tears streamed down her face as she leaned against the wall and stared at his naked form lying across the bed. She quickly clasped her hand over her mouth to avoid screaming.

Oh God, what have I done?

But God didn't listen to her anymore. He hadn't been around for years. She'd gone and made a real mess of her life. Gramm. What would Gramm say? She'd be mortified. Gramm wouldn't even know her anymore. She didn't know herself.

She'd become a murderer.

Trembling overwhelmed her. Stomach flip-flopped. She wanted to allow the eruption of the contents, but that would leave too much DNA evidence behind. Samantha fought the effort – and won.

Samantha wiped her eyes. Had to focus on the job at hand and get out as quickly as possible. The sun would be up in a little more than an hour. She had to escape to the hell-hole, escape back into the darkness. It was where she belonged anyway.

With effort she rolled Warner's body onto one side of the bed and covered his form with the comforter. Maybe if they happened to look inside when she left, Warner would appear asleep and they'd not disturb him for a few more hours. That would give her opportunity to be long gone before anyone discovered his body.

One more performance. You can do one more performance, girlie.

Samantha avoided staring into her own eyes as she adjusted her make-up and hair in the mirror. The body condom appeared ominous in the moonlight as she slipped it from her bag. Nuclear power and nano-technology combined to make atomic hosiery. She'd never activated the thing. Maybe she wouldn't have to, but she'd take no chances.

After pulling it on, the fabric seemed to melt into her skin like lotion. She could hardly make out the weave. Quickly she threw the skirt and blouse over it and stood at the door, her hand poised above the knob. A shiver passed up her spine. She couldn't think of what lay behind her. All she needed now was to escape.

In more ways than one.

When she opened the door, the agents didn't even look

at her.

"Gentlemen," Samantha said, her voice solid and firm like Alexandra's.

"Ma'am," they spoke in unison.

The long walk down the hall, she focused on keeping her legs from collapsing beneath her. They felt like overcooked spaghetti as she descended the stairs. As her shoes clacked on the tile floor below, Samantha felt eyes watching her. She glanced up to see the First Lady staring at her retreat. Their eyes locked briefly. Sweat dribbled down her back.

Samantha fought to keep her gait paced. The clack of her shoes on the tile echoed throughout the hall. She breathed deeply the moment the wind hit her face then set out across the lawn toward the waiting car.

***

Abbie Warner rushed down the hall toward the room the Alexandra woman had just exited. The idiot twins had the audacity to stop her.

"He's sleeping, Mrs. Warner."

"I seriously doubt that. Now get out of my way, fools."

She brushed past them and entered the dark bedroom. The table lamp glowed when she flicked it on and laid out the bottle and syringe. Had to act quickly before it wore off. Stupid girl stayed in here entirely too long.

Foam flecked the edges of his lips, his eyes wide and bulging. The poor man watched every move she made as she slipped on the gloves, but he could do nothing to stop her from finishing the deed. After penetrating the bottle, she drew long on the syringe. Marcus had better be right about this new concoction, better to have too much than not enough.

Abbie stood over him. "You were too good for me, Freddy. I'm sorry it has to end this way, but a woman will do anything for the man she loves."

With a stab, she emptied the syringe into his system. She looked at her watch as the minutes ticked by, felt for a pulse, then double tapped her ear.

"It's done. The United States is ours."

Then Abbie gathered up the syringe and bottle and deposited them into the trash can in the vanity. The rubber gloves disintegrated from her hands and melted away like candle wax.

"Guards!"

***

A shout drew Samantha's attention back toward the White House before she could reach the car. They'd found him.

Shots rang out. Samantha leapt out of her heels and raced across the grass while ripping off the blouse and skirt. Now or never. She jagged left then pressed her navel and felt a sharp stab.

In a split second, the air rushed away from her and out of her lungs. Warmth surged like an electric jolt through her body. Images wavered like heat off hot pavement before the world slammed back into place. Then she immediately cut right, leaving ricocheting bullets in her wake.

Curses and screams of horror faded behind her as she disappeared into the darkness.

***

The phone on the desk jangled. Hitchens picked it up, listened for a moment, then slammed the phone down with a curse.

"We're too late." The SAC ran out onto the main floor. "Get me a car around back now!"

While chaos reigned around him, Joe was drawn back to the grainy picture. Who was the redhead with Stinson? Something about her made Joe's mind race. Again he grabbed Laturno's arm.

"Do we have a name on this woman with Stinson?"

"Alexandra Shuvinovsky, but that's likely a code name. We haven't been able to trace much on her except height, weight, you know – the standard stats."

"Is she 5'7" and about 125?"

Laturno's green eyes were filled with questions. "Or thereabouts. Can't talk anymore, kid. I gotta go."

Joe grabbed his piece and shoved it into his waistband. "Then get me a pair of shoes. I'm going with you."

CHAPTER 51 – REUNION

Samantha's lungs burned like they were filled with hot coals, reminding her of the last night in Gramm's house. Even though no one could see her, she still kept running. The stupid safe houses – she should've studied the entries and exits to the underground a little more closely. The Melrose Hotel entry was too close to the White House, plus it would look very strange for the front door to open all by itself. The doorman would surely have a heart attack at such a sight so early in the morning. She might feel like a ghost, but she could never accomplish walking through walls even with this stupid suit on.

An entrance in the old warehouse district lay just down the road, but no way she'd be able to choose the right one from all those brick buildings. They looked exactly alike.

The sky deepened – the darkness before the dawn. The city would awaken soon and quickly turn into a nightmare trying to dodge people and cars. They'd never see her, but they could still bump into or run over her.

Samantha slipped into an alley between two apartment buildings and tapped her ear. "I need a corridor in the warehouse district."

Marcus' voice rang out in her head. "Four blocks east, building eight on the northwest corner, seventh floor, elevator bank two."

"So you've been demoted to COM duties now? What – couldn't get it up anymore?"

"Get moving," Marcus hissed in her head. "They've called it in and are bringing in heat sensors on search helicopters."

Not good. Not good at all. Four blocks. Time to crank up the speed. The pavement pulsated beneath her feet each time they slapped the concrete. The hosiery protected her feet from the rough surface like a cushion of air.

Sirens blared in the early morning darkness. The thup-thup of helicopters echoed around her. She wasn't going to make it.

***

"Shit – you mean she just up and disappeared right in front of you?" Laturno asked.

The Secret Service agent nodded. "One moment she was there and the next she was gone like a vapor."

Joe interrupted, "What direction was she running?"

"Headed east, then right before she disappeared she

turned north." The agent hesitated.

Laturno asked, "Was there something else?"

"The moment she disappeared, I glanced back toward where she'd been and that's when the vertigo hit me."

Joe intercepted the thought. "East again?"

"Yes."

Joe grabbed Laturno's arm. "I need the car."

"What kinda messed up ass-wipe shit do you have going on in that mind of yours now?"

"East – the warehouse district. Maybe their hideout is in the warehouse district."

Laturno cocked an eyebrow. "You've bat a thousand so far, kid, so it's worth a shot. But I'm going with you."

***

The area seemed strangely quiet with the radio silenced. Sirens had died down and the helicopters were flooding other areas of town. When would the message get to them to turn attentions to their location?

The sky took a breath as darkness began to lift. Laturno split off and jogged down one alley and left Joe to take the opposite side of the street. Laturno would never locate her at that rate. If the woman was invisible, they weren't going to find her by looking. They needed to listen. They needed to hide.

Joe slipped around the corner and edged into the arch of an old doorway before melting into the shadows. Closing his eyes, he willed his heart to slow, his breathing to still. He searched the surroundings with his ears and merely listened.

The pavement echoed with a steady staccato rhythm. Was that breathing coming up the sidewalk? An early morning runner or a runner from authorities?

The breathing moved closer, the footsteps nearby. They were close, so very close. Joe pulled the Glock from his waistband. It warmed in his hands.

Vertigo hit him seconds later. He fought to keep his wits about him as nausea swelled in his stomach. Then he leapt from the doorway and collided with the air.

***

The world rushed away from her as Samantha made contact with the ground. The impact stunned her until she realized a man stood over her, his gun trained on her form. She was no longer invisible. She was no longer alone.

Her breath escaped as she recognized her captor.

"Joe."

***

The woman lay half enveloped in darkness, her face hidden. But Joe knew that voice. He could never forget that voice.

"Sam?"

It had always lain as a suspicion in his gut, more a hope really, but something had kept Joe from fully accepting the reality of Samantha Bartlett's death. She'd remained alive in his thoughts, his dreams, and now she lay sprawled on the concrete in front of him. It was almost more than he could comprehend.

His Glock slid from his fingers and clattered on the ground as he reached for her outstretched hand. A jolt shot through him at her touch. He pulled her to him and enveloped her mouth with his.

"Joe," Samantha sobbed. "Joe, stop."

Joe ignored her pleas and pressed his lips urgently against hers. Anger, loss, love, sorrow, joy all coursed through him as he ravaged her warm mouth and poured all his emotions into her – all of the feelings he'd buried for over a year. He entangled his fingers into her silken hair. Like an arctic wave, reality came crashing down.

He gripped her hair and jerked her away from him. "How could you fake your own death like that?"

The arctic wave penetrated his core and left him breathless. Joe staggered away and stared at the stranger he'd kissed. Red hair, green eyes, high cheekbones, the woman didn't look like Samantha, yet the voice. His mind played vicious tricks on him as he remembered the woman from the cyber café, the hotel explosion. Similar – yet different.

Joe snatched the gun from the ground and trained it on the woman's naked form. "Who are you?"

Her glistening breasts heaved. Tears ran down her cheeks. Strangely enough, the woman smiled a familiar smile.

"I can't believe it's really you. You don't know how I..."

The woman looked down at herself and a slight blush crept up her neck. She curled herself into a ball to hide her nakedness.

"They've carved me up with plastic surgery. This body may not be totally mine anymore, but you have to believe me, Joe. I'm really Samantha."

Joe's mind whirled. "How can I know?"

That smile again. "Remember the night in the 'fraidy hole at Gramm's?"

The memory made Joe's heart skip a beat. He stared hard at her face, trying desperately to comprehend the differences in what he heard with what he saw. His mind raced until acceptance finally slowed it. The gun lowered.

"What's happened to you?"

Sam's face contorted. She stared at the ground. "I didn't think I had a choice." Her head jerked up, and she stared at him with cold eyes – strange green eyes. "They've killed everyone I ever loved. I couldn't let them do that to you. You've got to let me go, or they'll kill you too."

"Who're they?"

The thunder of helicopters filled his ears. Fear enveloped

Samantha's face.

"Joe, please, you've got to get away from me. If I don't get back soon, they'll press a button to blow me up and both of us will die."

The picture. The woman in the picture. "Does this have anything to do with Marcus Stinson?"

Confusion clouded her face until dust and debris swirled up in the air.

She grabbed Joe, her breath hot as she whispered in his ear. "Find the Elite and you'll find me." Her mouth found his for a moment and then she was gone.

Joe watched in bewilderment as Samantha sprinted off and dashed across the street. Vertigo hit him again when she disappeared. As he braced himself against the wall, he grabbed his radio and turned it back on. Traces of red tendrils curled around his fingers. An idea formed in his mind.

"This is Agent Roberts – get me SAC Hitchens."

CHAPTER 52 – THE RESCUE

The drainpipe creaked and groaned under her weight, but Samantha clung to it and pressed herself against the cold bricks. The searchlights passed over the building right next door. She had to hurry and get inside to the elevators. Just one more floor to go. Heights were never her forte.

Relief washed over her when she finally pulled herself over the ledge and up onto the roof. Lungs heaved as she crouched behind the air-conditioning unit. Samantha tapped her earlobe.

"I'm on the roof."

Marcus' voice crackled through. "Hold on a minute while I get your position. We're getting a lot of interference."

"I thought you guys had the best systems in the world," Samantha retorted.

"Satellite signals are still rather primitive, but it's all we have to go on at the surface. Now silence for a moment while I...wait a minute. Damn, you're at the wrong building."

"What?"

"You should be at the building straight in front of you."

The other building was four floors taller. There was no way – no way could she climb down and crawl up an even larger building. She didn't have the strength left to even try. On the roof or on the ground Samantha knew it was only a matter of time. Authorities were going to find her soon if she didn't get down from the roof, or Marcus would press the button to blow her up. Either way, she was never going to get back to the underground.

"I can't do it, Marcus. They'll find me before I can even get down from this building, much less crawl up the other one."

"Wait – go to the edge and look over the side. There should be a wire like a clothesline strung between the buildings. Check to see if it's still there."

Samantha stayed crouched in the shadows as she slunk along the wall like a cat. Helicopters buzzed all around the early-morning sky, sweeping their sensors – looking only for her. Of all the horrible things Warner had done, he'd still deserved better than the death-hand she'd dealt him. Her life was so condemned. No way could she extricate herself from the grip of evil. It enveloped her like a dark cloud.

The ground appeared six stories below as Samantha glanced over the edge. All she had to do was throw herself over. Death would be painless.

The wire glimmered in the searchlight. Samantha darted back from the edge and pressed into the lifting darkness.

"The wire is there, about two stories down."

"Good. Now you're going to have to gauge it just right in order to catch it."

Coldness gripped her belly. "What are you saying? You want me to fling myself over the edge and just hope I catch that thin wire in the dark?" Samantha laughed bitterly to herself. Wasn't that what she'd just been thinking of a moment before, sans the wire?

"You should be able to see it by now and gauge the distance by the windows on the other side. You'll have to jump at an angle. Or you could try climbing down the wall if you think you can accomplish such a feat."

"What about gloves? My hands will be sliced in half with the momentum."

"Just get moving. The suit will protect your hands like gloves. In theory it can withstand some force. Just be careful to put your feet out in front of you when you break through the window."

Samantha sighed. She had to close her mind from the potential pitfalls of what she needed to do. The darkness was rapidly lifting. The authorities would find her any moment if she didn't act now.

A sharp glance over the edge was all she allowed to align herself with the angle of the wire. She ran back a few yards along the roof then took off in a sprint toward the edge. The possibility of missing the wire, slicing through her hands, seeing the ground rise to meet her free-fall all pounded through her mind. As her heart raced and the edge neared, one thought rose up and penetrated all her fears.

She wanted to live.

The thought died away as she met the rush of air in freefall. The wire came into sharp focus. Being a trapeze artist had never been part of her training, but she instinctively knew the force of her free-fall could keep her from being able to hold onto the wire if she even caught it. Her heart rose in her throat. The wire neared.

As her hands made contact, Samantha gripped it with every ounce of strength she possessed. Every muscle in her body seemed to tighten around the wire as momentum slid her along it toward the other building. Her hands burned as the wire seared through the fabric and bit into raw flesh.

The window rose to meet her. At the last second Samantha remembered Marcus' warning about penetrating it feet first. Her muscles were slow to respond.

Glass shattered all around at the impact. The momentum carried Samantha across the floor as she released the wire. Pain gorged her leg. It flopped around like a rag doll. The impact into the far wall stopped her progress, and the world rushed back into stark relief as Samantha screamed in agony.

***

"Samantha! Samantha, what's your status?" Marcus yelled into the microphone.

Her screams echoed around the cavern and sent cold chills up his spine. The minimal staff all stared at him, waiting for direction. Normally he'd just press the button, be done with her and let authorities clean up after the Elite. They'd done it so many times before. Samantha had already completed the purpose of her mission. They didn't need her anymore. But Marcus couldn't bring himself to do it. The damned girl had engaged his heart.

Marcus pointed to a nearby subservient fool. "You – man the COM link. I'm going up."

"But Debrille…"

Marcus gripped the man's throat. "…is asleep, so I'm the one giving orders. Now man the COM link while I go topside."

The shafts felt so far away as Marcus sprinted along the hallway. What would he find? FBI was likely already swarming the building. Good thing he'd felt the need earlier to slip on his own bodysuit, but if anything happened Debrille would chew his hide for endangering the Elite.

Or worse.

Time dragged as he rode to the surface. Going invisible in the shafts was dangerous, but he had no choice. Marcus slipped out of his clothing and activated his suit. The rush of air expanded then compressed the tube before equilibrium was again reached. It held. The elevator bank greeted him as he stepped from behind the adjoining panel and entered.

Would he be too late to save her? What would he find? Marcus tapped his earlobe. "Can you still hear her?"

"The screams have died down, but she's moaning every once in awhile."

"Has she answered your status demands?"

"Negative."

The doors slid aside. The FBI clamor echoed from below as they searched for her. He didn't have much time.

Marcus whispered, "Which direction?"

"To your right, second hallway on the left all the way down to the end."

Marcus padded quickly along, careful not to draw unwanted attention. Let the bastards search the lower floors as long as they wanted.

The cavernous room opened before him at the end of the hallway. A rapid scan reflected the shattered window and scattered glass where Samantha had entered. Blood – so much blood pooled on the floor near the opposite wall. No body.

"Samantha," Marcus whispered. Had the FBI already removed her body? Impossible. They'd never outfox the Elite.

"Samantha," he called, a little louder.

A groan rose up from behind a series of stacked crates. She was still alive. A trail of smeared blood led him straight to her body. She was no longer invisible. A tap to his navel and he became visible once again.

Marcus gasped. Her leg had been severed clear to the bone, which from the contorted position appeared also to be broken. Blood continued to flow from the gaping wound. She'd bleed to death in a matter of minutes.

A tarp covered one of the crates. It would have to do. Marcus untied it from the crate then positioned the leg. Samantha screamed out then was silent as he wrapped the tarp around the leg to stabilize it and injected a sedative.

"You're going to bring the Feds down on us if you aren't quiet."

Samantha groaned and licked her lips. "I must be dead."

Her voice sounded far away. Time was running out. "Not yet, if I can help it." Maybe he could keep her talking.

"Course I am."

Marcus tied the rope very tight above the serration to help staunch the severe blood flow and hopefully numb the leg. "And why do you say that?"

Her speech wavered and grew thick. "Cause you're never nice to me." She almost smiled.

"Well I'm not going to be very nice to you now. This is going to hurt like hell when I pick you up, but you have to keep quiet."

"A brief reprieve from your whip, eh?"

Here goes nothing. Marcus tapped his navel then Samantha's. The tarp still showed. The fibers of the bodysuit must have been far too damaged to activate around the injured leg. Marcus gauged properly and slid his arms beneath her back and good leg and picked her up. Samantha sucked in her breath and had the presence of mind to bite her lips to keep the scream in her throat from filling the room. Then her body went limp.

Marcus rushed from the room back toward the elevator. Shouts and stamping feet echoed up the stairwell. They were coming.

The stairwell door slammed open and bodies rushed out into the hallway. Marcus slumped in a dark corner and tipped Sam's body toward the floor. Hopefully they'd only see a rolled-up tarp tossed into a corner, if anything. He held his breath as the Feds scattered and searched the floor. Someone surfaced from the stairwell and stared at the tarp heap – a face he'd seen before. Marcus hoped Samantha had only passed out, glad for the stillness.

A voice called for the agent and drew his attention away from their corner. A brief opportunity opened up, and Marcus made a dash for the elevator. He exhaled a sigh of relief as the doors closed and the elevator made its way down into the depths.

***

The monitor beeped steadily – slowly but steadily. Marcus kept the sound always in the back of his mind as he worked up to his elbows in the gore laid open before him. Samantha definitely had a strong will to live. Somehow he'd make sure it was a life worth living.

With careful precision, Marcus stitched each fiber in the leg back together. Hours ticked by as he worked not only to save her life but to ensure she'd maintain use of the leg. Maintaining blood flow to the muscle tissue was critical. The bag dripped low again.

"You there," Marcus muffled through his mask, "get additional blood ready."

Before anyone could move the surgical doors slammed open, and Debrille stormed into the room, his face a mass of twisted fury. He wore no scrubs, no mask – nothing to keep the germs at bay. Marcus fumed.

"What the hell do you think you're doing?" Debrille squelched.

Marcus moved aside. "I'm trying to save her life."

"Do you really think I care about your measly attempt to save her?" Debrille's eyes bulged. "You've wasted valuable resources and endangered a completed mission, that's what you've done."

Marcus stoically endured the fury. Debrille's anger would soon be spent, and he'd either be shot or left to attend Samantha. All the reasons for joining the Elite those many years ago no longer mattered. He'd perfected their age-defying formula, and for what? No prestige, not a single moment of admiration, only countless tongue lashings.

"I guarantee you they are pulling DNA samples and will have the names within days. I can't believe you did something so asinine."

Marcus glanced back to the leg. Precious minutes ticked by as Debrille paced and stewed. The monitor continued to beep, the bag dangerously low.

Debrille stopped and pointed his bony finger in his face. "Continue here, but the moment she is healed I want that girl sent to South America, you got that? I never want to see her face or hear her retorts again."

Marcus nodded. "Yes, sir."

As Debrille shuffled off down the hall, Marcus shouted commands. The bag was replaced just in time. The area was wiped down with disinfectant, and Marcus resumed surgery.

Then an idea struck him. It was risky. They had yet to test the powder on a live human being, but he had to give Samantha every possible chance.

A nurse held the handlink to his face and beeped the lab. "Bring me the vial in section J-6 marked lippo-proteins. We're in surgical two."

Marcus fully realized what he'd have to do. To accomplish it, he might have to get Samantha up sooner rather than later.

CHAPTER 53 – A DICHOTOMY

"That's impossible!"

Hitchens handed the DNA lab results to Joe. "See for yourself."

The name swam before his eyes as Joe stared in disbelief. Sure enough – Jana E. Sayers. The hair wasn't Sam's after all. The bitter pill didn't go down easily.

"But the voice, the things she knew. How in the world could she have known all that?"

The SAC shook his head. "Maybe this *Elite* group pumped Miss Bartlett for information before killing her – you know, use the identities of some of their victims."

"They blew up her house."

"But there was that portion of a tunnel remember," Hitchens reminded him.

The tunnel – he'd never be able to forget that blasted tunnel. It haunted his dreams nearly every night. The

RUNNING INTO THE DARKNESS

ground-penetrating radar hadn't picked up anything past the caved-in area. Was it possible it was only a fall-out shelter or something?

Then there was the lady in black at the cemetery. She'd been staring at her parents' graves – not Sam's. So many times he'd wished he could've gone back to that moment. Why hadn't he paid a little more attention to her that day?

"But why would this Jana Sayers have given me this Elite name then? Also, how could she have recognized me?"

The squawk box buzzed. "Sir, the other lab report just arrived."

Hitchens responded, "Bring it in."

Joe ground his teeth. Once again he ran through last week's encounter in his mind. The new results threw all his theories and hopes out the window, but there were still too many bells going off inside his head. The body definitely hadn't looked like Sam. Of course, he'd never really seen Sam nude before, but she was just the right height. The green eyes were easily explained – colored contact lenses. The hair could have been dyed, but then the hair was where the real problem lay. Was it really Sam's voice or had he just wanted so badly to believe it was her?

The agent brought in the packet and handed it to Hitchens. Joe waited for the confirmation of DNA from the blood samples they'd taken at the warehouse.

A low whistle emanated from the SAC. "I'll be damned." Hitchens handed the sleeve to Joe. "No doubt now. We've got an interesting twist on this suspect."

The name on the report screamed from the pages.

Samantha J. Bartlett.

***

The back room was in mass confusion. Digital images of Samantha flooded computer screens in various stages of reconstruction as multiple agents tried to piece together plastic surgery procedures used to alter her appearance.

Joe scanned the screens and clarified images. Her new appearance was seared in his mind from the shock he'd experienced in the alley of trying to bring together the familiar voice with the unfamiliar face.

"And she'd had, um...implants," Joe offered.

Several agents asked in unison, "What kind?"

The darkness of the room concealed Joe's blush. "You know – in the chest."

"Breast augmentation?" one asked.

"Yes."

Fingers flew across keyboards, the tapping creating a hypnotic drone.

"Would you estimate the cup size?"

Joe rolled his eyes. The line of questions was becoming almost humiliating. "I'm no expert in women's lingerie, guys. Maybe about here." Joe held his hands at about the right distance from his body.

The agents whistled.

"Looks like a G to me."

"Hubba-hubba."

"Did you get to touch them?"

Hitchens walked over and slammed a button. The images on the screens immediately switched over to a camera feed – the President's funeral procession.

"Who here does not understand that we are in a very serious situation? President Warner is dead, people. This woman is the only sure link we have to that sinister plot."

Silence filled the room. The feed showed the horse-drawn caisson slowly rolling down Constitution Avenue, a flag-draped casket resting inside on its journey to the U.S. Capitol Building. Minutes ticked by as the horses continued their deathly cadence. The silence continued even after the SAC switched the image back to Samantha's, save for the resumed clacking of keyboards. Hitchens pulled Joe aside.

"Has it occurred to you that with the level of blood found, your friend may not have survived this time?"

Joe nodded. "Then I keep coming back to the fact that *they* went through the trouble of rescuing her."

"Yes, that's where I end up too."

Her image across the screens seemed so unreal.

Samantha a killer? How was it possible? That just didn't compute. If those in her group had saved her, she was still a marked woman. When found, she'd be tried and executed. Even if he saved her, he couldn't save her.

Joe felt trapped, his allegiances divided. Memories of their youth together, her return to Kansas, their kiss. Bitterness waged war in his soul as reality crashed over him, drowning out any hopes of reconciliation.

Samantha was doomed.

CHAPTER 54 – FOR LOVE

The enormous agony lessened day-by-day. Samantha's waning strength gradually returned, but to what point and purpose?

Debrille never came to visit her – more of a blessing instead of a curse. Too soon Marcus started in on exercising the leg to the barrage of Samantha's curses. But it didn't compute. Why was he so concerned about rehabilitating her when she'd completed her deadly mission? Debrille had to have a new plan for her up his sleeve, however she wasn't going to stick around long enough to find out what it was. She had plans of her own, foolhardy though they were.

No longer would she continue being their little Barbie doll. No longer could she stomach being controlled by a crazed madman. She'd committed the most heinous of crimes – taken a life. As soon as she was able she would escape – or die trying.

The thought pushed her to work the leg when Marcus left the room, sometimes to the point of passing out cold.

Then as soon as the darkness cleared and the throbbing grew more manageable, she'd flex and bend it again. Always she massaged the muscles to keep them warm and ready, the blood flowing. Atrophy would be the worst possible roadblock to her plans of escape.

Marcus came in alone one evening after dinner. Silently he checked her over, paying diligent attention to the healing laceration around her thigh. Apparently satisfied, he reached into his pocket, took out a notebook and pen, and began to write. Sweat gathered above his lip and on his forehead. Samantha had never seen the guy break a sweat before except when training. Something was up.

After he finished, he ripped the page out and handed it to her. The paper trembled almost imperceptibly as she took it from his hands.

"What – testing my eyesight now?"

His face grew stern - fearful. He tapped the paper she held and motioned for silence.

The words leapt from the page and nearly stilled her heart.

Plan to escape. Get you walking without anyone's knowledge.

Samantha stared at him. Was it another mind trick? Was he setting her up? His eyes held a glimmer of truth, his mouth set in a firm resolve. This was no test.

She grabbed the pad and pen from his hands and wrote one word. *Why?*

Debrille sending to South American brothel. Worse hell.

Nausea gripped her belly. A sex slave? Wasn't that what she was already? She stared at him in bewilderment, her mind unable to comprehend a worse horror.

Marcus scribbled again. *Tied up – drugged – new john every thirty minutes until you DIE.*

Samantha's hand shook as she wrote. *Bone strength?*

New drug heals bone faster.

Ear chip?

Working on it.

Samantha nodded. Marcus grabbed all the pages, stuffed them into a ceramic dish, then poured a small sample of hydrochloric acid until the contents dissolved. The evidence of their plot disappeared.

Gently he lifted Samantha from the bed and propped her against him as she tested her weight on the good leg.

"Careful," he whispered.

Weight transferred gradually between her legs until darkness closed in around her. Before she lost consciousness, Samantha was aware of concern emanating from Marcus' eyes.

It wasn't until she regained consciousness and found herself alone in the dark once again that Samantha realized Marcus' eyes held something else – something so entirely foreign.

Love.

***

Abbie Warner peered through the dank darkness of the long tunnel. Where was he? Anticipation beat in her chest, longing rose. It had been so long.

Secret Service agents were probably already planning their strategy to come in after her if she didn't get back topside soon. Hopefully Ben could keep them busy. The chance that they'd find the shaft and then the corresponding tunnel did not bode well for future plans. They'd been in more dire predicaments than this though. Just a few moments longer.

A light suddenly glimmered in the distance. Hope leapt. The tram pulled near and stopped. She could barely contain herself when he stepped from the vehicle.

"Oh, Adolf." She buried her face in his neck and smelled his nearness. Tears rose in her eyes.

"You should not have risked coming down here now," he chastised in German. "Your days of mourning have not yet ended."

Through the sternness in his voice she still detected his tender regard. "I could not wait another day." The guttural language came easily to her lips. "Do not make me go back. I cannot bear to be away from you any longer."

"Just another year, my love."

Abbie's heart threatened to wrench from her chest at his

words. Her sobbing increased. She clung desperately to him.

"But it's already been two years since I last saw you, and that was brief enough," she choked.

Adolf's hands were warm as he stroked her hair. "There, there. You have done so well. No one suspects you killed him?"

"No. They are chasing down your Alexandra girl, or whatever her name was."

"Good. One year more, then all our plans will be fixed, and we'll never be apart again." He lifted her chin until their eyes locked. "I promise you."

Abbie stared at his face, devouring just one more look to last her another year. She swallowed her sobs and dabbed at her eyes.

"I will hold you to that promise."

"And I will fulfill it." He enveloped her mouth with his. "Until then, my dear Eva."

***

"So, Rookie, tell me more about this sex-goddess, murdering tramp friend of yours. Is she that good?"

If Hitchens hadn't grabbed his arm, Joe would have laid Laturno out flat on his back.

"That's enough, Laturno," Hitchens said.

Laturno stared at Joe and grinned. "So – even after all

she's done, you still love her?"

Joe seethed. "You're sick, Laturno, you know that?"

"I'm sick? Your girlfriend bucked him like a bronco then killed the President of the United States, and *I'm* the sick one?"

The SAC intervened. "I said that's enough. Now either cut the sarcastic comments, Laturno, or you're off the investigation."

Their voices echoed throughout the warehouse. At this rate they'd get very little investigating done.

"Hey, I've been the lead on this case four years. He's the one with the personal connection. The rookie should be off if anyone."

"Last I checked, I'm the one they call *Special Agent-in-Charge* around here. Therefore *I* lead every damned investigation in this division of the entire Bureau. Therefore *I* decide who is on what case. You got it?"

Steam almost belched from Hitchens' collar. Daggers practically glinted from Laturno's eyes, but eventually he backed down.

"As you say, sir."

They returned to pouring over the blueprints of the building.

Fact – Samantha had entered the building through the fourth floor window.

Fact – She'd not exited the building through normal channels.

Fact – No one else had been able to enter or leave the building to rescue her.

Fact – A trail of blood droplets led down the hallway to the stairwell where it ended in a small puddle. No footprints. Someone else must have carried her, but how did they get in, then how did they get out without being seen?

Joe had a thought. "Sir, what if we undertook a demolition project?"

Hitchens face held questions. "Where?"

"Here."

"We'd have to get the owner's permission."

"Not hard for the Bureau, I'm sure."

"Done. What perimeter area?"

"Around the stairwell."

Laturno interrupted. "Wait a minute. What in the world do you expect to accomplish by taking out a stairwell of an old building?"

"Not the stairwell itself, but the wall here," Joe pointed on the blueprints, "between the stairwell and the elevator shaft."

Laturno slapped the blueprints. "It's just empty space. There's not enough room there for anything."

Joe was about to lose his patience. "Look, they had to have a way to get in and out of the building without being seen – why else would she have done something so crazy as to have crashed through the window after crawling up the other building? She was obviously in the wrong place and needed to get over here."

Hitchens leaned back and lit a cigarette. "Keep going, Roberts."

"Okay, consider this. If these people are somehow connected with Hitler or Nazis or some other such..."

"Hogwash?" Laturno intervened.

"Sure, whatever. The Nazis were famous for their secret bunkers, underground labyrinths of tunnels, you name it. This building may be one of the entry points to getting to their hideout."

Hitchens flipped out his phone and barked orders. "I want permissions and permits pulled on this building ASAP. And get demolition out here pronto. We've got a duck to pluck."

CHAPTER 55 – LOST AND FOUND

"Samantha. Samantha, wake up. It's time."

The light pierced through the edges of sleep as Marcus flipped on the bedroom light. He'd already covered the camera with black tape. With a sweep of his arm he cleared the surface of her dresser and laid out an array of instruments.

Samantha bolted up in bed. "What is it? What's wrong?"

"We've got to get you out of here – now."

"I'm still limping."

"I know, but we've run out of time. I can't believe they've figured it all out so fast, but they've linked Alexandra to Samantha. They know you are you. They know for certain you didn't die in the explosion a year ago, and now they're searching. Debrille's been briefed on the FBI's knowledge. He's on his way back."

Samantha's stomach did a flip-flop as she got out of bed

and threw on some clothes. How could…?

Joe.

The realization gave her comfort followed by a fear and torment chaser. The memory of his kiss left bitterness on her lips. He was on her tail now. He knew what she'd done. Joe was an honorable man, and he'd make sure she was brought to justice for her crimes. If anyone could find her Joe would. Then he'd throw the book at her. But she was dead whether she stayed or left the underground. Anything was better than a life ended in a South American brothel.

The backpack lay right where she'd hidden it in the closet. Comfortable shoes were going to be important, so she threw an extra pair in along with another change of garments.

Marcus slid a wad of cash out of his pocket. "Put this in your bag. It's only a few thousand but is all I could pilfer on such short notice. I didn't expect this to happen so soon. How's the leg?"

"Doesn't hurt as much anymore. Still a little weak, but it's okay."

"Hold still then – this will only hurt for a moment."

The shot near her ear was necessary. They couldn't risk getting too close to the ear chip and setting off a signal. Otherwise they'd both be blown to bits. Still they had to get close enough for the medicine to work where it was needed.

After he finished the injection, Marcus pinched her ear

chip then outlined it with a black pen. "Once numbness takes effect get it over with as quickly as possible. I've brought plenty of gauze. Just dress it quickly and put the rest in the bag, but most importantly be careful."

"What about you?"

"While Debrille is up in arms sweating it out over your escape, I'll follow within twenty-four hours – no more, you hear?"

"Right."

Marcus reached into the other pocket, pulled out a map, and handed it to her – the National Cathedral. Samantha nodded.

"If I'm not there in the allotted time, get out."

"And go where?"

Marcus smiled. He had a nice smile. She wished she'd had the chance to see it more often.

"You're a smart girl. You'll manage to stay one step ahead of them if you have to."

No time for tears. No time for introspection. Samantha stared into Marcus' blue eyes as if truly seeing him for the first time.

"Why now?"

"You still haven't figured it out?"

He grabbed her and kissed her deep – so simple, so

much less than everything else they'd done before, and yet it held so much more.

Marcus looked hard into her eyes as he pulled away and whispered in her ear. "Just make it out, you hear? Bank three, shaft eight – I've disabled the camera and set the controls on automatic. Twenty-four hours. Hurry."

With one more kiss, Marcus left her alone. So alone.

Adrenaline rushed through her body as she picked up the hole-punch, stared in the mirror, and lined it up with the pen marks drawn on her ear lobe. She had to be firm. She had to be quick. She had to sever all lines from the ear chip at exactly the same time or there'd be one big mess for them to clean up.

Samantha exhaled. Closed her eyes.

And squeezed.

***

The demolition claw pulled back panel after panel of sheet rock. Dust swirled in the air like tornadoes during a Kansas spring before settling in a fine layer on the stairs. Then the claw bit more carefully into the wood panels positioned behind it. Minutes turned into nearly three hours. Joe knew immediately when they hit metal by the unnerving screech.

Heads gathered near the open wall as the debris settled. Steel tubes and chalky sheet metal lay cocooned in a narrow slot.

"Is it part of the elevator shaft?" Joe asked.

The dusty foreman pulled down his goggles and spoke up. "No – no elevator shaft I've ever seen. The blueprints don't show anything here but a narrow space."

"What's behind it?" Hitchens asked.

"We'll see in a minute." The foreman clicked his radio. "Bring up the radar, boys."

The SAC continued, "Can ground-penetrating radar see through metal?"

"We got us a new mechanism here, sir. Worked with the techies myself to come up with something brand new. Figured now would be a great time to test it out."

Three guys came lumbering up the stairs with the boxy contraption.

"She ain't none too pretty to look at, but she just might show us what we want to see."

After adjusting the setting, the foreman grabbed a wide paddle and leveled it against the metal. The minutes ticked by until the radar started a feed. All eyes were on the readout.

The foreman let fly with a low whistle. "Well isn't that just something else."

Joe butt in. "What? What's there?"

"Boys, looks like we have some sort of separate shaft butted up behind the main shaft here. Doesn't stop at ground level."

Hitchens eyed the foreman. "Well where does it stop then?"

"From my readings – it doesn't."

CHAPTER 56 – SINS OF THE PAST

"I want her found!"

Marcus had never seen Debrille lose it like this. Maybe he'd actually have a heart attack this time and save so many lives. At least Samantha had gotten away. Timing his own escape had to be perfect. Forcing his normal expression in the meantime – key to his survival.

How had he ever been sucked into the Elite's mindset? If only he could go back…go back to before he'd lost Iris and the baby. Their deaths had left him too distraught to think clearly. So much death surrounded him. Perhaps now he'd have a chance to make a new life and live once again.

Debrille shook as he strode up to Marcus. "Search the north chambers. Find her and find out who else is behind this. A damn hole-punch? Someone had to have helped her. She couldn't have gotten far on that leg."

"Rest assured. I will find her."

"Report to me immediately whatever you find. I'll be

reviewing video feeds in the COM."

The teams were divided up and sent into various sectors of the labyrinth. Marcus kept his boys busy for a couple of hours searching every square inch of every room, waiting for just the right opportunity to slip away to his own quarters. He'd have to be quick with the hole-punch – no time to numb the pain. They'd be watching the monitors closely as well. He could only hope to get to the surface before they caught onto him.

One of the men called out, "Dr. Marcus, I found something."

"What is it?"

"Just a blank notebook, but it looks like someone may have left indentions from writing on the previous pages."

Marcus swallowed the tremble of concern and had the presence of mind to keep his calm demeanor. "It's just a notebook. Probably nothing."

"But sir, it was in the trash, and you know what a stickler Debrille is about wasting anything around here."

"Hmm, yes. You two," Marcus called as he snapped his fingers, "go with him to take this notebook to Debrille. It could be a very important piece of evidence."

"Yes, sir."

After the three left the room, Marcus continued his pretense of searching the quarters with the remainder of his team. Inside he sweat over the notebook. He was screwed, so screwed and backed between nothing but barricades. If he had any chance of getting out with his life, he had to act now.

"Men, I've an idea to discuss with Debrille. I'll be back in ten."

The tile echoed his footsteps as he stepped into the corridor. He wanted nothing more than to take off in a sprint but merely satisfied himself with a rapid walk. The sound of his heartbeat thudded in his ears. Debrille and his entourage were expected around every corner. When he closed his bedroom door behind him, he felt more exposed than ever. No need to waste time covering the camera. He flicked off the lights and felt his way around.

The hole-punch was right where he'd hidden it under his mattress. The painkillers were still in his medicine cabinet – he swallowed three. The ear chip lined up perfectly. He'd die either now or later if he didn't get out immediately. He bit his lip and squeezed.

The pain told him he was still alive. It was more intense than expected, but he'd experienced worse. The gauze bandage slopped over the entire ear – couldn't be neat in the dark. A quick rummage through his closet produced a full backpack. He pulled out the pistol and stuffed it in the small of his back. Then he slunk out the door and headed for the surface shafts.

The closer he neared increased his desire to run for it. Finally he could stand it no longer and took off in a sprint. The technicians were as surprised as he was when he rounded the corner.

The backpack hit the ground as he pulled the 9-mm from his waist. Two shots neatly through the temples and all was clear. The ride to the surface would be agonizing, minutes like hours. The tube pressurized after the door slid shut.

No movement.

The door slid back. Debrille glared at him, surrounded by his entourage. Marcus' heart sank, but he remained stoic. No escaping the inevitable.

"I never would have suspected you."

Marcus stared down the barrel of the Glock. A report – then darkness.

***

Twenty-four hours come and gone. Still no Marcus. The convenience store hadn't been the most ideal place to do it, but she'd managed to crop her hair and color it black. After successfully making it to the cathedral, Samantha had changed the dressing of her throbbing ear with delicacy and her hiding place every two hours. She was rapidly running out of unseen nooks in the gigantic cathedral, but fear kept her moving. Just a few hours more. Maybe he had to spend more time covering her tracks. Or maybe he needed to disable the camera on a new shaft.

Even though she kept mostly to her hiding places, Samantha couldn't help but appreciate the beauty of the cathedral. She hadn't stepped into a church since Gramm's funeral. There'd been no peace then, but something about this place stirred a sense of awe. Memories of home came flooding over her, of her mother, of comfort, of belonging, of being loved.

Oh Marcus, where are you?

Had he set her up? No – she'd begun to see a completely different Marcus over the past weeks, a man with feelings, a man of compassion, a man who'd wanted to escape almost as much as she did. What if…? She couldn't allow herself to consider the possibility.

The hours ticked down. Twenty-four hours dwindled away. The ache in her heart grew. The more hours that ticked off the clock the more she came to the inevitable conclusion. Her heart echoed the fears of her mind.

Marcus was dead.

The realization brought tears coursing down her cheeks. She curled up on the floor of the confessional, her latest hiding place. She almost didn't care any longer. Nearly two days since she'd had any sleep. It washed over her in her grief.

***

Samantha's heart nearly stopped. Someone had entered the confessional. Silence – then a clearing of the throat. The man's gentle voice called softly.

"It's a bit early, but we work on God's clock not our

own, eh?"

Samantha stayed put. She didn't know whether to stir and make a run for it or to respond.

The priest called again. "I'll be happy to hear your confession when you're ready."

It slipped breathless from her mouth before she could stop it. "Confession?"

"It must be a terrible burden to carry to bring one in at such an hour." His voice held no disdain, only concern.

If he only knew the weight of the baggage she carried. "I'm not Catholic."

"God created everyone. He hears all His children."

"But I'm not anything. I don't even believe in God anymore. Not sure I ever really did."

"That doesn't change the fact that you're still right here – right now. Maybe it's right where you need to be."

The pressure built in her heart and mind like an old steam engine about to burst at the seams. It spilled from her lips in a torrent.

She told him of her death and rebirth, of the Elite, Debrille and Marcus. Sex, lies, death and murder. Warner. Gramm. Momma. Her life was laid bare until as far back as she could remember. The hours melted away like the wax of a candle. The wall around Samantha's heart crumbled until there was nothing left to say. Decay was spent. Life flickered.

The priest released her with the words *go in peace*. As Samantha stepped from the confessional, she felt as a butterfly emerging from the cocoon after a long winter. She stood at the top of the cathedral steps and let the night wind blow through her hair. The sun would peek out soon.

Closing her eyes, she breathed the air of freedom. How long she would have that freedom she didn't know, but she'd hold onto it for as long as humanly possible. Fear dropped like a weight from her shoulders. She descended the steps, chose a direction, and ran off into the waning darkness.

***

He watched from the shadows as the girl descended the steps and ran off into the night. The collar nearly choked him. He pulled it off and tossed it into the alcove over the body of the priest.

Eric Laturno double-tapped his ear as he stared into the darkness then spoke softly. "Don't worry."

"I've found her."

Stay tuned for the sequel

Piercing the Darkness

ABOUT THE AUTHOR

Sometimes life emulates fiction.

Life is filled with tragedy and Ms. Bale's writing reflects this reality. However, there is always a silver lining...even if one must spend their entire life searching for it.

In her previous career, Ms. Bale traveled the United States as a Government Relations Liaison, working closely with Congressional offices and various government agencies. This experience afforded her a glimpse into the sometimes "not so pretty" reality of the political sphere. Much of this reality and various locations throughout her travels make it into her writing.

She dreams of the day she can return to visit Alaska.

Connect with D. A. Bale online
Facebook: www.facebook/pages/D-A-Bale
Twitter: @DABale1
Blog: http://dabalepublishing.blogspot.com
Email: dabalepublishing@att.net

Made in the USA
Charleston, SC
20 May 2014